LOTTE JEAN ELLIOT

Eastern England who was a
a pen and using her creative mind to conjour a new universe
like the ones in her favourite books. Through literature, Lotté
has seen a whole new world open up. Diving into the deepest
realms of the mind to inspire readers through poetry, or
starting an adventure with a new character.

When she isn't writing novels, poetry, or screenplays with
her sister Francesca, Lotté finds inspiration in art, films,
music, exploring museums, and learning languages. She loves
to explore the deepest meaning behind ideas and gain new
perspectives of the world in which we inhabit.

Follow Lotté on Twitter @lottelauv

LOTTE JEAN ELLIOTT

THE MONSTERS CLUB

Northodox Press Ltd
Maiden Greve, Malton,
North Yorkshire, YO17 7BE

This edition 2022

1
First published in Great Britain by
Northodox Press Ltd 2022

ISBN: 978-1-915179-05-0

This book is set in Caslon Pro Std

To Leonard 'Tan' Kerridge and Jackie Kerridge.

My biggest supporters took away far too soon
but their belief always now lays at home within these pages.

This is for you.

```
 🗗                                              _ □ ✕
File  Edit  Search  Help
┌──────────────────────────────────────────────────┐
│                                                  ▲ │
│   ANONYMOUS70: [HOW DID YOU BECOME THIS WAY?]      │
│                                                    │
│   HEYJUN: [HOW DO WE BECOME ANYTHING? I'M A        │
│   BEING WHO CHOSE A PATH AND WENT WITH IT.]        │
│                                                    │
│   ANONYMOUS70: [IS THAT ALL YOU THINK THIS IS?     │
│   ONE CHOICE?]                                     │
│                                                    │
│   HEYJUN: [WHAT ELSE COULD IT BE?]                 │
│                                                    │
│   ANONYMOUS70: [THAT SOMETIMES WE DO THINGS WE     │
│   DON'T UNDERSTAND. BUT WE'RE SO FAR IN NOW,       │
│   HOW DO WE TURN BACK?]                            │
│                                                    │
│   HEYJUN: [I'VE MADE FRIENDS WITH SO MANY          │
│   DEMONS, WHAT WOULD IT MATTER IF I BEFRIENDED     │
│   ANOTHER?]                                        │
│                                                    │
│   ANONYMOUS70: [ONE DAY YOUR NARCISSISTIC WAYS     │
│   WILL CATCH UP WITH YOU. YOU CAN'T HIDE           │
│   BEHIND THAT PERFECTLY CRAFTED LIFE FOREVER.      │
│   YOUR GAME OF LYING WILL GET YOU ONE DAY.]        │
│                                                    │
│   HEYJUN: [I'LL WAIT FOR THAT DAY. I DO LOVE A     │
│   GOOD GAME. NOW I'VE TO GO, I HAVE SOME           │
│   PEOPLE TO PLAY.]                                 │
│                                                    │
│   ++ HEYJUN HAS LEFT THE CHAT ++                   │
│                                                    │
│   ANONYMOUS70: [YOU LOVE GAMES? THAT'S GOOD TO     │
│   KNOW, HOW ABOUT WE PLAY ONE NOW?]                │
│                                                    │
│   ++ ANONYMOUS70 HAS LEFT THE CHAT ++             ▼│
│                                                    │
│ ◄                                               ► │
└──────────────────────────────────────────────────┘
```

Chapter One

I'll tell you one secret, okay?

When a new season arrives at Dallington Academy, you had better hold onto your secrets. Each new season, the school implodes with anticipation at the announcement of the greatest event of the season: the grand party. And along with the arrival of a new season comes a time-honoured game. One person, unknown to most, is chosen to navigate the threat list. The cost: the humiliation of a student at the school. The prize: ascending the popularity rankings until the next party and immunity to the threat list themselves.

It had been a sport at Dallington for generations and I knew the heightened activity was partly due to its arrival this morning. You could truly feel the party approaching. My least favourite time of year. Exposing secrets wasn't my idea of fun. It was a nightmare.

I was sitting at one of the lunch tables in the main hall trying to ignore the pandemonium, distracting myself by writing out a new source code, when I felt a hand latch onto my right shoulder. A familiar voice layered with anticipation.

'Junie, Junie! The news is out. Have you seen it?'

Ela Allard emerged from the lunch hall and sat at the front of the bench ahead of me, clutching her maroon toned designer bag to her chest alongside a slip of paper. Her face wrinkled with excitement at every crease.

'What news?' I asked, knowing fully well the only words coming out of my best friend's mouth that week would be an interlude to the revelry currently consuming the school.

'The party leaflet has been passed out alongside something else. Something very important. First, look at the new season's style. The theme this year is amazing!'

Ela tossed over the slip of paper with an image of our gothic English manor school and a message welcoming the next season's party. An image of luxury stared back at me; this year it seemed the tone of choice was gold and rose. All the styles that would decorate the grand halls this year seemed more Christmas-themed than Autumn ball.

I forced a smile, throwing the paper back to her. 'Oh, that's great.'

These parties were the least of my interests. All they did was flaunt their parent's wealth and carry on the witch-hunt to burn down someone's reputation. It was not my favourite pastime to watch. However, at a place like Dallington, where parties and prosperity meant everything, if I didn't show some interest in the hunt, I would become an outcast and soon find my own name on the list.

She slouched into the seat, sighing. '*Great,* is that all you can say? Don't you get why I'm even more excited than usual for this year's grand gathering?!'

'You're always excited about these parties.' I shrugged.

She slammed her hand on the table. 'I know, but this time it's different.'

'How so?'

A smirk curled at her lip, but she kept her voice low. 'I'm the one in charge of destruction this season.'

Hearing those words creep out of her made me want to flee. Ela bit her lip with excitement, seemingly glad she'd been given the key to the social death of a student.

'You? Great. Who's the target this season?'

Ela leaned forward. The fact she'd been chosen didn't seem to bother her at all. Destroying someone's school journey would've been hell for anyone else. But I knew Ela was glad she'd been given the honour as it meant whoever had handed her the title deemed her worthy enough to give a good show of public humiliation.

She glanced across the room to a group in the corner of the lunch hall. Dillan and his friends, a group of popular football boys laughing at something playing on one of their mobiles. It took me by surprise, Dillan Smith had been Ela's crush since the beginning of time.

I narrowed my eyes, turning back to her. 'Dillan? The love of your life; he's the one whose reputation you're going to destroy?'

'Destroy?' She rolled her eyes. 'No, not Dillan...'

'Who then?'

'Who do you think? The one person I've been trying to take down for months.'

I should've known what was coming. 'Lucinda Darson. You've got something on her?'

I turned back to the group to see Lucinda, Dillan's current girlfriend, sitting by him, all smiles and happiness. They'd been dating for the last few months and ever since Ela had been trying to cut them apart, but Dillan was too attached to Lucinda. As sourced by Ela, his relationships usually lasted a month at best, which was why she seemed to have a harder time getting rid of Lucinda. Dillan appeared to want Lucinda to stay around, and now Ela had the chance I knew she meant business.

'I've been waiting for this day for weeks now.' Ela let out a little cackle. 'I found something out about her that will shock everyone. I can't believe I was chosen to do the shaming this time. I must've gone up in popularity.'

'You've always been popular?' I laughed. Which was true. Our group was pretty much untouchable in many stakes given we sat at the top of popularity rankings, if such a thing existed.

She smiled with pride at the comment but continued. 'Anyways, I've already got my plan ready.'

'Wait, who made you the destroyer this year?'

'I don't know who picked me, we never do. I just found out after the list was posted like everyone else,' Ela handed me another piece of paper with her coded name. I recognised Ela's code from her previous attempts at becoming the *chosen one*.

'What do you have on Lucinda? Is it enough to take her down or break her up with Dillan? It would've been pointless targeting her elsewhere.'

Ela leaned closer. 'She's been having an affair with Mr. Hawthorne.'

I gasped. 'Are you kidding me? Our English teacher?'

She sat back, smiling ear to ear. 'Nope, not kidding! Don't you get what this means, Dillan will finally be free for me. This has to work. Once and for all, I'm not gonna let another girl get ahead of me. It's my time.'

I turned to Lucinda, in shock that she wasn't this perfect girl, all bubbly and cute. I never would've thought a girl as innocent and doe-eyed as Lucinda would be capable of something so extreme. We all held our secrets. Some darker than others, it seemed. Mr. Hawthorne, on the other hand, didn't surprise me, given I knew our teacher's secrets very well.

My brow twitched with the realisation as I turned back to the coded name on the paper Ela had shown me. If it came out that our English teacher had been having an inappropriate relationship with a student, I had a problem of my own. I could be in a bad situation this term.

'You've thought of this fast, haven't you?'

She nodded. 'I've prepared for this all summer, just in case. Now the party's here, I'm going for it. Goodbye Lucinda Darson.'

'Surely you could pick someone other than Lucinda.'

'Like who?' She tutted.

'I have no idea.'

'Lucinda it is.'

'Do you have to do this?'

'Why wouldn't I? I'm the chosen one.'

'Still...'

'Why? Did you want it, Junie?'

'No.' I sighed. 'It's just if you don't get this right, it could be worse than being shamed yourself. What if you don't manage to humiliate her enough and Dillan stays with her? What would've been the point?'

'We've been going to these parties for years now. I know what to do. Don't worry. Do you really think he'd give up his popularity for Lucinda? I don't think so. He may like her, but he loves attention even more. I've known him since we were children, nobody gets him better than me. It may have taken me this long to finally be with him, but I'm determined to use the threat list to my advantage.'

I seethed inside. I hated the threat list. Every season it came around, when you found out who'd become the next target and watch someone humiliated at the party, I wanted to burn the dumb thing to the ground.

It was the first time a friend had received the role and it put me in danger. Mr. Hawthorne, the teacher Lucinda was having an affair with, was the teacher I'd paid to keep up my grades at the height they were in all my classes by switching the grade papers for me. I'd made this arrangement with him over the last two years. I knew exactly what he was like. I'd threatened to expose the secrets I'd discovered after accidentally hacking into his email.

I had my own secrets to keep and faking my grades helped with one of them. If it leaked that I was a cheater, I was toast.

Knowing Ela, she would make sure the whole school knew she'd been the one to discover the affair, and there was a chance

Lucinda and Mr. Hawthorne would use me as payback against Ela after their public exposing. A friend who paid to keep their grades up would reflect badly on Ela. They could use my lie to shame us both.

In that case, I would be the one dying of social suicide and since I wasn't prepared for that, it seemed I'd have to play Ela against her own game.

Too bad for her I wasn't going to lose since I was the Dallington's unofficial queen and keeper of secrets. I didn't want to be a part of this party hell, but it seemed I had no choice this year. I was going to have to ruin Ela's plan and as she sat there all smugly, I began plotting myself. In this school, you had to protect yourself and I wasn't going to fall to save Ela Allard, the biggest gossip at Dallington.

I cleared my throat, pretending harder than ever to be on her side.

'Well, as long as you think it's right. I could never go to this much effort for the love of a guy though but it's up to you. I don't want you to make a misstep and get yourself hurt in the shaming.' I said.

'Don't worry about me, little Junie Han, I've been waiting for this day. Not only to climb even further on the social ladder but to get Dillan. I'm ready. Don't tell anybody what I've told you, of course. We've got a lot to plan.'

'We? You're involving Aisha and Maria?'

'Of Course, I need helpers and they're our friends, they should be here for me. I won't drag you into it since I know you actually want to do well in your exams and keep your grades high. See, I am a good friend. I want you to get into Oxford and live your best socialite life.' She patted my head and stood up.

'Thanks,' I say.

'Well, I better go and find them. I need to put my plan into action. We only have two weeks till the party!'

'Good luck.' I smiled, looking down at my notebook and the

code I'd been working on all morning.

'What are all those symbols?' Ela said, glancing down at my journal.

'Ah, it's just an equation for maths class.' I lied.

'You're even studying during your lunch break? How I wish I had that enthusiasm to learn. See you later; we have lots to get ready!'

She rushed out of the lunch hall and I began constructing a fresh source code. Coding was my thing, and it was going to be the tool to save Mr. Hawthorne, Lucinda, and myself. Faking grades was grounds for expulsion, and as much as I hated Dallington, having it on your list of achievements meant that the world could be yours. I wasn't going to lose that for Ela trying to secure some boy.

As Ela had her own secret going on, it seemed I had my own destroy mission too. One to save me. It was a shame I hadn't become the chosen one this year because the skills that I would use to make Ela fail her mission miserably would have made for a lot more fun. Then again, the last thing I wanted was to be popular at this school. I wanted to exist and that was it. To hide the part of myself that could cause so much chaos if it leaked. I was blackmailing my teacher to upkeep an image and if it ever collapsed, it could cost me my private world. Which was only one of my secrets, of course. But one that could destroy my image.

'So, a new game begins. It's been a while, nice to have some fun again.' I muttered to myself suddenly excited by the new work I'd have to start. I hadn't played anybody in so long, something I only did when my secrets were threatened and oddly it felt good to be playing with people again. I liked it once in a while, it made me feel alive.

I looked down at my notepad and evaluated the coding. A combination of well-crafted and formulated directions that could take down a city bank if I wanted it to. I'd solved my latest code breaker just in time for the start of the new season's game. Now I could use it to bribe a certain someone to help me on this party project. I was going to name it, *the save my ass*.

My eyes lit up at the thought and I soon pulled out my phone. After a few rings, a sleepy voice replied.

'Junie, I told you not to call today...' Yamazaki said, through a long yawn. 'I'm busy trying to take down some government official. I need full concentration.'

I rolled my eyes. 'Yamazaki, I've finally cracked our code.'

His voice soon brightened up. 'For the major American project?'

'Maybe.'

'Send it to me now!' He demanded.

'No.'

'No?'

'I'll give it to you if you help me out with something else.' I teased.

'You're threatening a hacker? A dark web hacker at that! You have some nerve.'

I laughed, lowering my voice. 'You won't get this code if you don't help me frame a friend.'

'Frame for what?' He grumbled.

'Let's just say I'm saving my reputation. If I don't do something about it, a secret could be leaked. Can you do it?'

'Do I have a choice? When it comes to your little secrets, I know you mean business whenever you call to ask for help'

'No, you have no choice, but I like to let you pretend you do.' I smiled to myself.

'What do you want me to do?'

'We'll talk tonight, but this code will be your reward if you help me out.'

'The usual, is it; saving your pristine reputation from something or someone?'

'Of course. Now I have to go. I'm in school and if I'm overheard talking to a Japanese hacker; well, you know how it could look.'

'I'll await your mail and your code. I can't believe you've played me again to do something for you for nothing but a damned code...'

'I'm the queen of coding for a reason, Yamazaki. Just one of the many secrets I'm trying to keep hidden alongside my fake grades.'

As I put down the phone, I looked around the cafeteria to see everyone still buzzing with excitement. Little did they know the only chosen one wasn't sat far from them this season and was about to cause destruction herself. On the threat list or not. I would be turning the tables to save myself. That was how I played this game, after all, living the rich life. We all had to protect ourselves to keep our secrets and I wasn't even going to let my best friend ruin it for me. Even if it meant I had to ruin her instead.

Sorry, Ela. The only one being humiliated at the party is you. We all have our secrets to keep at Dallington and you're in my way of getting out of this lie of a life.

Chapter Two

The screen's electrified and I'm ready to kill.

'In two seconds, I'll send you a link and you'll have one minute to hack into the site and take the information we need, can you do it?'

As Yamazaki spoke into my headset, I scoffed at his lack of belief in me. 'Why would you ask me that when I always say I'm the *Queen of Coding* as a reply?'

He scoffed back. 'Okay, *Queen of Coding*. Let's see how fast you are! But take it seriously, this will be our biggest joint project yet, with lots of money at stake. I'm not talking to you through our headsets for no reason.'

He was right, it was strange to be hearing each other's voices in such a manner since we usually only communicated through a chat box when it came to our joint ventures. I soon forged ahead, ready for attack.

After making sure all my tools were set up - the security walls that defended me from leaking my own information, and my own perfectly crafted virus ready to bleed into my next victims' site - I got to work.

'I'm ready for the link,' I said.

Within seconds a closed-off HTML box arrived. I clicked onto it and hacked into the site of a government agency we were being employed to take down. I then let a virus out into the system to give me freedom, I dug through the pages with a complex scanner, got the information our client wanted, and soon removed all my details before closing down another task.

'It's done,' I said, sighing after a mere few seconds of tapping some codes into my keyboard. Even though I knew my hacking skills were top quality, it still never could stop the sick feeling filling my stomach that came each time we did something high profile like this.

Yamazaki let out his usual long drawn eh out of surprise. 'Fifty seconds, a new record... How do you do it so fast? What program did you use for this, Epicstar?'

I laughed as he swore in Japanese under his breath. 'Epicstar is for baby hackers. Yamazaki, don't you create your coding tools and programs?'

'Of course. But I still use a program and none of them are that fast!'

'What can I say,' I laughed, proud of myself. 'Why do you think I'm the number one hacker on the Serpan Pin Leader board? I'm in top place for a reason.'

Yamazaki scoffed. 'Hey, I'm number two and I'm not even that fast. Anyway, just tell me your secret. How was that possible?'

'What kind of dark web hacker would I be if I shared my secrets with you? I'm not telling anybody anything. You need to study more. I don't get how you don't know what I did to be that fast.'

'Someone helps you, don't they? Or I do know you're good at creating viruses and sending them to infect the site as a fast distraction for the moderators of it, so you don't have to battle so much while they fight off the bug and you get the information. There is no way you can do this all so fast any other way. You hear me, one day, I'll find out what is going on and knock you off the top spot that used to be mine!'

It always made me laugh when Yamazaki and I worked on projects like this because it would frustrate him that I was faster. Though he was right in thinking of the virus trick since it was the most effective way to give you enough time to get what you wanted. While the operators tamed the beast I had infected their site with, I worked quickly and got out without being traced. I always loved these moments as he tried to figure out how I was so good when he already knew the answer

'Forget it. You'll never know. Maybe it's my virus skill or that I'm just a better hacker than you. Anyway, we've completed another task together. Another agency hack for a fee, completed. How much did we make in Yen from this when we split it?'

'About two million yen each and I know what I'm buying from this.' He said excitedly.

'What? Another figurine?'

'No! I bought all those the last time we made this much money. This time it'll go towards a new higher-tech coding set because I need to learn how to do this faster than you. I'll beat you one day and take my rightful place at number one like before you came along to Serpan and ruined everything!'

'Keep saying it, not going to happen. Try all you want but you'll never get it back while I'm around.' I teased. He never failed to amuse me because I knew he hated being beaten.

Even though we were close friends, when it came to hacking, it was both a game and a business, and no hacker that used the dark web as their main hacking space liked to be beaten. It was why they brought their skills here; to challenge themselves on the edgy and risky side of the web.

Serpan was a place where we all fought for the top place each month. Compiled by how many people had been successful at hacking into the site listings Serpan posted each week on the forum space. The site was not only a place where we could all talk about the hacking world but also where, each week, a compilation of strange sites would be posted that we would hack into. The deeper a person got into, the higher they were on the leader board. These sites weren't just for any lone hacker, you had to have the best skills as some sites on the dark web were heavily manned for good reasons, it was all illegal stuff here. The more sites you could break into, the higher you would rank.

'You just watch, I'll do it!' Yamazaki snapped back, sending me a gif of a guy fist-pumping the air in determination to win this lone game he played through our chatbox. 'Anyhow, what time is it over in England? It took us so long to finally get into that site. It is always weird when we're done in seconds.'

I sat back in my chair and stretched. 'It's about three in the morning here and…'

As I sat mid-stretch, my amusement was soon paused when I heard familiar shuffled footsteps on the landing outside my bedroom and knew trouble was ahead.

'Oh crap, my mum's here,' I said, lowering my tone as I worked quickly to close some of my screens that had tabs open nobody needed to see. 'I have to go, talk later.' I saw her shadow illuminate under the doorframe and began to panic.

Yamazaki made a grumbling sound. 'Oh, you better hide. Don't want your mother to know you're a sociopathic hacker stealing information from the government. Better put on your angelic act. Anyway, I'll send the information to our client. Sayonara, Pachi-san!'

'Pachi-san? If you call me that again…' I was about to rage as he knew I hated him calling me that. A Pachi was a famous hacker who had been caught lying about their skills and were framed as being the biggest hoax in the hacker community. But he soon hung up and I threw off my headphones and closed the program to a more normal-looking screen.

'Junie, it's three in the morning. What on earth are you still doing on the computer at this time?'

Light flooded into my bedroom as mother's voice poured inside the dimly lit space. Since I always worked in my room by nothing but the screen light of my computers, it took my eyes a few seconds to focus on her body illuminated by only the hall light. Her usual stance when she was angry, placing her hands on her hips. She threw on my bedroom light a second later and I recoiled at the sudden light breathing into my room, immediately covering my sensitive eyes. Given I'd been sat at my computer since I got home from school at six; it was hardly surprising it felt like the sun had slapped me.

'Please, switch it off...' I groaned. Managing to open them slightly to see her come further into my room.

She stepped forward and analysed everything, scanning over my computer and me as if I was hiding some hidden tale. Which I was, but she needn't know.

'No, I won't switch it off. Not until you go to bed. I could hear you typing away at that keyboard as I walked past your room to get a drink of water. Why are you up, Junie? You have school in a few hours.'

I let out a sigh and slid off my headphones, blinking a few more times before turning to face my mother who stood in her fluffy pink dressing gown and dishevelled red bed hair, glaring at me with a scowl. I needed to get a new keyboard, learn to type more gently and talk quieter when I wore my headphones. But when I got in the zone, I couldn't help myself, and sadly, it had caught me out.

'I'm finishing some of my art class project.' I lied.

I scanned her face, hoping she believed me. Lines continued to grow on her forehead. 'I would like to believe that.' She huffed. 'But I saw your screen was on some social media site. If you're studying, where are your supplies, and why have you left it till this late?'

She looked over my messy desk, covered in food wrappers and discarded drink cans. Not a study material was in sight.

I shrugged. 'Nothing and because I was too busy. It wasn't on a social media site; I was closing a tab. I didn't need my supplies because I have it all online. I'm finished now though. I promise.'

She scoffed. 'You're done the exact time I come to find you still awake. Why do I smell a fishy situation here, eh?'

'What do you have to be suspicious of, mum? I'm hardly a criminal or anything.' I half laughed.

She shot me a quizzical gaze. 'I was going to say you were chatting with some boys, but what is with you saying something criminal related?'

I internally rolled my eyes. This was my mother. The kind of person who always had to know what was going on, no matter whether it counted or not. Even though she had no clue I had just hacked the government and stole highly secret information, and been awarded over ten grand for doing so, she still acted like this. It was annoying, amusing, and sad how she still treated me like a kid using the internet for the first time, even though I was seventeen and knew right from wrong. I could almost drive and would be going off to university to live by myself next year and yet she operated every minute of my life like a military operation. Parents are strange creatures indeed and the lack of trust was frightening.

I pretended to close off my computer to please her, before going over to throw her out. 'I'm going to sleep now, I promise. Goodnight, Mum.'

She didn't keep up the talk and I managed to push her away, I listened for a while to make sure she went back to her room before sliding back into my seat and switched the screen back on from black. Even though I'd just completed a client's work with Yamazaki, I still had plenty more to do. I was in the middle of a huge coding project right now. Sleep wasn't allowed.

I put my headset back on and called back Yamazaki, quietly. 'Mum is gone. Let's do another project.'

'You're back?' He laughed through a mouthful of food.

'Yes. Since it's early in Japan. We might as well do another one.'

'Don't you have school soon?'

'Yes, but forget about it. You know I have my teacher to fix my grades. I fail everything so I don't need to worry. You have school as well but here we are, being criminals and hacking weakly manned government sites. I'm in the zone to make even more money tonight after that. Talking of money, how about a proposition for you instead, what I was telling you about earlier today?'

'So, it was a virus you used to be so fast!' He scoffed. 'And when you say the word proposition, why do I get a bad feeling?'

'I need your help with something. I told you.'

'Let me guess, another cover-up of your wild secrets being exposed to your privileged world?'

'Wow, you know me so well!' Asking for help from Yamazaki wasn't a new concept. Over the years, when times came that my secrets could be revealed, I always asked him for help to fix things. As much as I said his skills were bad, he was good at extracting the information out there for me to make a mockery of another person. I was good at making viruses; he was the king of making people look dumb.

'Because in all these years we've known each other, that is the only time you ask for my help. Normally you're saying I'm a terrible hacker and yet you need me! What is it though?'

'Well, this time it seems the fact I pay for my high grades could be exposed, so I need your help to take down my friend and humiliate her. I found out that Ela plans to use a video of this girl that has a crazy secret. I have a crazy video of Ela to switch it with; I just want you to put it on a USB drive. How about it?'

'And you're giving me the code from earlier as a reward?'

'Yup.'

'Fine, deal. You and these schemes. You sure are an evil kid for doing this to your friend. Why're you so obsessed with your societal image that you'll do anything to keep yourself from being exposed? All you are is a hacker, what is the big deal about getting exposed.'

'It's not just about that. The fact my teacher fakes my grades could be leaked. That could get me out of every school, idiot.

You have no idea what it's like at this academy. I have to threaten him to keep up my grades, I have to hide that I'm an evil bitch and a hacker. They use everything against you and if I don't keep up the act, well, goodbye me escaping this damned place.'

'All you have to do is study and be good, can't be that hard?'

'If it was that easy, I would be doing it. You have no idea what this wealthy society is like. Everything runs on lies and secrets. Besides, I'm doing all of this to get out of England and into The University of Tokyo, to see you, aren't I?'

Yamazaki scoffed. 'Yes, let's not pretend it isn't to get away from your parents and high society once and for all. Not for me.'

'Forget what I said and let's go. Can you do it or not?' I joked.

'Send me the code and it'll be done in seconds. What are you planning to do to this girl to save yourself though, what's this video of your friend that could shame her instead?'

I smiled to myself that once again I was using his skill to save myself. 'This video contains something that will embarrass her enough to never humiliate someone again, a secret video that was taken on my hacking phone and I need you to place it on this USB the moment she plugs it in that night at the event. Thank you, Yamazaki. Now, let's take on another project!'

'That school sounds wild, but you always do what's best for yourself. You want to get back to work now? You're crazy, Junie. Any normal hacker would be exhausted from what we've done. We've been at it all night!'

'Yes, but we aren't normal hackers. It seems the excitement of this public humiliation to save myself is fun. Now are you up for it, or do you want to remain in the number two spot forever?' I challenged him. 'This is good practice for your skills, the more you hack means the better you will get at hacking into those crazy sites later. See, where would you be if I didn't get you to do these little games once in a while? I'm training you!'

Yamazaki huffed at me for bringing up such a thing, but I knew his competitive nature would make him unable to refuse.

'Firstly, you don't do these tasks in case you were caught at school, and that is why you get me to do it; and second, of course, I'm ready. Let's get hacking, Pachi-san!' He teased back.

'Stop calling me that!' I half yelled before we fell back into another hacking scheme that night.

That was my world. My true world. It was only a shame that when I left that room, I couldn't be this girl. The coding queen of the dark web. If my mother found out, it would do more than shock her. All she and the world outside saw was the pristine girl that did as told through the day. The girl who was kind, and unassuming. The world had many parallels, and this was my own. To survive this crazy planet and get what I wanted from it.

To have two versions of myself, was the only way for me to survive in a society that hated people being themselves. When the computer shut down, so did my personality for the evening. When morning struck, Miss Pristine awoke as she did every day. To survive, we had to play for ourselves and nobody was going to ruin my future of escaping this toxicity.

Chapter Three

The beginning of my two parallel worlds always started with a knock on my bedroom door. No words. No morning call. Just a simple knock by my mother to make sure I hadn't slept at my desk again. I waited for her slippers to shift away across the landing carpet before my eyes split open and I greeted the world with my usual sigh for waking so casually. I looked over to my window and once again I'd forgotten to close my curtains after a late night of hacking, so the morning sun streamed an image of light onto the end of my bedsheets, making my eyes squint with annoyance.

I wallowed there for a few moments as my aching body from the late night caught up with me. Another day of pretending I hadn't just hacked a government website. It had to be a record for how long I've sat and hacked in one night straight and I knew today was going to be hell because of it. However, it was time to be my normal self again, whether I liked it or not. The night hacker girl was about to go on pause mode for a few hours till she sat back in her desk chair for another evening.

I lifted myself from bed a few moments after the awakening that I should've been used to by now, given this was my usual alarm. I recoiled when I walked into the light shining from my window. As I stood right in the view, it streamed into my sensitive eyes, almost making me slip on a can of soda I'd discarded onto the floor the previous evening in the process.

This was the only problem I found when staying up all hours and staring into a computer screen, it completely messed up your vision. I stood and let my eyes adjust for a few seconds before bracing the day and storming to my bathroom to get ready for the day and mask the monstrosity I'd become from lack of sleep.

After washing, I put on my school uniform. The hideous yet expensive mash-up of a tartan patterned green skirt and matching tie and an ugly long green blazer that did nothing but cover you in a mound of unappealing itchy fabric that I had to wear for seven hours straight each school day. And pretend to be happy about it.

Fixing my tie in place and trying to get over my disgust for the uniform, I gazed towards my appearance and lightly pulled at the bags that lay heavily under my swollen eyes. My dark circles were terrible right now, I was staying up later than usual because I had gotten a sudden influx of hacking work alongside the government tasks, and I couldn't resist the money that came with it. It made me reach for my concealer, knowing if my mother saw me looking this dead, she would suspect even more that I wasn't using all my free hours of the day to study.

She'd been doing that a lot lately. Pouncing on me at random times to check on me. I knew she was up to something and I'd a feeling it was because the end of my final year was coming soon. She was making sure I was prepared to keep the high fake grades needed for admission to Oxford. I had to be careful right now. Not that she would suspect my hacking life, but still, I couldn't risk her breaking down the mask of normality I'd worked so hard to build. Exam season always brought out her intense side but she'd never been so insistent, making sure I was doing the best I could at all times of the day.

I placed a ton of the concealer under my eyes as well as one annoying blemish below my chin and blended my sins away. I brushed the tangled mess of my long black hair and straightened my fringe. It now covered half of my eyes and needed cutting, but straightening it managed to solve that issue for the moment. I took one last glance before heading downstairs, smiling to myself. I looked as normal as usual today. That was all that mattered. I would walk down these stairs and black-haired, blue-eyed, average height Junie Han would become me, with a fake, warm smile permanently etched across my mouth.

After a usual breakfast filled with trivial conversation at the dining table with my parents, I was soon sat in the back of my mother's car. She took me to school before heading to work, where I would see neither her nor my dad for hours after. I didn't see them much, but I didn't mind. I wanted it that way. The less effort to upkeep this image the better.

'Are you feeling ready for your exam this morning?' She said, much to my surprise, as we never usually spoke at this time. She liked to focus on thoughts of her meetings.

I lifted my gaze to hers as she looked through the rear-view mirror, forcing a slight smile. 'Yes, it should be okay.'

I sighed internally at the thought. I had to sit there for an hour to take an exam knowing that a few hours later a fake score would be overwritten. It was a plan I'd put together a couple of years ago after I found our teacher had been having a relationship with another student like he was now with Lucinda. I used it to my advantage as I did with everything, threatening to expose him if he didn't switch every paper and test I took with a better grade. All so I could focus on hacking rather than studying. The last two years that had passed and it had worked like a treat. He continued to change my grades and we never spoke about it again. Nevertheless, it was boring to keep having to take an exam that I'd pass regardless.

'You know, after last night, I'm thinking about taking your computers away from you.'

My eyes darted towards her, confused by the sudden topic

of choice.

'Why would you do that?'

'Since you're using the internet to study and not your books. Not only will you be damaging your eyes but there's more chance of distraction and that's not something you need right now.'

Out came my mother's obsession with studying like some student from the nineteen hundreds. She hated me using screens to study and ever since I could remember she'd forced a book into my hands. She eventually let me get the computers and little did she know, I'd never studied on a day in my life. Both my parents had graduated from Oxford and believed books had all the answers we needed and lead to less distraction than using a computer. I never understood her obsession.

'Are you talking about last night? I told you, I was finishing an art project. I don't get distracted. How else would my grades be this high? You search things up on the internet, why won't you believe me? That is all I am doing when I'm using them.'

She tsked. 'Not just about last night but these last few months you've been on them far more than ever. I'm only saying this to help you. More than just studying, you're doing something else. You seem to be on it whenever you're at home.'

'Have you been spying on me?'

'Not spying, just making sure you're focusing. It's your most important season right now. I want to make sure you're focusing on the right things. I didn't get into Oxford by slacking, Junie; I studied every free moment I got. You don't just need to study for exams, but your interview as well to get in. That is a huge task which you should be working towards, but don't seem to be.'

'What's with this suddenly?'

'Nothing. I want you to succeed and you can't if you're on the computer all hours.'

'By suggesting taking away the computers that I use to study?'

'You know how I am during exam seasons. I'm always like this. I just believe books are better than those technological boxes.'

I dug my nails into my palms and looked out the window. My online persona was screeching profanity in my mind. She would die if she knew what I was thinking but as usual, I bit my tongue.

I replaced my angst with a usual sweet obedient reply. 'I'm sorry, Mum. I'll try harder from now on. I suppose I've been too lazy if you feel this way. Not putting in as much effort now, the end of term is coming soon. I won't let it happen again.'

She nodded back. 'Be sure to. You do want to get into Oxford, after all. That's the only reason I'm being this way. I know what it takes to get into that school. I'm only looking out for you. Both your father and me. So, get your focus back or I'm taking away your computers and you'll be back to books. I don't know why you need so many computers as it is. Your room right now is like some technology hub.'

To hack multiple things at once. That's why.

We ended our conversation when we arrived at my pretentious private school that hid neatly at the edge of a country estate. I slammed my way out of the car without uttering another word. After she drove off, I walked around the corner and kicked the side of the entrance gate hard, before composing myself and walking inside the manor-style property that filled me with nothing but irritation.

School was important, I knew that, and I had to make it seem like I was trying even harder than usual. I cared so much that I threatened a teacher for these fake grades. I knew how privileged I was to be able to complain about going here and not being able to be myself in the real world. However, it didn't mean things couldn't be hard. Still, I knew I'd have to cut off some jobs to equal things out. I needed to refrain from staying up so late and making it look like I wasn't working hard or was spending too much time on my computer.

I couldn't wait to get out of this household and school. Playing a role was not fun. But I had to be careful about how I handled this. How I reacted to my parents. Because if they found out the true me, it could jeopardise my plan of escaping this world when I graduated, and nothing was going to do that. I had to cut back on the hacking and pull on my mask again, even closer than before. After all, I wasn't only doing this to keep up societal appearances, but also to hide my escape route, and get into The University of Tokyo secretly, and live my best life with Yamazaki. Even if on fake grades. Nobody knew this plan and it was going to stay that way. I wanted out of this world and away from these people.

As I stood at the grounds, dreaming of my secret plans, I felt my phone buzz in my blazer, meaning it was time for today's mission to begin.

'Have you got the video yet?' Yamazaki said a moment after I'd accepted the call.

I clicked my tongue, annoyed at the lack of a simple hello. 'Nope. But I will do it soon. Calm down, you don't even need the video till the day of the party.'

'I want it now so I can be ready for the day of the party. Hacking into USB drives isn't easy, you know. I need you to send the location IP information as well as where it will be. Where is the video right now?'

'On my hacking phone. I left the damned thing in my locker yesterday because I was figuring out that coding hack for some site I wanted to break into.'

'To break into a site? This isn't the code you told me was for our American project. Is it?'

I laughed, him knowing I'd conned him again. 'I can work on two codes at once and no, I do still have the other.' I lied. The only code I had was one to get into a new site posted on Serpan, which everyone was having trouble getting into. I'd been working on it for days and finally cracked it.

'Well, you better not be lying. What is this video exactly?'

I laughed under my breath. 'I told you. It's just of Ela exposing a secret of hers. It will end her in seconds, but she'll be fine in the end, popular kids always are. I just need to send her a message strong enough to leave my teacher and this scandal alone, to never shame someone again so she can leave me be.'

'Whatever. It sounds intriguing, though you're weird for having such a video in the first place. Just send it over and I will do the switch of videos. How long will you be, I need to head out soon?'

'I have to do these weird things in case of stuff like this happening, don't I. Not long anyhow. I just need to get my hacking phone and then I'll send it over.'

'Alongside the code!'

'Okay, okay. I have to go. If I'm seen talking to you like this it could end me. Now, bye.'

'I will await your mail, Pachi-san. How I do love a good destruction session with you sometimes.'

I hung up, ignoring his comment, and deleted his name from my phone. Having him on my normal mobile was never a good idea in case people asked questions. I regained my composure and headed into school, to put on the mask and get the video that would make sure it was glued back on forever. Yamazaki was right though; although I hated the risk of my secrets being exposed, once in a while I did love a good secret destruction game. Playing with people without them knowing could be fun. If it all went well, of course.

Chapter Four

When Dallington wasn't hosting luxury parties for the wealthy, it was an average prep academy in the middle of the Northern English countryside. The school was well known for how many established people had graduated from its ancient walls, and even though it was twenty miles from my home, thanks to the prestige, my mother didn't care about making the tour each day to take me there.

As I stood in the locker-lined halls and the abundance of rich faces passed me, I wanted to pixelate into the floor and sit back in my computer chair away from this irritating academy. It was hard work keeping up an image. Especially in a place where the people made you go crazy every five seconds for the stupid things they said. My online self would respond with such sharpness, so it was hard to hold my tongue when people talked about the world in such a futile manner. But I had no choice.

When I arrived, I was known as the preppy girl who always loved to help people, who was always kind to those around her. Not many people had a negative thing to say about the Junie Han who was presented to everyone outside my computer. I was part of a popular group of friends and being the good girl of the group made me seem unthreatening, yet no one would mess with me, as my friends would end your social life if you dared try them. A thing I purposefully looked for in friends was an extroverted nature so I could fade into the background a little more.

'Junie, are you ready for the exam today? Looks like I'm about to fail maths!' Ela Allard said appearing by my side with a lacklustre expression.

'You could say that again. Me and Maria ended up staying up late last night chatting with some guy from Anderson Wood Boarding School, so it looks like we're in the failure zone too.' Aisha sighed next to her.

'Nothing new. We always fail.' Maria added. The final member of our clique, leaning against the locker beside mine.

I looked at my friends and forced out a fake half-laugh in response. Ela Allard was my oldest friend, a girl I'd known since the start of primary school and one who'd always been the same. Blonde, tanned, and sure of herself. The only things that had changed were her height, and her love for boys had grown even more. Or one boy, Dillan Smith, who she loved enough to embarrass his girlfriend just to get him.

Then there was Aisha Kaminski. A glowing goddess who every boy wanted. She was quick-witted, sharp with her words, and had more boyfriends than I could count. Finally, standing at four-foot-nothing, boisterous Maria King. The loudest of the group who never failed to humiliate herself at least twice a day and had the greatest mound of curly hair you'd ever seen. Nothing much fazed her.

There I stood, in between them all. My friends, thinking I was a calm and quiet person they could speak with about anything, as I was apparently such a good listener. When in reality, I hated every second in anybody's company. I was a lone soul, and not because I hated people, but simply because I wanted out of this school and society. Or maybe I'd never found a good enough friend to match Yamazaki. That was why I'd chosen to surround myself with these girls. Because I wasn't the best at performing as an extrovert without them, a popular image at this school.

It may've seemed like I was using them, and I suppose I was. But didn't we all to some degree, to coast along in school and life? We used people for everything, no matter the stage of our lives. I just wasn't open about it. To myself, yes. To others, not so much. In order to survive in society, that was sometimes the way it had to be. We had to use people to both hide and receive things. That was the way it worked and if you couldn't handle it, then be prepared to lead a miserable life.

'I don't even know why I asked you.' Ela sighed towards me, flicking her hair over her shoulder. 'You never fail at anything.'

'That isn't true. I fail at having a boyfriend.' I joked. Since their favourite topics were boys or beauty, it kept me normal to them when I shared interest in these occasionally.

'That's true. However, we'll fix that soon. I'm still on the lookout for a guy for you.' Ela came and placed her arm around my shoulders. 'Don't worry, I'm working on it.'

'Good to know.' I lied.

'At this moment though, our main focus alongside securing you a boyfriend, is to take care of Lucinda. I can't wait. Honestly, it may sound evil but the thought of this public social execution has me itching with excitement. Nobody will see it coming!'

'I still can't get over you telling us you're the chosen one...' Aisha cackled with delight. She always did like a good secret.

'Shush, Aisha, don't say it so loudly. But yeah, I'm pretty excited, myself. However, I couldn't do it without you guys, that's for sure.'

'I still don't understand why Junie isn't involved in the plotting; all we've done is tell her what is going to happen on the day. Shouldn't she have been doing something more?' Maria added.

'We've already got the plan ready so there's no point now, and I told you, she's studying. You know how hard Junie works; I didn't want to involve her in this. I'm a good friend, you know. Besides, you and Aisha love scheming so much. Who else would I need?'

'That's true.' I said and we all laughed. 'How has the plotting been? Are you ready?'

'Oh, yes. Everything's in place now.'

'Have you got the USB drive ready with this video of yours?' I asked.

'Yup.' Ela smirked. 'That video will kill her. I still can't believe she's having an affair with Mr. Hawthorne though. I never would've guessed such a thing, I'm so glad I caught that moment of them. It was meant to be!'

They all laughed in chorus like a bunch of cackling witches, and it almost made me feel better about my own evil actions and myself. These guys didn't care about anybody but securing what they wanted and would go to great lengths to do so. Maybe this would teach them all an unintended lesson: to not be so ruthless.

It wasn't long before we began our classes for the day. Those three continued their excitement about the event of destruction. I was back to hours of droning on about subjects that hardly interested me. If I wasn't hacking, I wanted to sleep. However, before I headed to my class, which was the first exam of the day before lunch, I made a quick detour to my locker to get my burner phone.

I only used it in emergencies or when I needed to give out a fake number to clients. I quickly took it out and hid around the corner of the locker line, to sift through the videos I had and find the one I needed that I'd taken of Ela weeks ago, exposing her very own secret that I was going to use to save my future.

I often did this to people. I would gather information on them, and maybe I would never use it, but I did so anyhow in case one day they tried to expose me. I usually only did this to my close friends. I'd so much stuff on them that if I wanted, I could burn their reputations to the ground like they were going to with Lucinda. It may seem evil, but I only ever touched stuff like this video when I needed it. Like at this moment.

I attached it to an email to send to Yamazaki and quickly sent it off. He replied a few seconds later with a devil emoji and thumbs up. Plan destroy Ela's reputation for five minutes to save my own would soon be ready for the party this Friday. I smiled to myself, before hiding my phone in a secret pocket in my blazer. I could rest assured I was safe, because Yamazaki and I never failed.

As lunch came around after classes, we sat in our usual spaces in the lunch hall and it wasn't long before the conversation turned to boys again and I was back to pretending to care.

'Should I tell her now, or what?' Ela suddenly sparked up as I took a gulp of my drink. Lunch was normally a time I let them talk but today it seemed I was the topic of choice, so I had to zone back in for a change.

'Tell me what?' I asked, trying to make myself seem engaged.

The three of them looked at each other before nodding. 'About project find Junie a boyfriend. I think I may have found you a guy.' Ela continued.

'Who?' I laughed, internally sighing.

She turned and pointed to a group in the corner of the lunch hall by the old manor windows. 'You know Theodore Hawk-Silberston, right? It seems he has a big crush on you.'

Theodore Hawk-Silberston. The name was familiar to me because I'd known Theodore as a kid, but we hadn't talked for so long, so it surprised me now to hear such a thing. I looked over to the group to see his face, laughing beside his friends. I didn't know how he was as a person these days but given the football group he hung around with were hyper guys and always causing mischief, I didn't hold much hope.

'And you'd know that how?' I directed back to Ela, hoping to squash the fact.

'Because Ela has a big fat crush on Dillan, how else? He's Dillan's best friend and he told her Theodore has been talking about you a lot lately, all so suddenly.' Maria replied.

'Dillan told you that?' I asked Ela

She nodded. 'Yeah, he did. So, if you want a boyfriend, there you go.'

The thought was too weird to conjure up. 'I knew Theodore as a kid, but we haven't talked in years. No thanks. It's kind of weird he's been watching me and I didn't even know it.'

'Oh, come on, that is even better.' Ela prompted. 'Don't you think it will be nice for us to be dating friends when I expose Lucinda, and I finally make my move on Dillan? It will be so exciting.'

'I love that you're excited to think your plan will work, but the fact that he watched me? No way.' I scoffed.

'Well, should I tell Dillan to tell Theodore you're thinking about it?'

I narrowed my gaze. 'No.'

She held up her hands. 'Fine! I'll keep up the search elsewhere. But you're crazy, Theodore is cute as hell. I would go for him if I wasn't into Dillan.'

'Well, he's all yours.' I laughed. 'Go for both of them like Aisha would.'

'Hey...' Aisha pouted but we all laughed, knowing she rarely only had one boyfriend at a time.

Looking over at the group made me think about Yamazaki, if anything. My best friend, who was closer to my heart than anyone. Which was strange given we'd never met in person, only heard our voices and chatted over webcam. We weren't exactly in a relationship, but we knew it would happen eventually, so even having this conversation was funny to me.

As lunch ended, Dillan walked past with his group. Theodore smiled at me. It was weird, and sudden. I'd never even paid attention to them before, other than when they were playing pranks in the halls on people. I wondered how long Theodore had been watching me. I ignored them as they passed, elsewise provoke an invitation to talk to me. Dating rumours weren't something I needed right now. I was trying to save my teacher from having his secrets spewed out everywhere.

'You sure you don't want me to tell Dillan?' Ela said as we all got up to throw away our lunch trays.

'Trust me. I'm working on finding someone myself. It'll be worth the wait.' I replied as she linked Maria's arm.

'Okay, whatever you want, then. I'll continue the search elsewhere. This isn't the end. Who knows, after my fun destruction match at the party this Friday, you could leave with a new date, like I hopefully will with Dillan!' Ela assured me and as the group left, my burner phone pinged and I smiled to see Yamazaki's name.

Yamazaki always knew how to save the day and make me feel better, even for five minutes when I had to be in this exhausting play. I scanned the message with intrigue.

I got the video; task be ready to destroy your friend's reputation through an evil turn of secret events is ready to act out on the day. I watched that video though and all I can say is your friend sure is obsessed with this guy. Going through all of this just to get rid of his girlfriend, what a waste of time. This video will embarrass her. You're so evil for doing this!

Of course, I'm evil, but everyone at this school is, I'm just silent about what I do. Anyhow, well done Mr. Yamazaki. I will send you over the code I promised. But, I'm sorry to say, it was actually a code to hack into one of the Serpan board sites. I'm sure you'll enjoy looking at this hard to hack site though, right? It could get you your number one spot back if you are the first one to get inside the site before me, better hurry!

Junie... I'm gonna kill you!

Chapter Five

A Dallington Academy party was comprised of two things: to flaunt themselves and share gossip about the failings or amusements of other wealthy families. Because money seemed to hold no meaning. These families battled to throw out as many pound notes as they could in the school auction held alongside the party. To beat each other in the buying department for items they'd soon toss away just like their disposable income and all so that the money could go to another new chandelier in the cafeteria so they could say they bought it at the next gathering.

But tonight, this party was sweeter than ever. The air held a tone of vengeance to those that knew what was going to happen. That it was here a reputation was about to be burned to the ground to save another's.

Before the destruction began, the clock struck seven and my limo pulled up outside the academy. It was a strange sight returning to the place I'd been only a few hours before, to see it bright and ready for some grand event. You were stunned by the glowing affair, bombarded by light from every angle. Given the usual bland gothic stone, it now looked far more appealing hidden away behind a barrage of warm lights and fake flowers. As I pulled my studded stilettos onto the gravelled path below, it took a moment for my eyes to adjust to the flamboyant setting. A whole season had passed since the last Dallington party, after all. A statement had to be made.

'It's as bold as ever here then.' I said pulling myself out of the limo, standing to face the front entrance. 'They never fail on making it look like a fancy Parisian hotel. Do they?'

'Of course not.' My mother replied beside me, smoothing out her silver diamond encrusted dress. 'These parties are the highlight of each season. We don't go half-hearted at a place like Dallington.'

'Of course, we don't.' I replied, raising a smile as she walked ahead of me and handed her coat to the attendees. A smile that was as fake as every other adult there. Pretending they were there other than to brag.

'This is going to be another eventful party.' I sighed to myself, handing my coat over, before following my mother.

I had reason to sigh, and not for the bragging match that I'd have to be a part of that evening. It lay deeper than anything my parents even knew of. The only reason teenagers attended their adult affairs. Those parties never came without the annihilation of something or someone. Every time I had to pretend, like every other student who hadn't become this season's target, that I enjoyed watching someone burn to the ground. That time however, I knew, because for once I was secretly involved, even if by my own doing. Anything that made me need to protect myself and see if I could pull off what I'd planned oddly gave me a sense of thrill. Elite Academies were very strange places. I had to pretend I liked it here to survive. But then so did everyone else.

Taking off my coat upon entry to reveal the luxury dress, I could feel eyes shoot my way. Gazing at all the designer fabric that apparently meant so much to them, enough to comment on as I passed through the crowds, I headed to the main hall.

The hall that normally occupied our daily movements between classes had been transformed from the average, dull brown panelled walls and antiques, to a haven of warm lights, glowing objects, and beverages. People were crammed in every corner, brimming with enthusiasm for the night's get together, talking over glasses of champagne.

'Wow, it's even grander than last season. I've never seen it look so pretty in here.' My mother said, as awestruck as usual. Nothing ever changed in these parties, but as usual, keeping up appearances was the order of the day. And not just for me.

I nodded my agreement. I wasn't the biggest fan of school. Though, in truth, the décor so beautifully masked the usual dull aesthetic. I had to admit, it was pretty.

'Yes, well. Talking of beauty, it seems the whole Darson family is waiting to judge your outfit. You better go over right away.'

The Darsons were related to Lucinda Darson, the girl Ela thought she was taking down tonight. They'd been friends of my parents since their Oxford days, but I'd always kept my distance. Too much talk of Oxford made me nauseous since I would rather sell my soul than follow in their footsteps. And everyone thought I'd end up going there. The less I talked about the fact, the better. So, I'd always kept my distance, frustrated at the mere talk of them trying to dictate my future and I wasn't going to risk letting a rude comment and ruining things.

'You're going so soon?' My mother sighed.

I knew she hated pretending as much as I did, but she had no choice in the matter. She had to remain with the adults and talk of how beautiful Oxford was and how they couldn't wait to visit me there.

'Yes. I'm sure they can't wait to start the gossip.'

She rolled her eyes at my statement. 'You better head straight to the student section then. You know they hate both sides mixing, even for a few moments.'

I nodded, feeling sick as I knew what lay ahead for me in the next party hall. The waiting destruction.

'Yes, I have to go and see my friends right away. I'll see you at the auction.'

'Enjoy the night.' She waved me off, dancing over to the Darsons, who greeted her with faux smiles as they praised her dress.

'Oh, I will.' I smiled; the only genuine smile of the soon to be chaotic evening.

I stormed through the adult crowd and headed to the second hall where the student party was held and looked for my friends. If I were too late Ela wouldn't be happy, and she was the one I needed on my side the most in the line of fire that night. I couldn't have her suspecting anything about me and what I was up to. She had eyes like a hawk so I had to work hard.

I gazed around the second party hall before spotting Ela, Maria and Aisha plotting in the corner of the room. They looked like a group of witches, huddled and ready for causing hell. I so wished I could've melted into the ground and pretended I didn't exist, all to avoid the night's hell, but I had to pretend to enjoy it. Every student did. It was the rule of survival.

'Here she is,' Ela said, waving me over before I could utter a sound. 'You're late!'

'It's just gone seven. I had to study before getting here.' I lied. 'We do have an exam on Monday.'

'And yet, I said to get here ten minutes earlier. So we could talk. Exam or not.'

'I don't know how many more times we could go over this...' I groaned as Maria passed me a glass of fake champagne, which I soon downed.

'Junie, this plan has to be bulletproof. We're about to take a girl down and I can't be found out.' Ela snapped at my lack of enthusiasm. 'I know I didn't involve you much, but I still want you to be here to support me.'

Ela turned to Maria. 'Did you bring the USB?'

Maria produced an evil smile. 'Of course.'

The USB shined in the air as she handed it over to Ela.

'Good one.' Ela analysed the key as if it held her life on it. 'Now, I'm going to get the real party started. Everything we need for tonight's mission is on here.'

'Don't you want us to do anything?' Aisha asked, looking at Ela with such hope and bad intentions that it scared me.

'No. You've done enough by simply being here. I'll finish this off. I'm the chosen one after all.' Ela's smile was so assured. Her plan was fool-proof and simply showing her evidence was enough to win. Little did she know.

I looked up to the clock near the main stage. Even though little time had passed since I'd entered the room, I had to leave to put my plot into action. I knew Ela's full plan, alongside what she'd told me. I'd followed her and overheard what she was scheming. That was how I knew about the USB. At the opening of the student auction, she had planned to get on stage to start the event with the showing of the video of Lucinda and Mr. Hawthorne, who'd both be stood in the crowd and ready to shame.

I had to leave the room and head around the back of the property to watch this unfold from outside as I secretly called Yamazaki. He would then hack into the computer using the IP address I'd given and break into the USB key, which was easier to do than people realised. Once he'd made the switch, the video would be replaced by Ela's secret instead and all would be complete. I'd be safe because Ela's secret would shame her so much, she wouldn't be able to utter the truth about Lucinda to anybody. I knew how she was when it came to shame. She didn't mind humiliating others but if she became the target, it would crush her into never doing such a thing again.

I soon made my excuses to get away. 'I'm just going to see my mother a moment, I forgot to ask her something. Be right back!'

'But you just got here!' Aisha replied, always the first to suspect something, as usual.

'I forgot to ask her something, is all.'

'Well, hurry because you're going to miss out on the crushing of Lucinda!'

'I wouldn't miss it for the world.' I lied, turning on my heel and heading back through the crowded dance floor, my trio of friends having no idea that the only person being ruined tonight was Ela Allard.

The crushing of Lucinda had been the only topic those guys had talked of for ages. She was the bad topic of the season. The one to be taken down by a public humiliation. And all because Lucinda was Dillan's boyfriend. The guy Ela had been in love with for years and just like being here, I'd to pretend to care and be a part of the pathetic game. Because if you didn't pretend in Dallington, you'd become the burned girl or boy. Everyone there was fake. The adults, the teachers, the students. The difference was my fakeness was on a whole other level. What I was about to do that night was going to demonstrate just that, sabotaging the very plan my friends had put together.

Before I floated back into the adult's lounge area, I looked back into the hall and could see the group in the outer corner, Lucinda smiling with her friends and Dillan with his, neither having the faintest idea what we had plotted.

I headed back into the adult's lounge and as I scanned my eyes over the familiar faces, of families from every rich lineage of London, my mother came to my side, holding a porcelain dog in her arms. I couldn't help but groan.

'So, you fell for the showman money battle as usual.' I said. My mother tutted. 'Can't say I'm surprised, even if we only just got here. I thought the first auction was being held in the student area?'

'No, actually, the Darsons sold it to me.' She gave a proud smile as she stroked the head like a real pet. 'Excuse me, I can spend my own money on what I want, thank you. Besides, the money goes to the upkeep of your school, so you should be thanking me.'

'Yes, thanking you for another grand piano in music class or another painting of the headmaster to line the already filled halls. I'm so thankful.'

My mother's sparkly eyes flicked my way, not used to my sharpness that only appeared at these parties.

'What's up with you tonight?' She snapped. 'Ever since we got into that limo this evening you've been in a very shifty mood.'

'You know I hate these parties.'

The eye roll soon arrived. 'I forget you act this way every time one of these parties is held. I don't understand what you have against them. Every other teenager here seems to love an excuse to have the party hall to themselves for a few hours. You're the only one that seems to hate it.'

I soon delivered the lie that would cover up the actual truth for my hatred. It was a trick I'd created to hide my true annoyances. After all, complaining wasn't something I was used to doing around my parents, and I knew if I let that image slip too far it could expose a side of me I didn't want anybody to see. I put my curated mask back on.

'I have an exam on Monday. You know I wanted to study and yet they held this party during major exam season? It is crazy, Mum.'

My mother sighed. 'I know that's frustrating, but we'll leave a little earlier. I can't help when they hold these, but we have to come.'

'I know. Sorry I'm complaining. I want to do well is all.'

'And you will!' She smiled, placing the porcelain dog under her other arm and another around me. 'But for now, just go into the main party hall and enjoy yourself. You shouldn't be in here with all the adults. Go have some fun!'

'Okay. You're right. I'll go. I'm gonna get some air first.'

'Yes, well. Be back soon, the student auction will start soon, and you need to bid up a storm, as I heard people are battling tonight. I need you to back me up later.'

It was perfectly timed as she said it. The clock read seven

thirty, not long before the opening to the student auction, my cue to put my counter plan into action.

'Back you up for what?' I quizzed.

'The usage of your father's credit card. I need an excuse, as I'm about to blow a lot of money. There are so many great items here tonight!'

'What, splurge money on another porcelain dog?' She rolled her eyes at my negativity and I soon made my way out to the back of the school.

What a stupid thing it was to try and humiliate someone on a screen by playing a recording of them, when a person can so easily delete the proof before it is played. That person being me. I felt sorry for Ela. Her plan had been to stand on the stage, play the unflattering video of Lucinda and the teacher and denounce the girl from popularity, and hopefully secure Dillan. But without the video nobody would believe Ela if she tried to talk about it anyway. She would be known as the girl who lied, so much so that the plan would work like a gem. My grades would be saved, alongside the teacher who was faking them.

As I secretly made my way around the back entrance, where I would monitor the event from outside. I ducked past all the open windows on my way, heading to the back of the patio area where the student party was taking place. Everything was ready for the night, and what I was about to do was for a good cause. For myself. I just couldn't get caught.

However, after slipping on the side of a bush and managing to save myself, I didn't succeed in saving my secret plan as I fell right into the path of two figures making out by the patio doors. My face went bright red. Even more when I recognised one of them as my old childhood friend and Dillan's current close friend, Theodore Hawk-Silberston. He was the last person I needed to see right then.

Our eyes met and I gulped.

Chapter Six

'Oh, sorry.' I said, quickly getting back up, cringing to myself before brushing off the debris and turning on my stiletto.

'Hey, Junie. Wait-' Theodore started, rushing over before I could make a getaway.

Not only had I discovered his make out session, but he'd found me sneaking out back like some lunatic.

'Uh, I won't tell anyone.' I said as he came to my side.

Theodore laughed. 'Yeah, I'd rather you didn't. Why are you out here?'

'Why are you?' I snapped and soon realised how dumb it was given I'd just seen the reason. 'Never mind. Let's say I got lost. Bye.'

'You got lost at your own school?'

'Well, what can I say...'

I rubbed my palms to give me time to think. The situation could've ruptured at that moment. My plan had been to stand out near the patio doors and make sure everything ran smoothly. But now this guy was in my way, and worse, I'd been spotted. Nobody came out back here. It looked suspicious. I tried to think of a way to get rid of them but thankfully the girl he was with made the decision for me. Loretta Finch, a member of our school's opposing clique. She looked at me with a stern glare for interrupting them.

'Theodore, are we gonna stay here all night or what?' She

sighed, wiping down her dress. 'We may as well go inside and see the auction now.'

'You want to go inside?'

'Sure. Now we've been interrupted.' The girl huffed and Theodore turned to me with a laugh.

'So, you coming out back here to find a guy?'

'No.' I replied plainly. If I'd have said yes, a rumour would've soon began that I was dating someone which was an even worse fate than being at that school. Loretta Finch was the crowned queen of rumours, bad ones at that. 'I just came to get some air. I have a headache. It's so noisy out front.'

'Oh, okay.' He laughed sarcastically as he and the girl began to pass me. 'I'll see you inside then, eh?'

'Sure.' I breathed back as they disappeared around the side of the building and rushed to the patio doors.

The student auction was in full swing now and as our headmaster welcomed the event, I knew it was time for the shaming. I slid by the patio doors and pulled out my burner phone, but there was one thing I had to do to get it right.

It wasn't long before his voice answered. 'JunJun, what's up?'

'What do you mean what's up? Did you manage to do it?'

'Do what?'

'Don't play me, Yamazaki. Did you hack into the USB and change the video?'

He yawned. 'Of course, I did. Why're you even asking? I did it as soon as she put the drive in.'

I sighed. Yamazaki was always so cool about things. I investigated the patio doors from the corner, and soon enough, the black screen was illuminated by the video of Ela. Shock poured into the hall as everyone heard the plan she'd had to take down Lucinda and get Dillan. I knew this filming Ela discussing her plan would come in handy. Ela stood at the podium, looked at our friends in shock before rushing out as the video continued playing. Lucinda and Dillan stood in the

Lotté Jean Elliott

corner, stunned by what had happened. It was dramatic but it'd saved me and my teacher.

I leaned against the wall and stood with relief that my image was safe for another night. The secret world where I was my true self with Yamazaki was safe. But nobody in my normal life could see that and I would do anything to keep it that way, even if it meant destroying my friend's image for a few days. It had to be done. She would be okay. She was Ela Allard: Queen of Lies, and it would stay that way once all the fun had blown over. It always did for popular students.

'It worked.' I beamed.

'Told ya.'

'Ah, what would I do without you Reo Yamazaki?' I sighed.

'Eh, did you just compliment me? Since when was that a thing? And don't say my full name, it feels weird.'

'Well, I may be a better hacker but you're good at doing stuff like that.'

'Everybody watch out! Junie Han has admitted to being a hacker in real life, her secret is out that she is a warped psychopath that steals money from the government.'

His words made me look around before I rolled my eyes. 'Yes, well. I'm hiding my other life with good reason. Not only because we do illegal stuff, but because I also want to escape this place. If you lived my life you'd understand.'

'Understand what? That you hide it because it will jeopardise your plans to leave in the future. More so, if your parents find out your grades are fake and you're using that time to hack the world, you'd never get the chance to come to a good university in Japan and see me.'

'Shut up.' I pouted. Even though he spoke the truth.

'It's the truth.'

'Whether it is or not, you hide your hacker life as well.'

'Forget about this now. What time are you coming online?' Yamazaki asked. 'We have a lot of work to do tonight.'

'Oh, damn. I forgot about that. I won't be long. I intend to leave early, as I know Ela will be mad at me for not being in the auction and the others will be getting the blame for what went wrong.'

'Well, hurry. You know the time difference kills me here in Japan.'

'I'll be online soon. Prepare yourself; I think I'm ready to take on a few client projects tonight. This evening has drained me, and I need to relax. You don't know how hard it is pretending every day that I give a damn about anything here. All this role-play has been getting to me lately. I can't wait to escape to Japan. It's getting so close.'

'It's so weird that you find hacking and destroying people's lives relaxing.'

'Hey, I did a good deed today for a change, even if it was for myself. What can I say though; I'm not ashamed to say my strong suit relaxes me? Besides, Ela will be unscathed for the most part. Popular people always are. It'll just be embarrassing for the next few weeks given Dillan now knows she's madly in love with him. I'd better go now, my mother will be scoping the grounds for me.'

'Yes, you had better go, don't want to let her down. Just don't be late; we have a lot to do tomorrow night!'

'Oh yes, we do. Let's conjure up a storm!' I smiled to myself before cancelling the call.

The thought of hacking The Monsters Club boosted my happiness. Thursday evenings were one of my favourite evenings of the week, the only time when I could be myself and pretend that privileged world was anything but a wild dream. I would go on Serpan, the home for all of us dark web hackers, and choose a site to play with. There was one on the list that everyone was having a hard time breaking into and I had just managed to get a new code to try to break down a barrier their site seemed to hold.

The Monsters Club? What a dumb name. I thought to myself. The site was allegedly run by a group of killers who posted images of their victims. Like every site on the dark web, I took it with a pinch of salt. If only everybody knew I had the fates of everyone in my hands but at the same time, they had mine as easily. Welcome to the rich world, where money will get you destroyed if you don't put on their mask.

Dallington Academy was full of secrets just like the dark web, and so were all the people who frequented both places. However, my own secrets were on a level not a single person at Dallington would see coming. One that went beyond ego and riches, and no matter what, they were going to stay secret. No matter who I had to destroy to keep it that way. No one was going to destroy my plan to leave England. The lengths I'd go to till I graduated and got into The University of Tokyo were unending. I would get what I wanted, and nobody would stop me. No matter how low I had to go.

Chapter Seven

Waking up without a morning text from Ela was strange. Every morning she would message me the gossip of the day or drone on about Dillan. But today and for the rest of that week, it was silence, which was how I knew my plan had worked, and why she would be silent about Lucinda and Mr. Hawthorne. I knew what I'd done would make her feel so embarrassed she'd never take up the offer of the threat list if presented to her ever again.

I decided to call her after school, to make sure she knew I wasn't with her on the night's aftermath since I'd gone home to keep away from the drama, that something had happened, and I had a pretend reason for it.

I'd tried calling her a few times that week, but she'd never picked up to any of us. However, after a few moments, she picked up and her voice had never sounded so quiet.

'Junie.' She mumbled.

'Ela, how are you?'

'Oh, Junie... I'm ready to burst into flames.'

'So, what happened to you wasn't a dream then, was it?' I sighed.

'Afraid not. Though I keep trying to hope it was. But then I wake up and see it play all over again in my mind.'

'What happened?'

Ela let out a huge groan. 'I have no idea where that video

came from or who took it of me but evidently, I was wrong about being the chosen one.'

'What do you mean?'

'I think someone chose me as their fake target, they must've found out what my code was and used it to pretend I was in charge and then turned it against me. It's the only reason I can think of as to how this has happened. I played all along. I was never the chosen one.'

I smiled. What a good reason it was to use. I didn't even have to come up with an answer as to who could've done it when she'd given such an idea.

'I guess that seems like the most likely thing. You went about so excitedly while waiting for this list, maybe the real chosen one saw it by chance when you weren't looking and created all of this.'

'I think so, and I'm so embarrassed. Why would someone choose me? People rarely pick the popular kids to humiliate. They sure have the balls to pick me, given I could ruin them.'

'It may have been another popular student, but you're right, people normally target unpopular kids. How are you feeling? Are you coming to school soon?'

'I don't know.' She huffed.

'Come on, everything will be fine. Nobody will even remember that night now.'

'Talking of that night, where have you been? I never saw you at all after that spectacle.'

'I had to go home, I needed to study. I was going to come back but I realised I'd some important things left to do. I'm sorry for not being there.'

'It's okay, I'm glad you didn't witness the mess it was. But anyway, I don't know if I'll come back.'

'You'll be fine, Ela. Although we think that list is serious, it isn't for popular people like us. Nobody will even care now. Somebody was shamed and even though it was you, unlike unpopular students, you'll be fine. A few days have passed, and nobody will even care. I've never heard a student mention it.'

Which was true, even though I'd truly embarrassed her and while normally the person that was shamed in those events lived a life of hell afterwards, Ela was so popular it never lasted long. Mainly because people were too scared to play a person like Ela. Not only because she was popular, but also because her parents donated to many of the major universities in England, so students wouldn't dare play her if they wanted a chance of getting in.

'Here I was, so excited to get the destruction role and someone played it against me. But Dillan will care...'

'I doubt he cares. If anything, you've probably given him an excuse to break up with Lucinda.'

Her voice lightened at the thought. 'How is that?'

'You know what type of girl he likes. Not the innocent and restrained people like Lucinda. He likes people like you. The wild and bold, those who don't care about getting what they want.'

'What, the crazy kind?'

'Yes!'

'Junie!' Ela laughed.

'I'm just being honest. I know you're embarrassed by what happened and whoever changed that video, I'm sure they'll pay one day. But come back to school. Really, nobody gives a damn about what happened.'

'Really?' She sighed.

'Yup. I've not heard a word about it and normally whoever is shamed is gossiped about for weeks. And I know the true reason why you're ok.'

'How?'

'Because Dillan told people to leave you alone.'

'Really?'

'Yes, that is why I'm telling you this. Come back.'

'He hasn't called me though!'

'I'm sure he just needs time. But trust me, he's saved your reputation. You're both popular; of course it will be fine.'

'Thanks, Junie! But why would he do this for me? After he heard me plotting to take away his girlfriend like some monster in that video.'

'Because he likes the crazy ones.'

We both laughed before she finally seemed to agree. 'I suppose you're right. I'll come back to school. I'm embarrassed but I'll do it and find this person who swapped that video and filmed me. I still don't understand it. Who would have the nerve to play me like this?'

'Forget about it and come back. I'll see you soon, eh?'

'Yes, I suppose. Thanks, Junie. As usual, you always help me out.'

'No problem.' I soon put down my phone and knew it was mission clear. My teacher, grades and Lucinda, lucky for her, were safe for another day because I knew Dillan had actually done this. He'd saved Ela from drowning in social suicide; it wasn't just her popularity or rich parents. Which would help her keep her mouth shut about Lucinda and Mr. Hawthorne, because if she could get Dillan, she wouldn't need to leak it.

Another mission to keep my image clear was complete. As I sat back in my bed, feeling happy with myself, another message pinged at my burner phone. Yamazaki seeming rather eager for so early in the morning.

Lotté Jean Elliott

■■■■■

‹ Messages   **Yamazaki**   Details

I've got some cool news,
Jun. That code you used
worked; you know, to get
into that site everybody
has been trying to hack
into like crazy, The
Monsters Club. Text me
when you come online
tonight. I have something
to tell you, it's a wild
place! Even wilder than
what you just did to your
friend. Don't be late!

 Text Message   Send

Chapter Eight

As the screen illuminated, I put on my headphones, opened my coding source and started work again. It was what I always did after coming in to our empty home, since my parents worked till the late hours. The uniform would come off, my pyjamas would become my second skin and my true self emerged.

I started work for a company somewhere out in America, who needed me to hack into some business local to them, steal some information and hand it over. They said they were trying to oust a company who had opened a store near their own and were selling similar items. Since their arrival, they had been stealing their clients because they charged lower prices for items. They wanted me to either find some dirt or plant it on them to make them leave. They weren't doing anything illegal, this rival shop, so planting lies it was. Placing such information was one of the harder tasks, so I had been up longer than most of my usual jobs. I half-laughed to myself as it was like I was starting a new shift.

I spent the next two hours planting some false information on this business, before finally finishing it and sending over the information to my client. They mailed me back straight away and thanked me for my help, before I banished all our connection into my coding dustbin and face planted into my keyboard, exhausted from another night of making money. Ruining people's lives because they needed stronger security walls.

I did not see myself as ruining people's lives per se. I was doing what people paid me to do. Humiliating ex-lovers or friends, killing politicians' profiles, destroying businesses, generally, whatever people wanted me for, and could do online, within reason, I would do for money.

I needed to go to sleep. I had an exam at school in four hours, not that it mattered if I aced it or not since all my grades were fake, but I still had to keep up the illusion that I looked like I was serious. I had planned to go to bed when I let out a huge yawn. However, a chat message popped up on my desktop, gluing me to my seat for a few more moments.

YAMAZAKI: JUNJUN, WHERE ARE YOU? HAVE YOU SEEN IT YET?

HEYJUN: HEY, I WAS ABOUT TO LOG OFF. I FORGOT TO SPEAK TO YOU, SORRY. WHAT HAVE YOU BEEN DOING OVER THERE IN TOKYO?

YAMAZAKI: YOU KNOW, IT'S ALWAYS SO ANNOYING WHEN YOU DO THAT, BYPASSING MY QUESTION. ANSWER MY OPENING STATEMENT!

HEYJUN: SORRY, TOUCHY. WHAT IS IT THAT I AM SUPPOSED TO HAVE SEEN?

YAMAZAKI: DON'T PRETEND YOU DON'T KNOW WHAT I AM TALKING ABOUT. I KNOW YOU ARE ONLINE WAY MORE THAN ME! THE THING I'VE BEEN TELLING YOU EVERY DAY, BUT YOU'VE IGNORED ME. I WON'T STAND FOR IT ANYMORE!

HEYJUN: I KNOW. I HAVE AN INTERNET OBSESSION AND IGNORING YOU TOO IT SEEMS. WHAT CAN I SAY?

YAMAZAKI: BE SERIOUS! HAVE YOU SEEN THE NEW SITE YET?

HEYJUN: OF COURSE, I HAVE. I ALWAYS BROWSE ON SERPAN BEFORE I START ANYTHING. THAT AND YOU'VE TALKED ABOUT IT AT LEAST TWENTY TIMES THIS WEEK SINCE I GAVE YOU THAT CODE.

YAMAZAKI: YOU'VE SEEN IT AND ALL YOU CAN SAY IS THAT YOU HAVE?

File   Edit   Search   Help

HEYJUN: YOU DIDN'T ASK ME TO EXPAND. BUT YES, I KNOW WHAT YOU ARE GOING TO SAY, IT'S SOME CRAZY STUFF.

YAMAZAKI: SO, YOU MANAGED TO HACK INTO THAT SITE IN THE END WITH THE CODE YOU GAVE ME AS A GIFT FOR HELPING YOU. THAT WAS SUPPOSED TO BE FOR THE AMERICAN PROJECT, BUT YOU USED ME AS USUAL. WELL, I'M FORGIVING YOU FOR DOING SO THIS TIME BECAUSE THAT CODE ACTUALLY HELPED GET ME INTO THAT SITE. CRAZY IS AN UNDERSTATEMENT. ALL THE TIME I HAVE BEEN ON THE DARK WEB, I HAVE NEVER SEEN ANYTHING SO BAD. THE GORE IS ON ANOTHER LEVEL. DO YOU THINK IT'S REAL?

HEYJUN: IT WAS EASY ENOUGH TO HACK INTO ONCE I CAME UP WITH THAT CODE THAT I GAVE YOU, STOP ACTING AS IF YOU GOT IN YOURSELF. AND, WHO KNOWS IF IT IS REAL? YOU NEVER KNOW WHAT LURKS IN THE DARK WEB OR IN ANY OF THOSE SITES WE CLICK ON FROM THE PIN BOARD. I SEE WHY IT WAS SO GUARDED THOUGH; PEOPLE OBVI-OUSLY DON'T WANT US TO SEE THEIR WEIRD FETISHES.

YAMAZAKI: WELL, THIS SITE IS THE ONE I'VE BEEN GOING ON ABOUT ALL WEEK! I'M GOING TO EXPOSE IT SINCE NOBODY SEEMS TO BE AWARE OF IT, OTHER THAN A FEW OF US HACKERS.

HEYJUN: DID I READ THAT RIGHT?

YAMAZAKI: I DON'T LIE, JUNJUN.

File   Edit   Search   Help

HEYJUN: HAVE SOME OF YOUR BRAIN CELLS BEEN
FRIED WHILE LOOKING AT THIS SITE? WHY WOULD
YOU WANT TO EXPOSE SUCH A THING? THERE ARE
PLENTY OTHER GRUESOME SITES, YAMAZAKI.

YAMAZAKI: DID YOU EVEN LOOK AT IT? THAT IS
BY FAR THE WORST SITE I HAVE EVER SEEN. YOU
DON'T BELIEVE IT IS REAL?

HEYJUN: OF COURSE, I BELIEVE IT!!!!!! WHY
WOULDN'T I????? LIKE MOST OF THESE THINGS
THOUGH, IT'S JUST A BUNCH OF INTERNET TROLLS
OR BORED PEOPLE TRYING TO SCARE OTHERS. IT'S
NOT REAL. A CLUB FOR MURDERERS AND SERIAL
KILLERS TO SHARE THEIR DEAD BODIES LIKE
TROPHIES? REALLY?

YAMAZAKI: YOUR NAIVETY SCARES ME, JUN.

HEYJUN: I'M NOT NAÏVE. JUST USED TO THAT
PLACE AND SUCH THINGS. I HACKED INTO THIS
THE MONSTERS CLUB PAGE AND YES, IT WAS
GRUESOME AND DISTURBING AS HELL. A SITE FOR
SERIAL KILLERS TO MEET UP AND POST THEIR
ANONYMOUS KILLINGS AS IF IT IS A FUN FORUM
OF SHARED INTEREST, PRETTY WEIRD, BUT SO IS
ALL THE DARK WEB. BUT, WHY EXPOSE THIS PAGE
OF ALL THE GRUESOME THINGS OUT THERE? DON'T
YOU REMEMBER THE CANNIBAL CAFÉ OR HANN'S
HOME FOR THE BROODY THAT SELLS LITERAL
PLASTIC VERSIONS OF BABIES TO PEOPLE WHO
CAN'T BE MOTHERS?

File Edit Search Help

YAMAZAKI: I KNEW YOU WOULD MANAGE TO HACK INTO THEIR PAGE. ONLY ME, YOU AND ONE OTHER PERSON SEEMED TO HAVE BEEN ABLE. AND, BECAUSE, WHY NOT EXPOSE THEM? THAT CAFÉ AND HANN'S HOME HAVE NOTHING ON THIS!

HEYJUN: BECAUSE, MONEY, RIGHT? YOU'LL GET PAID FOR SUCH AN ARTICLE. YEAH, I KNOW ONLY THREE OF US MANAGED TO GET ON. THOSE GUYS ON SERPAN NEED TO UP THEIR SKILLS. THOUGH IT WAS ONE OF THE HARDEST WALLS I'VE TRIED TO BREAK, MUST ADMIT.

YAMAZAKI: OF COURSE! I'M NOT GOING TO EXPOSE SOMETHING FOR FREE, REAL OR NOT. AND YES, THE WALL WAS INTENSE, WHICH MAKES ME THINK IT'S REAL. WHY WOULD THEY HAVE SUCH HIGH SECURITY IF IT WAS FAKE?

HEYJUN: DAMN. DON'T YOU MAKE ENOUGH MONEY FROM HACKING?

YAMAZAKI: SURE. HOWEVER, MORE IS ALWAYS WELCOME!

HEYJUN: YOU'RE REALLY GOING TO RISK YOUR LIFE TO EXPOSE THIS NEW SITE? WHAT IF YOU CAN'T GET TO IT AGAIN? THAT CODE WILL ONLY BE A ONE-TIME THING, BECAUSE I'M SURE THEY'D HAVE REALISED WE'D GOTTEN IN AND CHANGED EVERYTHING AGAIN. IT WAS SUPER HARD GETTING THROUGH THE LOOPHOLES THEY'D PLACED AS IT WAS. WHAT IF YOU FAIL TO FIND IT AND BE MADE OUT TO BE A PHONY?

File   Edit   Search   Help

YAMAZAKI: I CONTACTED AN ENGLISH NEWS OUTLET, THEY AGREED FOR ME TO SHARE THE STORY OF THIS PAGE. I DID IT TODAY. I HAD TRIED TO TELL YOU, BUT YOU WEREN'T ANSWERING ME BECAUSE YOU'RE TOO OBSESSED WITH SAVING YOUR IN REAL LIFE IMAGE! I'LL EMAIL YOU THE LINK WHEN IT'S UP, WHICH SHOULD BE IN THE NEXT FEW DAYS. SOMETHING LIKE, INTERVIEW WITH A YOUNG HACKER EXPOSING THE TRUE EVIL OF THE DARK WEB. I DID LAUGH.

HEYJUN: I REALLY DON'T THINK THIS IS A GOOD IDEA. LOOK, STICK TO HACKING PEOPLE AND GETTING PAID FOR DOING SO. THINGS LIKE THIS ARE ABOVE US. THE SITES ARE POSTED TO LOOK AT, NOT TO SHARE OUT OF SERPAN. DON'T MESS WITH THE DARK WEB, EVEN IF I BELIEVE IT'S REAL OR NOT. IT'S NOT WORTH IT. WHAT IF THESE GUYS FIND YOU? WE WERE THE ONLY THREE PEOPLE THAT GOT ON BEFORE THE LINK WAS TAKEN DOWN. THEY MAY BE ABLE TO TRACK US, GIVEN HOW STRONG THE SITE WAS SECURED.

YAMAZAKI: YOUR LACK OF FAITH IN ME IS REALLY SAD, JUN. YOU SEEM TO FORGET I AM ONE OF THE BEST HACKERS IN THIS GAME. NO ONE WILL BE ABLE TO TRACE ME, IF THAT IS WHY YOU'RE WORRYING.

HEYJUN: IT'S NOT JUST THAT. ONLY THREE OF US MANAGED TO GET INTO THAT SITE. THEY COULD TRACK US ALL, YOU NEVER KNOW. IF THEY REALLY ARE KILLERS, IT MIGHT BE FUN TO THEM. SERPAN POSTS THESE LINKS FOR FUN, IT'S NOT MEANT TO BE INTERFERED WITH.

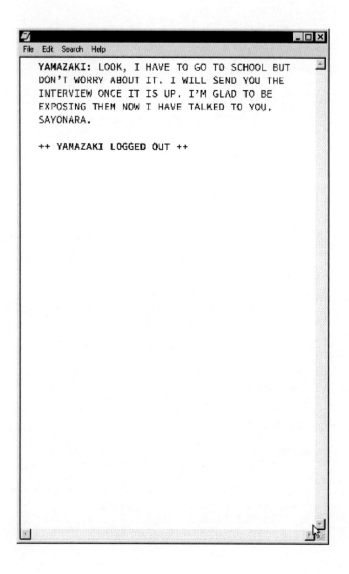

YAMAZAKI: LOOK, I HAVE TO GO TO SCHOOL BUT
DON'T WORRY ABOUT IT. I WILL SEND YOU THE
INTERVIEW ONCE IT IS UP. I'M GLAD TO BE
EXPOSING THEM NOW I HAVE TALKED TO YOU.
SAYONARA.

++ YAMAZAKI LOGGED OUT ++

I slid back into my seat and stared at my computer screen, annoyed he had left me like that but also slightly concerned as to what would happen. The more I thought over it, the worse I felt. It wasn't like we hadn't been on gruesome sites before. But it was in the Serpan's rules not to share these sites with anybody out of the forum. Mainly because these were dark web sites for a reason, and didn't want to be shared.

This guy was playing with fire. Yes, we went on the dark web and it was always dangerous, however, this site was more hidden and protected than any I had seen before. When the link to the site had been posted on the pin board, only three of us, one being the guy who discovered the site in the first place, managed to get past the many barriers, and I actually wished I had been one of the many that had not seen it. Gruesome scenes of dead bodies on a whole new level. Something I did not want to recall just yet, as I had managed to bury it to the back of my mind three nights after seeing it.

Yamazaki claimed he wanted to expose the place for so-called good reasons. I didn't believe him one bit. He wanted attention. He had always been like this. Trying to not only outdo me by getting more hacking jobs, but by trying to hack into the most barricaded of systems. My only interest when doing this was money, but his was that and fame in the hacking world. He really needed to fix that ego complex of his.

I hoped he knew what he was doing. This site was only meant for certain eyes, and the world's media were not those. I went to sleep soon after with a knot in my stomach.

Chapter Nine

The next few days passed by and my mind couldn't shift from Yamazaki. Even when Ela came back to school and managed to integrate as easily as I said she would, I found it hard to focus on anything other than the fact he was exposing this well-guarded site that did not want to be shared. That, and it was against Serpan's rules to share them out of the board. If they found out he was doing this article, he could be kicked out.

During my lessons, I was itching to get back home to check my hidden email box and see if the article was out yet. I only hoped he did not give too much information away. Sites that lay in the very deep parts of the dark web were hidden away for a reason; to be accessed by select groups of people. And since we weren't killers, we weren't supposed to be able to access this Monsters Club site. We only hacked into these shared links to browse, but never play with them.

I wondered what the head of the Serpan pin board, who also hacked the site, would think about Yamazaki doing this. I had only ever spoken to him twice, but I doubted he would be happy with Yamazaki for going against his rules. Especially as the rules were in place to protect us, and himself.

Yamazaki liked causing drama. That was how we initially met. He had somehow traced my IP before I could cover it up after leaving a particular site, and threatened to expose me, as I was one of the top hackers in the league. However, I soon hacked him back, and found stuff on him too. From then we continued to mail each other and a friendship had grown between us. Two hackers, both competitive, from opposite sides of the globe, became friends. Who would have guessed that outcome?

I tried not to think about it for the rest of the day. I didn't want to get to lost in my own head, as people would be curious as to why I was not as devoted to my studies as I normally was. I lay my head on my desk whilst my maths teacher droned on about equations I didn't understand. Then, midday, I got a text.

I sneakily pulled out my phone from my hidden blazer pocket. My school friends were all in classes, and my family rarely texted me during the day. After unlocking the screen, I narrowed my eyes as I looked at the unknown texter. It was out of area. For a moment, I thought it could be Yamazaki, even though he rarely texted my normal phone. I opened the message.

WELCOME TO THE MONSTERS CLUB, THIS IS A MESSAGE TO CONFIRM YOUR JOINING OF OUR SITE. THIS IS A HAPPY PLACE FOR THE KILLER'S MIND. ENJOY YOUR STAY AND REMEMBER OUR ONLY RULE, TO SPREAD CHAOS AND DEATH WITHIN THIS BORING WORLD BUT NEVER TO SHARE WHAT GOES ON INSIDE IT. COMPLY AND BE HAPPY.

HAPPY KILLING!

All in capitals, what read ahead, shook me to my core.

The secret club had somehow gotten my mobile number. I froze, and my phone dropped to the ground. The teacher turned round, and I quickly assumed the pose of an attentive student. Thankfully, the teacher turned back to the board, and I quickly picked up my phone, thinking I'd gotten away with it. However, Mr Franklin soon placed down the white board pen and faced my way.

'Did you drop something, Junie?' He said with a frown.

'No...' I muttered back, cursing under my breath.

'I saw your phone, Miss. Han.' He came and stood beside me, placing out his hand. 'Hand it over. I never expected to see this sort of behaviour from you.'

An odd corner of laughter emerged around me. I couldn't give him my phone, so quickly began to put on a performance to get out of class and process this message. My body fell to my desk as I faked a sickness.

'What on earth is wrong?' He gasped.

'I don't feel good.' I cried. 'Can I go to the bathroom?'

'Of course. Do you want someone to go with you?'

'No, thanks. I'll be fine.' He helped me out of my seat, and I placed my phone discreetly into my skirt pocket before I left class.

After seeing him off, I ran out of the school and hid around the back in a quiet area, the cold air sweeping my skin. My mind was racing. But, before I could process it, a familiar voice called to me from my side.

'Junie, what's up? You went pale back there.' I turned to see Theodore looking at me with concern, hands in pockets.

I let out a sigh as he approached me. He seemed to be showing up too much lately, and it was beginning to irritate me, accidents or not.

'I feel oddly sick.' I replied, internally sighing. I needed to be alone. I slid down the wall to the ground, clutching my now tainted-feeling phone. He did the same and fell beside me. He glanced between my face and the phone screen.

'The teacher told me to follow you. Do you want me to get the nurse or something?'

I shook my head. 'No. It's not that sort of sickness. Look, Theodore. Just tell the teacher I'll be right back.'

'I'm concerned about you, is all.'

'Why? We don't even talk.' I scoffed, though I knew he apparently liked me.

'Look, are you okay?' He was genuine, but I wasn't in the mood for pleasantries.

'I'm going back to class in a moment, and I need to get my head together. Will you go away, already?' I snapped and his face flushed at my reaction. I knew it was too sharp, but that wasn't something I could worry about right now.

He did back off then. I sighed with relief and looked down at my phone to look at the message in better detail. The same words in all capital letters stared right back at me.

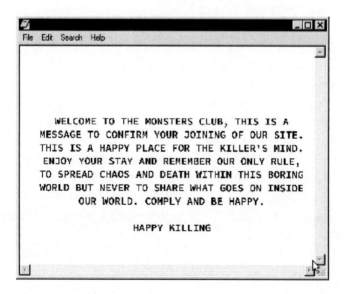

WELCOME TO THE MONSTERS CLUB, THIS IS A MESSAGE TO CONFIRM YOUR JOINING OF OUR SITE. THIS IS A HAPPY PLACE FOR THE KILLER'S MIND. ENJOY YOUR STAY AND REMEMBER OUR ONLY RULE, TO SPREAD CHAOS AND DEATH WITHIN THIS BORING WORLD BUT NEVER TO SHARE WHAT GOES ON INSIDE OUR WORLD. COMPLY AND BE HAPPY.

HAPPY KILLING

A cold chill that was nothing to do with the weather grew heavier on my body. This was either Yamazaki messing with me, or this site had found my personal phone number. But both were impossible. I was known for having the best protection out there. I was untraceable. This had to be fake, but it felt so real, seeing the same sharp letters only a few eyes had seen on the site's front page looking back at me. I didn't know how to take this in, but I knew I needed to get home and talk to Yamazaki.

Chapter Ten

My body trembled at the words as I read them again. How did this site get my phone number? It was not linked to anything in my coding world, and the walls I used to protect myself when I went onto any such place were the most secure you could get. Besides, I was barely on that site long enough for them to have been able to break down the security since it had been way too gory for me to handle. I didn't understand.

I went back to class and convinced Mr. Franklin that I was sick so I could get sent home a little earlier to talk to Yamazaki about this, and see if he had released his article yet. I was not concerned just yet. More so unnerved how they had gotten my dead phone number. If this was Yamazaki, he was dead meat, and his computer would be flooded with another virus of A-ha's Take On Me on a loop if he'd dared to play me with something as crazy as this. It was both mocking my skills and making me freak out.

When I got home, there was the usual note on the fridge to tell me to call for takeout for my dinner because my parents wouldn't be home till late. I crumpled up the paper and threw it into the trash. I never understood why they kept leaving them when it was so part of our routine now. They never were home and I didn't need reminding of the same thing when nothing had changed.

However, right now, the last thing on my mind was food and

I ran up to my bedroom, booted up my computers and began to check my mail and message Yamazaki to see if he had received this strange text message too.

As I opened my email, there was a message in my inbox from him. But it was only related to his article.

Jun. Here is the link to the article. It was so funny to see my name on such a famous page. I'll be on chat later, be there!!!!!

I clicked on the link to the article and stared at my computer screen, transfixed. The glare bounced against my eyes, and normally if I left it this way without any other light in the room they would start to hurt. However, I was too captivated by the glowing words to even realise that was happening. It had happened. He had done it.

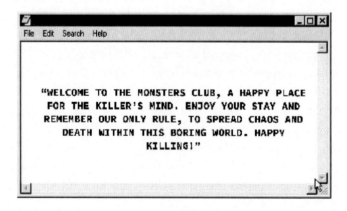

"WELCOME TO THE MONSTERS CLUB, A HAPPY PLACE FOR THE KILLER'S MIND. ENJOY YOUR STAY AND REMEMBER OUR ONLY RULE, TO SPREAD CHAOS AND DEATH WITHIN THIS BORING WORLD. HAPPY KILLING!"

Renka News Interview with a Young Hacker:
Investigating The Dark Web and The Truth of What Happens in it's Murkiest Layers.

These were the words plastered onto a website, hidden away in the deepest depths of the dark web that probably never would have come to light, if it had not been for one young man from Japan. We have conducted an interview with this young hacker, who cannot be named for obvious reasons but he, on one of his tours of the dark web, which we do not advise you ever enter, came across a site that we can't believe exists, but sadly does. The young hacker named only as Yamazaki, tells of what he has seen on the site and why you should stay away and never delve into the dark web. This interview was conducted over email.

Hello, please can you introduce yourself and what you do?

I go by the name Yamazaki in the dark web. I'm a hacker from Japan.

What got you into hacking?

I was young and bored, in need of control in another place and hacking was the thing that gave me everything I wanted and now, too much. It also helped me learn English.

Where do you venture to in the dark web?

When I'm not doing a paid hacking service, I'm there to check out these strange web pages. Mainly to sites where I can buy things I can't on the normal web. You know, dark stuff.

This site you wish to bring to light, what is so special about it? We know there are many gruesome and strange sites lurking on the dark web, why this one in particular?

Well, I am usually not one to squirm away from gruesome things because, well, I have ventured onto the Cannibal Café once to see if it was real and even that didn't make me report it. However, this site... all I can begin to say is, it has really, really unnerved me.

What exactly is The Monsters Club?

It is a site for murderers to meet and share their latest victims and so on. They post terrible images of dead bodies and talk about how they have killed and stalked these people, and, in the comments, people celebrate everything, asking for advice for their next killing. It sounds like it would be fake, but after everything I saw, it seems very real.

Why, out of everything you've seen, have you decided to share this site?

Because this was the most heavily protected site I'd ever come across, and only three hackers managed to enter it. To me, that makes it seem even more legit than many others and if this is the case, and murderers are sharing these dead bodies, I wanted people to be aware. To make them stay away from the dark web, as sites like this exist and you don't know who you're speaking with.

Thank you, Yamazaki. Is there a closing statement you'd like to make?

Yes, to stay away from the dark web and say hello to my friend, Pachi-san. I know she'll be reading this. See, I did it!

There you have it. This strange site amongst many others lays within the dark web. It's a place many have an idea of but know so little about, and maybe it is best to keep it that way.

When the article came to an end, I didn't even have time to think and immediately went to our chat box.

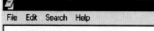

```
HEYJUN: YOU HERE?

YAMAZAKI: I WAS ABOUT TO GO TO SLEEP. YOU
READ IT?

HEYJUN: OF COURSE!

YAMAZAKI: WHAT DID YOU THINK?!

HEYJUN: NICE. YOUR WORDS ARE AS SHARP AS
USUAL. BUT WHY DID YOU SHARE YOUR NAME?

YAMAZAKI: IT'S NOT LIKE ANYONE READING IT
WILL KNOW WHO I AM. ESPECIALLY, IF THEY
DON'T KNOW JAPANESE GIVEN, I WRITE IN THAT
EVERY TIME. I ONLY REALLY SPEAK TO YOU IN
ENGLISH.

HEYJUN: THAT IS TRUE. DOESN'T THIS SITE
UNNERVE YOU THOUGH. LIKE, WHAT IF THEY FIND
OUT WHO YOU WERE FROM IT?

YAMAZAKI: THERE IS A ZERO PERCENT CHANCE OF
THAT EVER HAPPENING. WE'LL BE FINE.

HEYJUN: YOU SURE LOVE INFLATING YOUR EGO BY
THINKING YOUR HACKING SKILLS ARE THAT GOOD,
DON'T YOU?

YAMAZAKI: IF I DON'T, NO ONE WILL!

HEYJUN: ANYHOW, I CAME ON HERE TO ASK YOU
SOMETHING. DID YOU RECEIVE A STRANGE TEXT?

YAMAZAKI: DO YOU MEAN THIS?
```

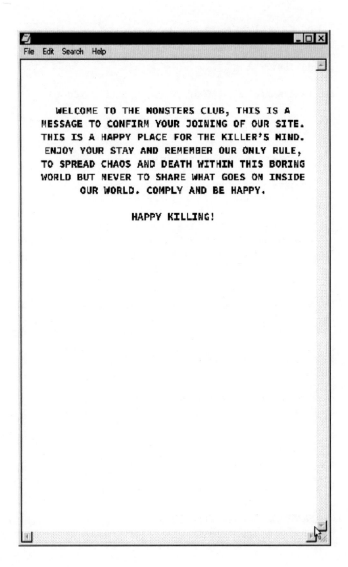

WELCOME TO THE MONSTERS CLUB, THIS IS A
MESSAGE TO CONFIRM YOUR JOINING OF OUR SITE.
THIS IS A HAPPY PLACE FOR THE KILLER'S MIND.
ENJOY YOUR STAY AND REMEMBER OUR ONLY RULE,
TO SPREAD CHAOS AND DEATH WITHIN THIS BORING
WORLD BUT NEVER TO SHARE WHAT GOES ON INSIDE
OUR WORLD. COMPLY AND BE HAPPY.

HAPPY KILLING!

HEYJUN: YES! I SAW IT AT THE START OF YOUR ARTICLE AS WELL. I WAS IN SCHOOL WHEN I GOT THE TEXT. I THOUGHT YOU WERE MESSING WITH ME. BUT IT'S REALLY FREAKED ME OUT. YOU'VE NEVER DONE SOMETHING LIKE THIS BEFORE, AND WE'VE PLAYED EACH OTHER A LOT.

YAMAZAKI: IT WASN'T ME, I SWEAR. BUT TO BE HONEST, I AM SURPRISED IT BOTHERED YOU SO MUCH, SINCE YOU DON'T SEEM TO BELIEVE THIS SITE IS REAL.

HEYJUN: IT'S NOT THAT I DON'T BELIEVE IT'S REAL. WHY ELSE WOULD IT BE THAT SAFELY GUARDED THAT ONLY THREE OF US GOT THROUGH TO THE MAIN PORTAL SITE. I GUESS I DON'T WANT TO BELIEVE IT'S REAL.

YAMAZAKI: I UNDERSTAND THAT. BUT IS IT THAT BAD IN COMPARISON TO SOME OF THE OTHER STUFF WE'VE HACKED BEFORE?

HEYJUN: OH, IT'S BAD. BUT I DON'T KNOW. I'M JUST NERVOUS BY THE FACT THEY GOT MY OWN PERSONAL MOBILE NUMBER. HOW THE HECK DID THEY GET IT?

YAMAZAKI: YES, THAT HAS HAPPENED TO ME. IT DID SURPRISE ME. HOWEVER, WITH THE SECURE FIRE WALLS THEY HAD, IT DOESN'T SURPRISE ME. I GUESS WE AREN'T AS GOOD AS WE THOUGHT. WHOEVER MADE THAT SITE MUST BE GOOD THEM-SELVES.

HEYJUN: YOU DON'T SEEM OVERLY CONCERNED THAT THIS SITE MAY HAVE MORE PERSONAL INFORMATION ON US. IF THEY CAN GET OUR PHONE NUMBERS LIKE THAT, WHAT ELSE COULD THEY GET?

YAMAZAKI: NOT CONCERNED MORE, CURIOUS TO SEE WHAT WILL HAPPEN.

HEYJUN: YOU SURE LOVE PLAYING WITH FIRE...

YAMAZAKI: REAL LIFE IS BORING. I HAVE TO FIND ENJOYMENT SOMEWHERE! YOU CAN TALK THOUGH, DAY BY DAY YOU PLAY WITH FIRE WITH ALL THOSE SECRETS YOU HAVE.

HEYJUN: THAT'S TRUE. BUT STILL, NO MATTER HOW BIG YOUR EGO IS, IT DOESN'T MEAN YOU SHOULDN'T BE VIGILANT. ANYWAY, IF YOU GET ANY MORE MESSAGES, LET ME KNOW.

YAMAZAKI: I WILL. HAVE YOU CHECKED SERPAN TODAY?

HEYJUN: NO. NOT HAD A CHANCE. I'VE BEEN TOO CONCERNED ABOUT THIS TEXT.

YAMAZAKI: WELL, YOU SHOULD, THERE ARE SOME COOL NEW WEIRD SITES ON THERE. REIGN HAS BEEN FINDING AMAZING SITES LATELY!

HEYJUN: SOUNDS GOOD. HOWEVER, I'VE HAD ENOUGH OF WEIRDNESS THANKS TO THE MONSTERS CLUB FOR ONE DAY. I'LL GO ON NEXT WEEK, AND HOPEFULLY NO MORE TEXTS WILL ENSUE.

File   Edit   Search   Help

YAMAZAKI: SERIOUSLY, DON'T WORRY ABOUT IT.
ANYWAY, SPEAK TO YOU AGAIN SOON. I'D BETTER
GO TO SLEEP; I HAVE AN EXAM TOMORROW AND IF
I SHOW UP LATE ONCE MORE MY TEACHER IS GONNA
GIVE UP ON ME GOING TO UNIVERSITY. AND I'M
NOT GOING TO BE THE ONE TO BOTCH OUR PLANS
TO GO TO TOKYO UNIVERSITY TOGETHER. I NEED
TO STUDY WELL IF YOU WANT TO COME HERE AND
LIVE WITH ME, WE GOTTA HAVE A ROOF OVER OUR
HEADS!

HEYJUN: I LOVE HOW YOUR EXAM IS YOUR MAIN
CONCERN AFTER GETTING THAT TEXT BUT
WHATEVER. TAKE CARE, YAMAZAKI. YOU'RE THE
ONLY PERSON THAT KEEPS ME SANE. THE ROAD TO
JAPAN IS THE ONLY THING KEEPING ME GOING
OVER HERE. BY THE WAY, DON'T YOU EVER CALL
ME PACHI-SAN LIKE THAT IN AN ARTICLE EVER
AGAIN!

YAMAZAKI: YOU TOO, JUN. HAPPY KILLING
PACHI-SAN!

++ YAMAZAKI LOGGED OUT ++

As the chat ended, I sat back feeling no less uneasy than before. Also, highly unamused at his last sentence. He had been fazed enough to bring this site to light beyond our pin board, however, he was not at all concerned by the fact this site had our phone numbers. I had no clue how they had gotten them and whether it was real or not. All I knew was we had to be careful.

Chapter Eleven

Two weeks had passed since I'd received the strange message from The Monsters Club, and the feeling of abnormality had yet to simmer. It was the phone number issue more than anything. It was gnawing at my mind as to how this site had gotten our numbers and I couldn't figure it out. It wasn't even that I believed the site was real. It was the fact someone had gotten my personal number, which meant they had to be a pretty good hacker. It annoyed the hell out of me since I prided myself on my protection skills.

I was stuck between belief and disbelief, and I didn't want to test it to see if the site was real. For once, I was glad at the fact I was going to a Dallington friend's birthday party. I needed distraction from it, even if for a few hours, because these ideas were all plaguing me with frustration.

The birthday I was attending was Ela's. She was already back on top form like I knew she would be. This girl was one of the most popular girls at school and no matter what people did to her, she couldn't fall for long. She was fine and back to her peppy self.

This party was another event where I would put on my mask and pretend to be a caring, loving friend, when all I wanted to do was sit at my computer and live in my virtual world. Ela lived in the same wealthy gated estate as me, in a lavish house at the very end of the community. Her father owned a tech company and her mother a high fashion chain, so it was to no surprise she lived in the biggest house on the lot. This was how fickle Dallington could be. For other students that had experienced such shamings in the past, their lives never would've resumed as quickly as this.

'I invited over Dillan's group of friends and they said they would stop by. Tonight, I'm determined to make him my boyfriend!' Ela said, as we sat in her bedroom doing our makeup for this evening. As usual, I sent her a smile back through the mirror, pretending I had any interest in her love for one of our schoolmates.

'It's so funny. You were shamed in front of him and you've soon forgotten about it. Well, he did too and actually loved it. Bizarre.' Maria replied, laughing in the background as she looked at her phone. 'I would've died if that had happened to me.'

Ela snapped her head to Maria as she laughed beside Aisha, who carefully was applying false lashes. 'Well, he clearly cares, since he agreed to come along. He's been talking to me more lately. So, it seems I'm forgiven. That and the fact I know he's broken up with Lucinda. Even without me ruining her, they've ended!' Ela jumped on her bed with joy.

Maria rolled her eyes. 'You have no shame. Not long ago you thought everything was over. Look at you now!'

'I agree.' Aisha chimed in. 'I can't believe you're suddenly this happy.'

'Dillan is now single and talking to me, why wouldn't I be happy?' Ela turned to me. 'Junie, are you ready to secure Theodore tonight?'

'No way am I going for Theodore.' I replied. The topic of Theodore wouldn't seem to end lately, and with him showing up in my life more, it was starting to annoy me. 'I told you, I'll meet someone else. On my own terms.'

Ela sighed. 'Oh, come on, Theodore is cool. I'm sure you will anyway. But it amazes me that you haven't got a boyfriend. You're so pretty! Do you just have high standards? Is that is why it hasn't happened?'

'No, I don't have high standards...' Just that all the guys at my school aren't Yamazaki. 'I just haven't met the right guy yet.'

She shrugged. 'Well, we'll see what happens. Either way, tonight we're all gonna have fun because after I was publicly shamed, I need this night of letting go. I'll find out who did that to me one day but till then, I'm enjoying myself. I'm never talking about Lucinda, the threat list, or taking someone down ever again!'

I rolled my eyes internally and we soon finished getting ready for the evening. It wasn't long before we were all standing around in our short, glamorous dresses. I was so bored barely thirty minutes into the event that I spent the first half of the party in the bathroom. Trying to waste the hours away before I ran out of excuses to hide and was dragged in a circle to dance. It had worked well as a distraction though, as I mindlessly watched all these teenagers prancing around and acting like they cared to be here.

It was funny because to some degree everyone held up a false image like I had been doing. Everyone wanted to fit in and would do whatever they could to do so. In reality, I wasn't any different from these people who forced themselves into relationships and groups they probably hated. I did that too, so I wasn't so odd in that manner. We all wanted to pass by and pretend we were normal. Whatever normal was.

It wasn't that I didn't like these people. My friends and the guys that were now trying to gyrate against every girl in the room just weren't for me. That was my own doing for not showing them who I really was. My online self. But it had to be this way because nobody would like that version of me in this society. Besides, nobody else showed their real selves so why should I? I didn't want to stay in this town, around these rich people who only cared about their next hair appointment, the latest dating scandal, luxury car or the current victim of embarrassment. I'd never been interested, and since I wouldn't be staying in England after graduation, I didn't need to show my true self. There was no point befriending people I would soon cut off.

It wasn't long before I'd had enough of all the guys trying to swarm me, and sneaked outside. Ela had finally gotten her wish and made out with Dillan as I passed the patio door to the kitchen. She truly had no shame, and it seemed neither did he. They were perfect for each other and I supposed I may have done good by doing what I did after all.

As I hit the back garden, the cool breeze felt beautiful on my skin. I pulled out a sneaky cigarette but was caught mid puff by a familiar voice that seemed to be appearing in my world more these days.

'I didn't know you smoked, Miss Pristine.' I turned to see Theodore smiling back at me. All six-foot, bronzed and dimpled cheek of him. When you haven't seen somebody up close for so long, it was weird. He'd gotten handsome. I'd not noticed this before now.

'Hey Theodore, you seem to be showing up a lot lately.' I replied sitting down on a bench near the doors, scanning his attire. He was wearing a sleek black suit that seemed far too clean and pristine for a party full of horny teenagers.

He came and sat beside me on the small bench, picked up a piece of grass and began tearing it up. 'Hasn't it only been once since you caught my make out session that we've been bumped into each other? But anyway, our paths never crossed simply because we never usually go to the same school parties.'

'Why, do you have something against us?' I taunted.

He let out a huff of cold air. 'Not you. It's Maria, everyone knows how overbearing she is. We tend to only go to football house parties.'

I looked back into the house as he said that and saw her laughing hysterically with a group of guys, the sound piercing out into the garden. 'True. Bit of a wild one. I thought guys liked that though?'

He laughed. 'Not all of us. We're pretty chill guys in the football squad.'

I laughed. 'The football team is chill? Aren't you the guys that pull pranks all the time?'

'Sure.' Theodore laughed, not denying the fact. 'It is strange to be talking to you though. It feels like a lifetime ago since we last spoke as kids.'

'It sure does.' I said flicking some ash off my cigarette.

'You know, you should come to some of our groups' parties.'

I turned to him and laughed. 'Why?'

He shrugged, keeping up his smile. 'I don't know. Maybe it would be nice to get to know you again. We were once very close.'

I looked at him oddly. It was strange to be talking to him again, and it felt so foreign being this close to him as an adult. We'd always gone to the same schools and had played together as children, but as we got older, we naturally grew apart as we found our own friendship groups. We were in two different popularity sides at our school, and that meant we would never usually mingle since neither side tended to keep to themselves. But that could change now Dillan and Ela had connected.

As nice as it would have been to get to know an old friend again, I didn't need it. I threw the cigarette to the ground and stomped on it. I already had enough of keeping up appearances with one group of people, and I didn't need more to add to my list. I opened my mouth to reply to him when I felt my phone buzz in my dress. When I opened the text, a chill shivered down my spine. It was them again.

Mistakes equal consequences. Even for members.
Be careful of the words you use and share.
Abide by our one rule and you will be safe.
Refuse and meet your end.
We are watching at every hour.

Be careful.
TMC.

'Are you alright?' Theodore asked, sensing my rush of discomfort. I nodded, shakily pulling myself up.

'Uh, yeah. I just got a text from my mum. It seems to be some family emergency. I have to go.'

'So soon? Oh, well. I suppose I'll see you at school then.' Theodore smiled.

I rushed away, not even telling Ela I was leaving, holding my phone to my chest and feeling sick. I had to get home and talk to Yamazaki about this. Whatever was going on with this site was starting to feel more real after this second text.

I ran home, heeled feet barely managing to keep my body stable. The text had sent a jolt of fear through me. This site shouldn't have my number. It wasn't connected to anything I did online. But it was this second message which now had me worried that there may be more to this than a joke. A thought I really didn't want to accept. But after Yamazaki had sent out the article and I'd received this message saying it was dangerous to share anything, I had to clear things up and make sure they weren't related.

I sprinted to my computer, threw off my heels and typed out a message to Yamazaki, but nothing came back.

Maybe he had gotten this text, and knew it bothered me, and he didn't think it was an issue. But the site stated not to share it with anybody, and I knew there was a chance it was actually run by killers. I didn't know what to do. Most of the sites we hacked were jokes, or at least posed no threat to us. Certainly, no one from these sites had communicated with us before. Something was starting to feel off about this.

Chapter Twelve

'Hey, where did you get to last night?' Ela collared me the next day after her birthday party as I stood at my locker. I turned to see her looking as pristine as usual, but not without a scowl.

I cleared my throat. 'I had to get home for some family problem. Sorry I didn't tell you.'

Ela sighed. 'It's fine. I'm just sad you missed such a great night. Is your family okay?'

'Yeah, everything is fixed now.' I said, taking my last binder out my locker. 'How are you today, feeling eighteen yet?'

Ela smiled with a huge grin, leaning against the locker as I shut the door. 'All I can say is this, I'm pretty much dating Dillan now.'

My brows raised. 'That's fast. Didn't he just break up with Lucinda, and you only just properly started talking to him again?'

'He said he'd loved me for ages but was too scared to tell me about it because he didn't want to lose me as a friend. The video he saw of me made him decide to just go for it with me since he saw how much I loved him. I can't believe it!'

'I don't know what to say to that. If that video had of been me, I wouldn't feel that way.' I laughed.

Ela narrowed her eyes. 'I do wonder how you know about the video though; didn't you say you had gone home before it played? How would you know what was on it?'

Oh, she's caught me out. I soon came up with an excuse realising I was making it sound like I had been at the event during her shame, when as far as she knew I hadn't. 'Oh, no. I'm just talking about what I've heard. It doesn't sound great.'

She nodded, buying my lie. 'I suppose not. But he likes me and that's all that matters. This has been amazing, whoever tried to shame me has truly failed. If that person was on the threat list, then it means they'll be in trouble for messing it up. Way for something to backfire, they actually brought us together!'

'You truly have no shame, Ela.' I laughed as we started to head to Maths.

'Well, if I didn't, I could have let the situation get to me forever. I didn't.' Ela suddenly stopped in front of me, looking at me with inspection. 'Are you okay this morning, you sound rather glum?'

'Glum?'

'Yes, you've no enthusiasm for me. This has been a grand event and normally you would be far more excited!'

I realised how blunt I did sound, but this morning had not been a good one. I'd not slept all night because I couldn't get in contact with Yamazaki, and after that text message, I was concerned. He always answered me, no matter the time difference or how much he would complain; he would never leave my messages hanging, even for an hour. I had to regain some composure, given I was probably over-analysing this.

'Sorry, I'm a little tired after last night. In fact, I might skip Maths this morning.'

Her brows raised. 'Junie Han missing a lesson? You really must be tired. Will you be okay?'

'Yes, just tell the teacher I'm not feeling good this morning, will you?'

'Sure, but I can come with you if you want.'

'No, thanks. I'll be okay.'

'Oh, Junie. Why did you have to be this way this morning, I

wanted to celebrate with my best friend about the fact I have Dillan now!' She taunted. 'I'll see you at lunch, just text me if you need me, okay?'

I nodded before we parted ways. I was going to head out the back of the school, but the chance of bumping into Theodore was not something I needed right now. Instead I went and sat in the girl cubicles for most of the morning.

I was at a loss. Even though it had only been a short time since he'd stopped answering me, with this text on the brain and nobody to talk about it, I felt really strange. I kept trying to contact him for the rest of the morning, but to no avail and with each passing minute I was getting more and more freaked out. What was he playing at, leaving me like this?

As lunch approached, I huffed my way out of the bathroom, trying to be more enthusiastic than earlier, and bumped right into Theodore in the hall as I did so.

'Oh, sorry Junie. We seem to keep bumping into each other like this.' He laughed as he steadied me from falling. When I didn't reply his smile was soon replaced with concern. 'Are you okay?'

'Yeah, I'm fine.' I replied, trying to get past him but he pulled me back.

'Hey, what's wrong? Is this about your family problem from last night?'

I sighed. 'No, it's not. I'm fine, Theodore, thanks.'

'Hey, you can talk to me...' He continued and a sudden rush of anger hit me.

'Just let me fucking go...' I groaned and he removed his arms right away. I knew I'd slipped up and was overreacting, but I was frustrated, and this was starting to scare me. I knew I had to get home, otherwise I was going to snap at other people.

I soon left school, not even telling my teachers. I didn't know if I was overreacting, it had only been a day since I'd gotten this message but hearing nothing from Yamazaki in all these hours was not normal. I felt sick to my stomach. When I got home and checked my message boxes, they were still empty.

I sat back in my seat, feeling helpless. A hub for serial killers had messaged me to be careful after Yamazaki had released this article and now he wasn't replying to me. I'd not thought anything of hacking into this site for the thrill of it when it was first posted on Serpan. Yes, it was disgusting and evil. However, that was nothing new for a dark web user. But this was new territory. Could this site be real? Could Yamazaki be in danger?

I shook my head to get rid of such thoughts and kept up that Yamazaki was either playing with me, his computer was broken or that something had happened to stop him getting in contact with me, but not him being in danger. I couldn't accept that thought. This site had taken him out like they threatened to do so for exposing them to the public.

It was an oath they had on the front page and now I was starting to believe it was real, the more the hours passed with silence. Hours that turned into days. I was about to lose it if he didn't reply to me soon. My image in society was so hard to keep up from the stress of this. All my friends thought I was acting strange, and even Theodore kept his distance.

Then one evening, six days after Yamazaki had gone silent, whilst refreshing my mailbox as usual and cutting off any hacking jobs while waiting for his reply, a chat box popped up on my screen, but not from the person I needed most.

Reign: You are Junie, right? I'm afraid I have some news for you. I've been trying to contact you for the last few days but I couldn't get through till now.

My eyes brightened as I recognised the name from the Serpan pin board, but I had no clue how he had gotten my information. It was Reign, the guy who owned and ran the board, whom I had spoken to very few times.

REIGN: YOU ARE JUNIE, RIGHT? I'M AFRAID I HAVE SOME NEWS FOR YOU. I'VE BEEN TRYING TO CONTACT YOU FOR THE LAST FEW DAYS BUT I COULDN'T GET THROUGH TILL NOW.

HEYJUN: REIGN? YOU ARE THE GUY WHO RUNS SERPAN, RIGHT?

REIGN: YES! YOU SURE USE SOME DAMN SECURE STUFF TO HIDE YOURSELF. EVEN HIDING YOUR DETAILS ON SERPAN, IT TOOK ME AN AGE TO GET TO YOU!

HEYJUN: HEY, ARE YOU HACKING ME?

REIGN: NO. WELL, NOT HACKING YOU. I HACKED YAMAZAKI TO GET TO YOU.

HEYJUN: HUH?

REIGN: HAVEN'T YOU SEEN THE FORUM TODAY?

HEYJUN: WHAT ARE YOU TALKING ABOUT?

REIGN: ME AND YAMAZAKI OFTEN TALKED. SO, I KNEW YOU TWO WERE FRIENDS.

HEYJUN: WHAT ABOUT IT?

REIGN: YOU HADN'T BEEN ON THE BOARDS FOR A WHILE, SO I JUST CAME TO CHECK UP ON YOU. THOUGH I AM GUESSING YOU HAVEN'T HEARD, GIVEN YOUR RESPONSE.

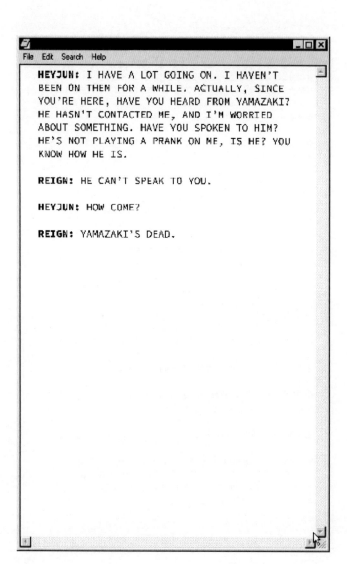

HEYJUN: I HAVE A LOT GOING ON. I HAVEN'T BEEN ON THEM FOR A WHILE. ACTUALLY, SINCE YOU'RE HERE, HAVE YOU HEARD FROM YAMAZAKI? HE HASN'T CONTACTED ME, AND I'M WORRIED ABOUT SOMETHING. HAVE YOU SPOKEN TO HIM? HE'S NOT PLAYING A PRANK ON ME, IS HE? YOU KNOW HOW HE IS.

REIGN: HE CAN'T SPEAK TO YOU.

HEYJUN: HOW COME?

REIGN: YAMAZAKI'S DEAD.

Chapter Thirteen

My hands froze over the keyboard as I looked over the words. They didn't feel real as my eyes glided over each and every letter and tried to process what Reign had told me. Dead. Yamazaki was dead? My whole body froze at the statement as the words together were unable to make sense in my head.

Reign: I suppose you're letting that sink in. I can't believe you haven't heard the news. I posted it on Serpan with my condolences the other day. You really didn't know?

After a few more moments of trying to force my fingers to type, I finally responded.

HeyJun: He's... dead?

Reign: Yes, sadly, and not in such a nice way.

HeyJun: What the hell happened?! I never saw the message on Serpan as I haven't been on for the last few days since I've been concerned as to why he hasn't been responding to me.

Reign: You really haven't been online, have you? He's been murdered, Junie.

HeyJun: What?! How would you even know this?

Reign: His mutilated body was posted on that site, THE MONSTERS CLUB. The site I posted on the pin board a few weeks ago.

It held a message underneath saying:

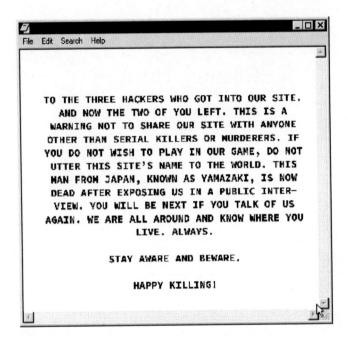

TO THE THREE HACKERS WHO GOT INTO OUR SITE. AND NOW THE TWO OF YOU LEFT. THIS IS A WARNING NOT TO SHARE OUR SITE WITH ANYONE OTHER THAN SERIAL KILLERS OR MURDERERS. IF YOU DO NOT WISH TO PLAY IN OUR GAME, DO NOT UTTER THIS SITE'S NAME TO THE WORLD. THIS MAN FROM JAPAN, KNOWN AS YAMAZAKI, IS NOW DEAD AFTER EXPOSING US IN A PUBLIC INTERVIEW. YOU WILL BE NEXT IF YOU TALK OF US AGAIN. WE ARE ALL AROUND AND KNOW WHERE YOU LIVE. ALWAYS.

STAY AWARE AND BEWARE.

HAPPY KILLING!

As I read the message, I slumped back in my chair and felt like my reality was falling into pixels. That every second was melting away. This didn't feel real. It couldn't be.

HEYJUN: THEY REALLY DO KNOW OF US...

REIGN: DID YOU RECEIVE THE TEXTS TOO?

HEYJUN: YOU DID ALSO? I DID, YES. BUT HOW DID THEY GET ALL OUR INFORMATION? US THREE ARE THE BEST HACKERS AROUND. THIS COULDN'T HAVE HAPPENED. IT HAS GOT TO BE A LIE.

REIGN: THEY ARE SEEMINGLY BETTER. IT'S NO MISTAKE, JUNIE. YAMAZAKI WAS MY FRIEND AS WELL. I WOULDN'T DO THIS. I WOULD NEVER MAKE UP SUCH A LIE.

HEYJUN: ARE YOU SURE IT'S HIM? THAT THEY AREN'T JUST PLAYING US WITH INFORMATION, THAT BODY COULD BE FAKE?

REIGN: YOU HAVE OBVIOUSLY NOT SEEN IT. THEY SHARED A PICTURE OF HIS MUTILATED BODY. I RECOGNISE THE BLEACHED BLONDE HAIR ANYWHERE. I'VE KNOWN THE GUY FOR YEARS AND SINCE NEITHER OF US CAN CONTACT HIM, WELL...

HEYJUN: YOU KNOW WHAT HE LOOKS LIKE TOO?

REIGN: YES, WE HAVE TALKED OVER WEBCAM MANY TIMES WHEN WE HAVE DONE CODING JOBS TOGETHER. MOST RECENTLY WHEN HE TOLD ME ABOUT THE ARTICLE. HE WAS ELATED TO TELL ME. I TOLD HIM TO BE CAREFUL. I SHARE THESE SITES FOR A REASON, THAT YOU ENTER WITH CAUTION BUT NEVER TELL PEOPLE ABOUT. THEY AREN'T SURFACE SITES; THESE THINGS ARE THE REAL DEAL. HOWEVER, HE DID NOT LISTEN......

File   Edit   Search   Help

REIGN: .....AND PROCEEDED TO SHARE TOO MUCH.
OF COURSE, THEY WOULD KNOW IT WAS ONE OF US
AND SADLY, IT HAS BACKFIRED ON HIM.

HEYJUN: I TOLD HIM THAT TOO. EVEN THOUGH I
BELIEVED IT WAS FAKE. THIS CAN'T BE REAL,
REIGN...

REIGN: I THOUGHT I WOULD TELL YOU, AND I WAS
WORRIED SINCE YOU HAD BEEN SO QUIET, I
THOUGHT YOU AND ME COULD SOON BE NEXT. WE
MUST BE CAREFUL FROM NOW ON.

HEYJUN: WHERE ARE YOU FROM AGAIN, REIGN?

REIGN: SWEDEN. YOU'RE FROM THE ENGLAND,
RIGHT?

HEYJUN: YES. DO YOU KNOW WHAT AREA THAT
NUMBER CODE SENDING US THESE MESSAGES IS
FROM? I HAVE NEVER SEEN IT.

REIGN: WE WILL NEVER KNOW. IT'S JUST AN
ILLUSION NUMBER TO DISGUISE ITS REAL PLACE.

HEYJUN: OH, RIGHT. OF COURSE, IT IS.

REIGN: THE CREATOR OF THAT SITE IS OBVIOUSLY
A VERY GOOD CODER TO BE ABLE TO GET TO US
LIKE HE HAS. THEY MANAGED TO GET OUR
PERSONAL INFORMATION, IT HAS AMAZED ME. I
JUST WANT TO SAY, WHATEVER YOU DO, DON'T GO
BACK ON THAT SITE. THOSE IMAGES OF YAMAZAKI
WERE BAD, JUNIE, AND I KNEW YOU TWO WERE
GOOD FRIENDS. HE ALWAYS SPOKE WELL OF YOU...

File Edit Search Help

REIGN: .....OF YOU, EVEN THOUGH HE WANTED TO
BEAT YOU AND BECOME THE BEST HACKER.

HEYJUN: I CAN'T BELIEVE THIS HAS HAPPENED...
I TRIED TO GET HOME AND SHARE MY FEELINGS
AFTER GETTING ANOTHER TEXT THAT ALARMED ME
BUT I WAS TOO LATE. HE NEVER RESPONDED.

REIGN: THIS IS A RARE REALITY.

HEYJUN: WILL WE BE OKAY?

REIGN: JUST STAY OFF THEIR SITE AND ANYTHING
TO DO WITH IT. THAT IS ALL WE CAN DO. I HAVE
TO GO NOW AND I WON'T BE HACKING BACK INTO
HIS STUFF AGAIN OR BE ON SERPAN FOR A WHILE
BECAUSE THE POLICE OVER THERE WILL PROBABLY
LOOK AT HIS THINGS AND COULD TRACK US, AND
ALSO, I'M NOT FEELING UP TO IT AFTER THIS.
IT HAS WELL AND TRULY FREAKED ME OUT.

HEYJUN: BEFORE YOU GO, WHEN WAS THIS ALL
POSTED? THE IMAGES OF HIM.

REIGN: I BELIEVE ONLY A FEW DAYS AGO.

HEYJUN: THANKS FOR LETTING ME KNOW. I DON'T
KNOW WHETHER ANOTHER HACKER WOULD HAVE BEEN
AS NICE AS YOU TO DO THIS AND TELL ME.

REIGN: I THOUGHT YOU SHOULD BE AWARE, AND I
WAS WONDERING IF YOU WERE DEAD TOO AND WAS
WORRYING ABOUT MYSELF AS WELL. I CAN'T
BELIEVE THIS HAS HAPPENED. I'M SORRY FOR
SHARING THAT STUPID SITE, BUT I DIDN'T......

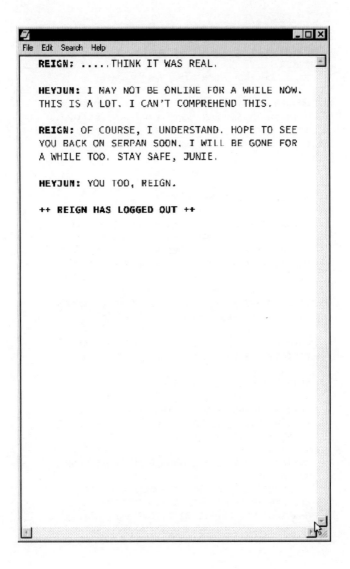

I sat back in my seat, stunned. What was I supposed to think of all this? Should I be terrified that this was a legit site and my friend had seemingly been mutilated? I believed Reign, he was not one to say such things and go to this length to contact me either. Was I supposed to feel so sick? I'd never met Yamazaki in real life but I felt like I knew him so well. We were close to something more than a friendship, but there was an unspoken understanding to not mention anything until we did meet. Despite our odd circumstances, we had each other. Not matter how much sarcasm or competitiveness there was between us, it was true.

Reign had told me not to go on the site, but I had to see this for myself. I needed to confirm if this was real or not, so I could take appropriate action. What action that was, I did not know. Because if I reported this all to the police, I would be arrested too. I was participating in illegal acts after all, and I'd have to hand over information about myself in order to share what was going on.

I turned back to my computer, still refusing to believe this had happened. I went straight to the Serpan pin board on the dark web and headed back to the original link. I was surprised it was still on the page. I hovered over the link for a few moments. I should listen to Reign and not go back on, not just because of Yamazaki's supposed death but all these messages. However, the need for confirmation was too strong, so I clicked on it and began to tear down their security again to get back through. I needed to see this for myself. I couldn't accept it until I did.

It took me even longer this time, however, I soon managed to get back through their defences and arrived at the familiar enter page where THE MONSTERS CLUB was written in red slash-marked writing against a black background.

I clicked enter and was taken straight to the main forum page, where the killers would post their images and blogs in different sections. All the posts were titled with things like, the girl I killed in the park todayy or Latest Catch. How could you believe such a thing would be real, that these people were sharing their victims, and for it not to have been discovered already by the police and eradicated? But then again, it was the dark web for a reason. People could get away with this stuff here. You could buy guns, hire a hit man, dead body parts and drugs. Anything was possible.

I looked around and found it dated back all the way to twenty eleven. I soon headed to the forum and began my search for Yamazaki. I would know if it was him, his face was so distinctive against his hair. I couldn't not recognise him. I'd known him for over five years now.

I scrolled for a while. There weren't that many posts containing recent dates and most had no dates at all, but I kept looking at the top of the page as it would have been recent if it was true. I was beginning to think Reign had played me for whatever reason, and maybe even Yamazaki too by not contacting me. However, when I came across the title, Late Night in Japan, my breath caught in my throat.

It took me an eternity to click on the post but when I did an image popped up straight away and it was for sure, Yamazaki. It was not gory at first and instead a screenshot of a profile picture of him from what I assumed was a passport photo. The blonde hair, tanned skin and sharp eyes. It was Yamazaki.

Below was a note, both in English and Japanese, that churned my stomach.

This guy was easy to catch. These three so-called hackers who broke into our site, this is the one who I found out tried to expose us in a recent article, and for doing so, we have had to re-wire our site again since an influx of people, not wanting to be killers, came here. This is a warning to anyone else who tries to share our site, keep your mouth shut or we'll be after you.

This site is for killers and killers only. This is our haven, and we will not have it being shared to people who aren't like-minded. Look at your friend below and take a word of warning from this: share our site with the wrong people, or come back here again, then this will be you. We aren't a showcase.

Just so you know, we have the strongest systems running, beyond any of your childlike coding or hacking techniques. We are the real deal, and we are in every country, ready to pounce at any second.

Stay away from places you do not belong.
Hope you enjoy the images.
Happy Killing!
TMC.

I knew if I scrolled down any further, the images were going to be of his dead body. However, I had to confirm it in my mind. For whatever reason, I had to see that this was not a hoax and it was real.

I braced myself as I scrolled down as slow as I could before the images began to appear. Reign was right. I should've stayed away. This was real. It had to be, his body was too realistic, and, with his limb's half hanging away, even more so. There, laying on the muddy ground, with a white plastic bag beside him and discarded groceries, was a human body. It was dark, but whoever had taken the image had switched on their flash and it picked up every horrifying detail. My mouth gaped as I saw the blonde hair stained with blood at the back of his head. Blood everywhere that slowly blended into the charcoal-coloured path below him.

My friend was dead. A guy who I complained about loads, but was my only true friend, was dead. Laid out and mutilated in front of me, and all because we entered one stupid site which he shared, thinking nothing would amount from it. I closed the screen and screamed.

I couldn't believe what I was seeing or hearing. I was in a

dream, I had to be. Living in some strange moment that I would wake from any second. But I didn't and instead my parents rushed into my bedroom after the scream had escaped my mouth. They frantically tried to calm me as I broke down, having no clue what was happening as I paced around my room with sweat gripping my skin like a blanket of agony.

'Junie, what has happened?!' My mother yelled through my tear-filled screams. 'What's with the screams?'

I so wanted to tell them, scream it to them, but it was too much for them to know. I managed to calm myself down enough for a few moments, to lie.

'Nothing, I just-' I had to catch my breath through each word. 'I fell asleep at my desk and woke from an odd dream.'

My mother's shoulders sloped as she rolled her eyes and let out a huff of annoyance. 'Is that all? I'm in the middle of a talk with my employers, Junie.'

'I've been busy studying and I fell asleep on the keyboard and woke from a bad dream-'

'Junie...' My mother cried out, and stormed out the room.

My father stood and watched my mother race off before turning back to me. 'Are you okay, Junie? You look a little pale.'

I wished I could scream what I was thinking, but if he knew any of what this was about, my life would be over. My insides hurt not being able to say it, but I kept the tears back for as long as I could.

'I'm fine.' I grumbled. 'I just got a shock.'

'Well, maybe it is time to switch of your computers and go to bed. Me and your mother have noticed you've been on them a lot lately.'

'What do you mean?'

'You seem to be spending a lot of time in here. I hear you into the early morning sometimes typing away at all hours.'

'I'm studying.'

'But you've completed most of your exams. What else are

you studying? Don't be too stressed about getting into Oxford, you'll be fine. Take it easy now.'

'Okay, I'll go to sleep.'

My father let out a heavy sigh. 'Switch them off and go to bed, Junie.'

After he closed the door, I sat on the edge of my bed and tried to remain calm. What I had just read, I knew it was real but not how I was going to accept this. What was I going to do now? Who was I going to talk to or grieve with? I felt frozen. I couldn't sleep that night. The images pressed on my mind relentlessly. The thought of him being dead because of this site, the images of his discarded body plagued every inch of my brain.

We all knew it was a risk lurking on the dark web. All of us coders who used the Serpan pin board; a place both created to share the creepiest and oddest dark webs sites that could be found, and as a place for us to gather, understood the risks of messing with this stuff. But nothing like this had ever happened in the five years I had been using this site. No site had been truly deadly; not simply a creation to creep out users of the dark web. I could never have imagined this would be real, but I knew it was.

I lay in bed for hours. Crying and thinking over the loss of my friend. I didn't know what I was going to do without him. As I lay there, I received a third message from the site. The most disturbing yet.

I was checking the three of you who broke into our site. You're a girl?

You're cute. I don't want to let you go after all. We were only going to harm Yamazaki for sharing the site, but now, I don't want to ignore you.

Hope to meet you soon, Junie Han.
Who knows? Maybe you will be my next victim.

Just like Reo Yamazaki.
But, unlike him, your death will be that much sweeter.
He muttered your name, by the way.
Too bad he never will again.
TMC Member.

I threw my phone to the ground as I saw the message end with a smiley face. I then set about destroying my technology. Yamazaki had physically died, now I had to virtually die. This was the truth about the dark web, one mistake, one wrong judgement, meant everything could come crashing down. I could do nothing but now await my own death, or be stalked by this site forever if I couldn't block them. I didn't know what to think anymore. My reality had mixed with the virtual world for the first time, and it was a bitter pill to accept.

With that message, my life changed in seconds. I'd gone from saving myself to destroying myself. The world felt empty without Reo Yamazaki.

Chapter Fourteen

Seven Weeks Later

For weeks after Yamazaki's death it felt like I was living in some strange paradigm. I couldn't get my head around the reality of things. Nothing as crazy as that had ever happened to me before and I didn't know how to process it. How was I supposed to accept my closest friend had been murdered by a dark web site for serial killers because he shared their website to the world? We all knew how crazy the world was but when it happened to you, you start to believe it was always that way. I was so used to being in control.

My parents saw the change as it was impossible to hide my shell-shocked state. My grades were falling since I wasn't sitting the final exams and I'd stopped blackmailing my teacher to fix them. I felt paranoid about leaving my bedroom and so my whole false demeanour had broken down. If my grades and appearance didn't return back to normal, I'd no longer be on track for university. I wouldn't be going at all. I was unsure whether I'd be able to wear that fake mask again when I'd nobody to comfort me at the end of the day. I couldn't put it on. I felt broken and lost without my only friend.

I had not received another message from the site in the seven weeks following Yamazaki's gruesome killing. I'd thrown away my burner phone and every piece of hacker-related technology I owned. My parents were not oblivious to the fact. While they'd seen my destroyed computers, they thought it'd been some act of rebellion against them and had ignored me. I didn't mind that, it was what I needed to try and come to my senses. But I couldn't come to terms with what had happened, and I was afraid to go outside, in case those crazy people had found me. Given they had discovered Yamazaki so quickly, I didn't see why they wouldn't do the same for me. Even if I hadn't exposed the site, it was evident by that final text to me that I was part of this now.

I'd locked myself in my room for weeks and since I was missing so much school it soon forced my parents to speak to me. I'd heard many of the phone calls my mother had with my principal. Everyone was so confused by my sudden change. Nobody understood my sudden depression. I knew my parents would think it was to do with the stress of getting into Oxford. It would be the only reason they could think of. Never guessing that it was something so much darker.

One day, however, they finally gave in and stormed into my bedroom. They both looked glum at the whole fiasco. Ready to end whatever had amounted from seemingly nothing.

'You have to go back to school, Junie. I can't believe we have allowed for you to be off for this long. Why have we, Juwon?' My mother said, standing by the side of my bed and turning to my father.

'Because she won't tell us what is going on.'

'Well, I'm here now and from Monday, you're back at school.'

'No...' I sighed, trying to pull my cover over my head but she tugged it away.

Talking to her was like arguing with a plank of wood. There was nothing to tell her anyhow because I couldn't reveal my secret life to them and what had really happened. For all I knew they would call a psychologist to try and work out why I lied so much, and they would never understand me, so it was all pointless. I had no choice but to live with the crazy hell that was happening. All this stemming from one article and a site that should have been fake.

'I don't know what has gotten into you lately. First, these late nights, and now, you're acting out this way for no reason, even getting rid of all your technology. Well, today, it ends. You are going back to school.' My mum soon stormed out of the room.

'Dad, please. I really don't feel up to it.' I said, feeling tears well up in my eyes.

He sighed. 'I'm afraid you have to go back. Whatever reason you are acting up these days, it must end. School, Monday, be ready to go.' My father finished before closing my door.

I slumped back into my pillow. They really weren't going to let me not go to Oxford. I had no choice but to live as my false self. It was going to be the hardest trial of my life. I would never get the chance to be able to be myself like I was with Yamazaki. I did not know even if my false self could be strong enough to deal without him to sustain me.

I had to try, though. I needed to get out of this house, and without my fake image, I would truly have nothing. My plan to head to Japan was dead alongside Yamazaki. I would have to think of another escape plan, but right now I needed to just slowly accept things.

I had to swallow the fact this had happened. That I was a hacker. The fact I met Yamazaki and that I had discovered a world that had made me feel alive. I had to let it go. Knowing that Yamazaki may never be found and that I could never properly say goodbye to him hurt me more than anything. However, I had to move on. I had to get the internet out of my life and pretend that it had all been a dream. I couldn't let thoughts of Yamazaki's death seep in because it would kill me.

I had to cut off my emotions before they controlled me, or there would be no escape plan at all anymore. I knew I couldn't let that go. I would have to bring back my false persona, the girl everyone thought was so perfect. It would be excruciating, but

I could do this, if not for myself and my sanity, for Yamazaki. I would get out of here. I had done too much to lose it now.

Chapter Fifteen

You'd think putting on my façade to people outside of my hacking life would be easy. To pull her back up as if it was a normal day, just like I had for most of my life. But because of what happened to Yamazaki, my mask had half fallen off and I wasn't able to put it straight back on. It was crooked because my heart was wounded, and as I got ready to go back to school two weeks later, after finally managing to drag myself out of bed, I was trying my best to numb my emotions enough to at least keep the mask half on.

Even though nobody knew of the true reason for hiding myself away, my mother had formed her own opinion and told my teachers that I'd fallen into a depression over some nervousness of the one-day Oxford application process. This fuelled me with rage, but it gave everyone enough of a distraction to help me hide my truth even further, so it was better than me having to come up with some excuse.

It was agreed I would only start at one day a week, which wasn't much but since they thought it was studying and exams that had me so stressed out, they let me slowly build myself back up so I didn't get overwhelmed. I didn't mind that in the slightest. Even if I'd rather be in my blanket cocoon.

Everyone around me knew something was off. I wasn't smiling like usual, or going out of my way to help people or generally being the do gooder they were used to seeing and controlling. I had things going on in my mind. The place I'd hidden from everyone had started to seep out into my daily life, all because I couldn't get those images out of my mind. Even though weeks had passed, I couldn't break away from it, and it was proving impossible to freeze them out of my mind.

Looking at the final message to me made my stomach turn, as did not knowing who was behind his murder. I hadn't received another text in weeks, and I hoped I never would. I had destroyed my phone, after all. Both of my phones. My life had to become nothing but school and focusing on my studies as much as I could. Not even for distraction, but rather to keep my parents and teachers off my back as to why my character had become so bleak. I knew I had to get my old façade back, but it was so hard, and it only grew harder the more I tried to pull the mask back into position.

'Junie, are you ready to go? I have to leave earlier this morning.' My mother called from downstairs for another day of school. It had only been three weeks now since I'd started going back, slowly growing into a new routine.

'I'm coming.'

I called back before looking at myself in the mirror, fixing my tie in place. 'I have to pull her back. All that I have worked for, I must find her and get back to normal.'

My words to myself were empty, and looking at my dull complexion reminded me of how false it was. All the makeup I had applied couldn't make me look any less of a lie. Even though I hadn't been online in so long, it still felt so fresh. It was so hard to hide my pain, and I was not used to feeling and looking this raw.

'Don't think of it anymore. You knew becoming a hacker wasn't a good job. Even though you didn't expect this. You have to get back to your old self. You're risking so much. You have to keep focused so you can leave this life. This is why you're doing this. Lying.'

I had already risked so much. Keeping up good impressions and stable grades was something I needed to do in order to escape as soon as I was eighteen. Because as soon as I did, I was out of here.

It seemed harsh, but my parent's expectations and lack of care for my actual needs were draining. The problem was I'd planned to go and stay with Yamazaki. And now I couldn't, that was another reason I was finding it hard to put the mask back on. I had no idea what I'd do when I was eighteen. I had so much planned and now it was dead. I knew I had to pretend that my plan to head to Japan was still on, I had to make myself believe it still existed to survive these next few months.

'Junie, come on!' My mother called again, and I soon let out a sigh, grabbed my bag and put on as much of the mask as possible before heading to face another day of pretending.

I greeted her with a smile as I got to the bottom of the stairs and she looked at me as if something was wrong.

'You seem happy this morning.' She said, as she wrapped a scarf around her shoulders.

'I am happy.' I replied. Wondering if saying it would send some pheromones into my body, but it failed.

'I'm glad to hear it.' She said kissing my cheek as we headed to the door. I held my phone in my pocket as I did so, the piece of technology I'd been forced to reintroduce into my life in case I needed to contact someone if I didn't feel good. I hated having it, but I had to make sure they thought I was resuming my normal life.

The trip to school was tense as usual but after a few chats to myself I managed to calm my mind down. Not trying too hard was the best idea. Focus on my studies and everything would be okay. I had to find a distraction.

'Mrs. Burns said you've been enjoying your lessons since you've been going back. Maybe this one day a week thing is doing you good.'

I broke myself out of my thoughts and smiled. 'I think so too, Mum. I'm just taking things slowly.'

'That's good. At least you're keeping yourself busy. Whenever you are ready to tell us what has been going on, I want you to know we're here for you.'

I turned to her at the remark, because in reality nobody knew why I had changed other than the suspected stresses of exams and Oxford. It was so hard to not debunk that theory. I hadn't even spoken to Mr. Hawthorne in weeks now, and I knew my grades would have felt the impact. But I wasn't sure if I was going to reinstate him to fix my grades either. Maybe failing everything would be the reason not to go to Oxford, but at the same time, I still wanted out of this town. For now, I wasn't going to do anything, I would just ignore Mr. Hawthorne when I saw him and let things develop naturally. I was in no state to think too far into the future right now.

'Actually, your teacher asked me if you wanted to add more days of going to school now. But since you seem to better this way, for now should we just keep it as is?'

I nodded, grabbing my bag. 'I think it is for the best. I will let you know when I'm ready. It is still a little early to throw myself back into things.'

'Okay, darling. Take care, and don't be hard on yourself.' My mother being kind like this was never going to not feel strange. I got out the car and she waved me off.

Growing up, she'd always been so strict, and niceties were few and far between. Maybe this had given my parents a wake up call. I hoped so. And maybe if it had, I wouldn't have to think about getting out so quickly when I turned eighteen. If they cooled the pressure for enough time for me to gather myself. I still would escape this life but right now, the thought had to go to the back of my mind so not to think of Yamazaki.

I let out a sigh and turned to my school, ready to put on the mask of normality for my teachers and friends. However, I felt a buzz in my blazer and soon opened a message that ripped off any comfort I had built up.

I'm back! It took me so long to get your new phone number. Have you been hiding from me? I see you. Trying to live in the real world. It intrigues me. You intrigue me. Now I have your attention, I may just play with you a little. Hacker girl. I didn't think I would. But I need a new game. And it may be you. Junie Han.

TMC Member.

The text sent a shiver down my spine, but I managed to keep myself together until I reached the girls' bathroom. I dug my nails into my palms as I ran. I really had clicked on the wrong pin board link. But I couldn't let this very first text after so long get to me. I had to pretend that world didn't exist. I had to let it go and bring back my false persona. I couldn't let my secrets slip out. I'd worked too hard for this. Taking so many people down over the years to protect my image. But with Yamazaki not here, the one person that always helped me keep up my lies, I didn't know how I was going to protect myself now. This was going to be difficult, but not as hard as missing somebody you can't openly mourn.

After the text, I wanted to do nothing but vomit. Any association with this group made me visualise Yamazaki's dead body, and I couldn't stand it. I hadn't had my phone in so long, I had forced them out of my mind, but they were still here. They'd found my new number. Waiting for me to return, and it chilled me to my core. I wasn't going to be left alone.

I splashed my face with some cold water to get some sense back into me. I returned to my senses before I allowed darkness to cloud my mind. Whoever was texting me was reminding me to keep my mouth shut. Well, they didn't have to worry. Because being silent on truth was one of my greatest attributes.

I forced the message to the back of my mind before heading to class. Greeting my friends like it was a normal day and heading to my first classes of the morning. It was only a short time that I'd been back, and I knew every student was wondering what had happened to me. Even my friends were trying to prize the truth out, but thankfully none of the teachers had mentioned anything, so it was up to everyone to guess.

'Junie, how are you feeling this week?' Mrs. Burns asked and I could feel every curious student's gaze on me as I walked into Science class. Even my friends stopped and stared since nobody really knew what was going on with me.

'Uh, I'm good.' Is all I replied before rushing off to my seat and not long after she got on with the lesson.

The morning classes passed by fast and I kept my phone switched off for every one of them to forget what was happening. Because if I kept getting bombarded with these wild messages every hour, it would have driven me insane.

'It is so unfair that she only gets to come once a week. Talk about privilege. I've had bad things happen and yet I'm forced to come to school.' I heard a group of girls say as we left our final class before lunch. Even though they had no idea as to why I had been off, people didn't care. All they thought about was their problems.

I ignored the girl's remark and said goodbye to my friends for a few moments, making them think I was heading to the nurse's office, but instead I went to my place of solitude at the back of the school away from everyone. I needed five minutes to myself. I needed to let out some frustration.

I pulled out a cigarette, still trying to ignore that text message and just about everything else right now. Frustratingly, my lighter wouldn't fuse. I shook the lighter as much as I could before I threw it onto the grass out of annoyance.

'Hey, littering is illegal.' A voice called from my side a few seconds later. A familiar one at that.

I turned to see Theodore, walking slowly to the side of the wall I was perched against. I hadn't spoken to him since the moment I threw some profanity at him during my last day at school before everything changed. He, however, still held his usual warm smile as he came and stood in front of me.

'What do you want?' I huffed, knowing I could get away with some sharpness around him since he didn't appear to have blabbed about my previous verbal assault on him.

Theodore shrugged. 'I saw you head out here and came to see how you were after hearing what those girls said in the hall. You seemed to rush off fast.'

I narrowed my eyes, confused as to why he was watching me, given we weren't even in the same class. 'You saw that?'

He nodded. 'Yeah. People can be dicks.'

I shrugged. 'They don't bother me. Don't worry if that is what you came here for. I can handle such things.'

'Actually, I only came to ask you how you were.'

'Why?' I sighed.

He came and leaned against the wall, placing his backpack by his feet. 'Well, given what has been going around the school about you, I thought I'd come and talk to you.'

'What has been going around?'

'Nothing major. Only that people don't have a clue what is going on with you and why you aren't coming to school as normal. Also, where the heck have you been? You left so suddenly, everyone was so confused. You were gone for weeks, not answering anybody's messages, either.'

I turned and looked out onto the frost field ahead. 'It's nobody's business.'

'It is only out of concern.'

I scoffed. 'I wish I could be that optimistic. But it's more that people are nosey. A trait of which I can't stand.'

'True. However, I don't need to know what's wrong. I just came to make sure you're okay. You don't have to tell me anything else.'

I turned back to him. I knew he had a crush on me, but I couldn't help but be irritated with him showing up so much lately. 'Why though, we haven't spoken for years?'

'Just because we don't speak doesn't mean I can't care about an old friend. We only grew apart 'cause of ageing; we've never been on bad terms.'

He was right, but I was in no mood to talk. 'I'm fine, Theodore. Thanks.'

'Are you sure? You're looking a little pale.'

I rolled my eyes. 'I'm always pale.'

'Are you okay?' He asked again and it annoyed me.

'I'm fine!' I spat and soon regretted my tone. I was supposed to be looking normal again and even though I could act a little wilder in front of him, I didn't want to let go too much. 'Sorry, I am okay. I just want to be alone, Theodore.'

Thankfully, he didn't take offence and smiled. 'Okay. But if you need anything feel free to talk to me. You can swear at me as much as you want, I don't mind it.' He replied before walking off as easily as that.

A kid I hadn't spoken to in years was showing random concern and a liking for me. Everything was so bizarre at the moment. But people were really watching me everywhere I went, it seemed, and I had to be careful. Nobody could know the truth. I took one last look out into the field before heading back inside and soon finished my weekly school session, saying goodbye to my friends before my mother picked me up and asked me about my day. I lied my way to my room before shutting myself inside and letting out a sigh.

Even though I only went one day a week, it was tough. Lying to everyone and myself about feeling better, even though they had no idea my dearest friend had been murdered, was the hardest thing I'd ever done. Lying used to be second nature to me, but now it was difficult. I was starting to feel numb, even with these high emotions though. It was like I was disassociating myself. But it didn't last long when I switched my phone back on, having forgotten about this morning's text after my conversation with Theodore had distracted me.

That evening, as I lay in bed, another message popped up.

We're finally in touch again. My previous text is the first I have sent to you in weeks. I knew you needed time to grieve and wouldn't answer. I didn't know if I would play with you either. I gave it some time. We are monsters. But after getting Yamazaki, I didn't know if you would be worth it. But like you searched my forum, I did some digging on you.

Junie Han. What I found, it pulled me in enough to want to add you to my list.

My list,
Of victims.
Do not worry yet.
You won't be harmed.
I just wish to learn more about you
and if you cooperate,
you will be safe.
I will get back in touch soon.
Stay safe, Junie.
TMC Member.

I didn't even know what to say. Whoever this guy was, I knew he wasn't playing, given Yamazaki's fate. They'd been watching me. Like I watched others. Simply for accessing this site, I was now a target of murderers. I had to wait and see what would happen to me. Staying strong was my only way out of this.

I refused to let myself panic. I had been hacking since I was twelve years old. Diving into the darkest and wildest of sites. I couldn't let this get to me. I'd played with so many people and done many bad things over these years; doing what I had to. Ela was nothing in comparison as to how far I would go to save my own reputation. But never had any of it happened in real life like this before, where I was so out of control of my life. I couldn't block my IP address in real life or put up a code to protect myself. If these people were watching me in real life and got my name, they knew where I lived. I didn't know what to do but stay calm and keep to a routine, all while watching my back. I would wait for the next text and then decide.

Getting this text made me look at my computers that my parents had forced back into my room after I'd tried to throw them away. The two lonely monitors sitting in the corner of my room that hadn't been touched in weeks now. They were thick with dust and memories of myself sitting in that corner, hacking into systems in every corner of the world. But I didn't know what to do about it. Any of this.

I couldn't show my parents the texts or what happened to my only real friend. I couldn't say anything about how I felt. Because if I shared this world, it would show my lies and illegal activity, and put people in danger if they tried to access anything. I would either be arrested or be harmed if they tried to find the person or people behind these texts. I couldn't escape, and I really had no choice but to accept these texts as they came. To save us all.

That night I sat in front of my computer and shivered. I so wanted to go on and look at the very site that had taken my friend's life. To uncover the layers behind it and see who was messing with me. However, I couldn't bring myself to do it. I had to keep away from that world as either I would do something bad or they would, and I couldn't risk my family's life for nothing. As much as I wanted out of here, I didn't want to put them in harm's way, and whether someone was watching me or not, I had to act accordingly.

'Oh, sorry. Are you about to study?' My mother said as she entered my room with a pile of clothing. It was good timing because it forced me to stay off the computer.

I nodded. 'Yeah, I thought I'd get some extra hours in.' I lied.

My mother came and threw me into a hug. 'How glad I am to see my daughter returning!'

'What do you mean returning?' I replied.

She pushed me back. 'Well, you're back to looking alert and talking.'

I soon shook her off. 'Well, I'm going to do some studying, then.'

'Okay, but don't overdo it. Get some sleep as well.'

'I will.' I fake smiled as she left the room and soon sighed onto my desk.

I looked at my computer knowing that studying was still the least of my problems. I'd already done most of my exams, so that would be fine. Whatever this person texting me wanted from me was my main issue right now, and trying to live as best I could without breaking down again was the other. Not going on my computer right now and trying to locate this person or people was the hardest thing ever. However, it was too dangerous to do it. They told me to stay away from the site, so I had to.

I knew I had to fix something. I didn't know what to fix or how to even begin to escape such a problem as this. I'd always been in control and had Yamazaki to help me, and now a stranger was controlling me from a website for killers. But that was because this was filtering into my real life, and I'd never been good at doing things in reality alone. I lived in the virtual world for a reason. It was the only place I usually did have control.

Chapter Sixteen

A week had passed since the last message and I still couldn't settle at all. My façade was slipping day by day, and I knew something had to be done or I was going to fall back to my bed and become a hermit again. I was so on edge, wondering if someone was watching me. They knew my real name, and I had never put that out on the internet in all my life. I had no social media that this person could find me on, and that freaked me out. However, at that point, I was less frightened than I was willing it to end, so I didn't have to think about Yamazaki anymore.

At lunch break, I headed to my usual place, for what was now beginning to become a bad cigarette habit to cope. However, it was the only tool I had to release some tension. I was hardly able to go to therapy, given I was not able tell anybody what exactly my problem was at this point. It would have a bad outcome, so it was better to live with it. That and the fact a murderer was watching me; who knew what they would do if I told anybody.

I let out a sigh of frustration along with my cigarette puff and it bled into a body in front of me. I looked up to see Theodore staring down at me with a smile.

'Hey.' He said, looking at me as if it was now a normal thing to be talking to me these days.

'Is it a regular thing now?' I asked.

'Is what?' He laughed sitting beside me on the wall.

'You coming to talk to me.'

He shrugged. 'I suppose it could be.'

I rolled my eyes at his smile. 'Isn't it obvious that I come here to smoke and be alone?'

'I'm just checking up on you.'

'What for?' I huffed.

'Well, whatever is going on with you, I just want to make sure you're alright. You weren't off for that long for no reason, Miss Study Queen who hasn't had a day off in years. Of course I'm going to be this way.'

'You don't even know why I've been away from school. It could be for nothing. I may have had a bad flu and have a weak body, so I don't have the energy to be here much.'

'Maybe so. However, I just want you to know you aren't alone. Whatever the reason.'

I turned to him. 'You make it sound like something bad happened to me. You know nothing. Like everyone else who thinks it's something crazy.'

'It doesn't matter. Good or bad, I want you to know I'm here for you. Besides, I have the right to assume it was something bad given how you left me that day in school. What am I supposed to think?'

I was confused by him. We hadn't spoken in years, and because I had been off for some time and only came to school once a week now, he was suddenly speaking to me like we were still kids playing outside. Whether he secretly liked me or not, for this to be happening so suddenly was both annoyingly timed and frustrating. He just couldn't take the hint that I wanted to be alone.

'Look, thanks for the kindness, and I don't mean to be rude, but you don't need to be doing this, Theodore. Pretending you care about me. Go back to your sporty friends and leave me be.'

Theodore leaned back and let out a half laugh. 'Okay, you caught me.'

'Caught what?'

'I do have another reason I came to see you aside from making sure you're okay.'

I rolled my eyes. 'What is it?'

'I want to ask you out.'

His words made the cigarette freeze at my lips. 'What?'

He looked away as he spoke, his face reddening. 'I know it's bad timing, to be asking this now given you're going through something. It's only, I was going to ask you at that party but then I've not seen you in weeks, and you left me in such a weird way that day at school. I've never had an excuse to come and talk to you, so, although I do care, what has gone on with you gave me a reason to finally speak to you again for long enough to ask you on a date.'

'You want to go on a date? We haven't spoken for years. Why do you suddenly like me now?'

'Well, don't think of it as a date. See it as a way to get to know each other again.'

'Why, Theodore?' I sighed.

'I'm not gonna lie. I've looked for a way to talk to you for years, but your friends are always around you and I've never had a reason to start a conversation again. I'm still shy, like when we were kids.' His face grew even redder at the topic, and as much as I didn't want to cause a scene, this was the last thing I wanted right now. Any form of attention.

He was right about my friends; they usually were always around me. However, I didn't know what to think of his secret crush on me finally coming out. He'd wanted to speak to me all this time and only did now he could get me alone. When I did think about our younger days, he had always had a hard time speaking to people out of his inner circle. I understood that fact had not changed, but it was still terrible timing to have something like this happen.

I didn't even know how to reply. 'I don't know what to say, Theodore. It probably couldn't have come at a worse time.'

'I know and I'm sorry, but it was killing me holding it in.' He laughed awkwardly. 'I thought I would take the chance to speak with you now and spill the truth.'

The mere talking of relationships made me think of Yamazaki, and I got up and stamped out my cigarette, trying to erase him from my mind before I broke down. 'You really have terrible timing, Theodore. I'm not in a good place right now. I can't be thinking about things such as this.'

Theodore looked at me, eyes full of guilt. 'I know. I'm the worst. But I don't know what is going on with you, so I didn't know that it would bother you so much.'

'What do you want me to say?' I sighed.

'I suppose, would you go on a date, or a friendship outing, at least?'

He waited on me with expectation. This was so out of the blue I didn't know what to feel, but then I realised something. As much as I wanted to be alone, maybe it would be good to go out and think of something else for a while. Forget about what was going on and just escape from my reality, even if for five minutes. It would be strange being with Theodore again but maybe it would do some good. I could be away from thoughts of Yamazaki and the killers playing with me. It would also be a good tool to have to distract everyone at school. If I started hanging around with Theodore, it would become the topic of the school's gossip, and would override my disappearance problem.

I shrugged, giving up. 'Since you went to all this effort, I suppose it wouldn't hurt to go out.'

'Really?' His eyes brightened.

'Sure. But where are you thinking?' I asked.

It seemed he had the answer ready. 'Do you like vinyl?'

'Yeah.' I shrugged.

'We could go to that new vinyl café in town, listen to some cool music and, well, reminisce. How about it this Sunday?'

His dimpled smile filled me, oddly, with ease. 'Okay. I guess it couldn't hurt.'

'Great!' He said jumping up and blushing when he realised he looked too eager. 'I'll see you then and not annoy you anymore today. Looking forward to it, Junie!'

He rushed off, and I stood there in disbelief at what I was doing. I was going on a date with Theodore. I hoped it would help, both as a distraction and as a tool to keep my mask of normality in place, and would not complicate things further.

'Where are you going?' My mother asked the following Sunday as I applied some mascara and got dressed to meet up with Theodore.

She came and sat on the side of my bed looking confused as I hadn't made any effort with my appearance for weeks now. 'I'm going to meet a friend in town.'

'A friend?' She said. Given I didn't go anywhere but school lately, I knew it would look like odd to her. 'What friend is this? Ela?'

'No, you know Theodore Hawk-Silberston, right? He asked me to go with him to a café in town. I agreed as I thought it would be good to get back to some normality in my daily life as well as in school.'

Her eyes widened. 'You're going on a date and never told me?'

I shrugged. 'I never thought about it, but it isn't a date. We're getting to know each other again. It has been years since we last spoke.'

'You sure about that? That kid has liked you since you were young. I'm surprised it took him all this time to ask you out.' I wondered how she'd known that, when I hadn't realised until Ela had told me. I brushed it off.

'It isn't a date.' I sighed.

'Sure. That is what all teenagers say at first.' She laughed. Speaking to my mother this way would never feel normal. She had been trying to act more like a friend than a parent. 'Anyhow, I'm glad to see you going out again. Will you be okay?'

I turned to face her. 'I will. I'm only going into town.'

'I'm glad to hear that. Do you want me to take you?'

'It's okay, I'll get a taxi.' I said and got up, dusting off my white dress.

'You look pretty. I'm sure Theodore will blush. He always was a shy child. How is he these days?'

'He's good. A nice guy, I suppose.' I said, forcing a smile. 'Anyhow, I'd better be off. I shouldn't be out that long.'

My mother got up and gave me a hug. 'Enjoy yourself, Junie. I'm glad to see you getting back to yourself.'

I smiled at her before she waved me off in my taxi. I let out a sigh, feeling oddly nervous the closer I got into town. It had been so long since I'd been out like this, and given my circumstances, I felt on edge knowing someone could be watching me. I had to be careful and aware of everything. However, I couldn't let these people scare me into hiding, so held my ground. To honour Yamazaki, if nothing else.

It wasn't long before I arrived in town and made my way to the café. I wasn't a person that ever got nervous for much, but this made butterflies float in my stomach as I drew closer to the café. When I did arrive, it took me a few moments of standing outside and swallowing my nerves to finally go inside. It was still strange to have Theodore so suddenly back in my life. But I didn't want to think too hard about it. I had decided to simply let it unfold. I didn't want to know anything. All I wanted for that day was to be free of the darkness following me.

As I looked around for him, Theodore called my name from the side.

'Hey, glad you came.' He smiled awkwardly as he stood in his casual clothing. A plain white t-shirt and dark jeans. It looked strange; I was used to seeing him in school uniform, or, more recently, suited up for a party. 'I'll get you a drink. What would you like?'

I hesitated for a moment, looking at the menu. 'A hot chocolate would be good.' I replied.

'That sounds nice. Think I'll get one as well. I'm sitting in the corner over there. You go and sit down, and I'll bring these over.' He smiled and brushed past me as I headed to the seating area.

I soon sat down in the corner of the café, taking in its pretty aesthetic. I loved listening to records, and the seventies music playing in the background made me feel relaxed. It was quiet, and the tone was so warm in here it made me feel lighter. I felt so calm that when Theodore came back and sat down facing me, it shocked me.

He was so familiar, and it was like the past had come flooding back all at once. It seemed natural, and didn't feel forced. Being out of an environment as stressful as Dallington made me see him differently.

'It is strange, isn't it.' Theodore said after sitting down, sending me back to the moment.

'What is?' I asked, grabbing my drink.

'Us being here together after so long. I don't think we have spoken since the beginning of high school. Not properly.'

I shrugged. 'Well, people grow up and part ways. It doesn't mean there's anything bad.'

'You're right, but still, it is nice to be here after so long.'

'I agree.' I smiled. 'You finally gained the courage to ask me out. It's funny to hear it, to be honest.'

'I know, you probably never guessed. I bet it's weird.'

'Not at all. I mean, I don't mind. But actually, I did know about your crush on me.'

His eyes widened. 'Was I that obvious?'

'No,' I laughed. 'Because Ela found out from Dillan, and she told me about it.'

'Huh, Dillan told Ela?' Theodore beamed. 'That's good, I suppose. Since I was taking so long. At least we aren't awkward. But anyway, now you're here, how have you been?'

'Fine.'

'Why exactly were you off school? I began to wonder if you were ever coming back.'

'It doesn't matter. I'm okay now.' I replied.

'I'm only concerned as you seem very quiet these days.'

'How would you know what I'm like? We haven't hung out in years, remember?'

Theodore sat back in his chair and shrugged. 'Well, you're pretty popular. People know your character well, and so they're curious about all of this.'

I shrugged. 'Look, thanks for the concern, but don't worry about it. I'm slowly coming back to school more, so let's just say the problem is ending.'

'Okay but if you ever need to talk…'

I broke in. 'Thanks, Theodore.'

I took a sip of my drink and he let out an exhale. 'You know, I really have liked you for some time.'

'Why didn't you say anything?'

He laughed. 'I told you, I was too shy.'

'And now my situation finally made you brave enough to say it?' I laughed back.

'It really did, as bad as that sounds.'

'It's funny, when we were friends as kids you were never this shy. In fact, you were pretty popular and played football and things. How come you are shy now? You don't seem it around others.'

'Yes, but that is different. When you like someone, you can become awkward. Well, I do anyhow.'

I sat back in my seat and smiled. 'Well, don't worry. I won't bite. I'm just as nice a person now as I was back then. I'm just going through stuff, that's why I have been snappy with you. Stuff you needn't know, but now you can understand things a bit.'

'Good to hear it. But don't feel pressured by me saying I like you. I understand if you don't. I just wanted you to know because you never know...'

I let out a sigh. 'I'll be honest. My head has been all over the place lately so I can't say I like anything right now.' He looked sad at that, so I continued. 'However, that doesn't mean I can't grow to like something in the future.'

'Well, that gives me hope.' His smile returned. He really did have a beautiful face when he smiled. I realised I was getting lost in his appearance, and it made my heart skip a beat. It made me feel strange, and guilty to be feeling this way so soon after Yamazaki's death.

I soon jumped up. 'Uh, I'm just heading to the bathroom. I'll be right back.'

He nodded, and I shuffled off, before closed the door behind me. I took a deep breath for getting annoyed at myself. This was meant to merely be a distraction, to allow myself to forget my pain and the mess I was in.

I took a few moments to get composed and to remind myself of why I was here before I went back out and sat down.

'You know, since I said I can grow to like you, how about we go for another date?' I asked.

His face lit up with both delight and surprise. 'I was just about to ask that. I would love to.'

We both smiled as we sipped our drinks. I wasn't going to let myself feel down, I had to disconnect from what was happening.

'Where are you thinking for next time?' He asked.

'How about the beach?'

'That would be nice.' I smiled.

'How about same time next week?' I nodded and we both smiled awkwardly.

I couldn't believe I was letting someone take me on dates when it was my hacking and coding that had been my focus for so long. But I had been thrust back into the real world, and this is what real-world people did. I couldn't hack right now, and since my old plans were dead, I had to choose my next path.

My phone buzzed and all thoughts of the future vanished. I opened the text and felt sick.

Having a nice day, Junie? You look pretty in that white dress,
It looks beautiful on you.
So would my knife,
Slicing your skin.
However, that is too soon to speak of.
Unlike with your friend
I want to take this slow
And play you gently.
Don't be scared.
I'm here for you.
My new love.
You hacking our site connected us,
It was your best mistake ever.
See you soon.
TMC Member.

The message almost made me drop my phone. I must have gone pale, as Theodore's expression instantly became concerned. My eyes darted around afraid, someone was there. I turned to him, unable to speak.

'Are you okay?' He asked, but I didn't respond. I felt like the whole world was watching me outside this cafe, ready to attack.

I ran out of the café as Theodore called my name, and got in whatever taxi I could, without looking back. Whoever was watching me had known where I would be that day, and had followed me. I had to get away; the thought of them being so close was terrifying. I now knew there was no hiding from them.

Chapter Seventeen

Theodore bombarded me with messages after I left him without explanation, but I couldn't bring myself to respond. Paranoia plagued my every thought. I panicked and went home, locking myself in my bedroom. The virtual world had forced its way into my reality. I didn't know how to handle these people messing with me like this.

I looked at my computer. I had to end this. I went at the site to see if I could trace anything. If I wanted to remain alive in the real world, I had to kill my virtual self and cut myself off from the club that was plaguing my phone. They'd gone too far, and I was done with it all.

But still, I didn't know what exactly I was going to do. If I went on the site again and tried to mess with it, something bad could happen. But if I left it, they would think I was scared, and would continue doing this to me. I had to do something. To start with, I could ensure all traces of my online self were removed.

As I logged in to all my portals, it was filled with so many messages my computer almost crashed. I had not been on for so long, and clients had been either requesting my services, or other Serpan members had been asking where I was. I ignored it all and deleted everything.

When it came to my conversations with Yamazaki, my hand froze, but I knew I had to get rid of it. Even if it meant eradicating all that I had left of him. I would do this to save my own life. I clicked delete and erased everything. Messages, the dark web, jobs, it all died in one click.

But as I did so, a new message popped up before I could delete the message portal itself.

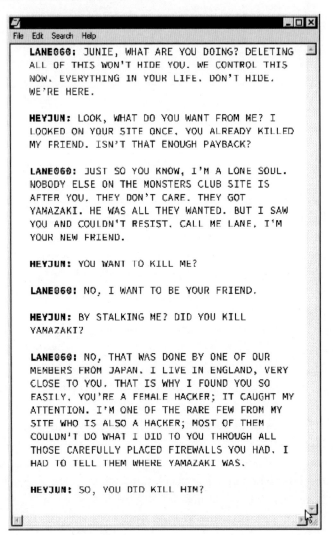

File   Edit   Search   Help

LANE060: NOT PHYSICALLY. I JUST SENT THE
COORDINATES.

HEYJUN: LOOK, WHAT DO YOU WANT FROM THIS? TO
SCARE ME?

LANE060: NO, LIKE I SAID, YOU FASCINATE ME.
TO BE HONEST, I DON'T KNOW WHAT I'M DOING. I
JUST CAN'T HELP BUT WATCH YOU AS YOU LIVE
YOUR NORMAL LIFE OUTSIDE OF YOUR HACKING
WORLD. YOU ARE SO DIFFERENT, AREN'T YOU?

HEYJUN: HOW WOULD YOU EVEN KNOW THIS?

LANE060: IT DOESN'T MATTER. I DON'T WANT TO
SCARE YOU, BUT KNOW I AM HERE AND, I AM
ENJOYING WATCHING YOU.

HEYJUN: YEAH, HOW CAN I NOT BE SCARED ABOUT
YOU TEXTING ME THAT YOU WISH TO SLICE MY
SKIN?

LANE060: I'M SORRY ABOUT THAT, I GOT CARRIED
AWAY. I WON'T HARM YOU. BUT THE WEBSITE YOU
HACKED IS FOR KILLERS, AFTER ALL.

HEYJUN: SO, YOU'RE A KILLER?

LANE060: IT DOESN'T MATTER. YOU WILL BE
OKAY.

HEYJUN: I'M SURE MANY KILLERS HAVE SAID THAT
BEFORE THEY THROTTLE THEIR VICTIM.

The Monsters Club

File   Edit   Search   Help

LANE060: YOU'RE VERY FUNNY. I LIKE YOUR WIT. THE CONVERSATIONS YOU HAD WITH YOUR FRIEND ON HERE WERE FUN. I SHOULD HAVE JOINED THE HACKING COMMUNITY MYSELF.

HEYJUN: LANE, PLEASE. IF YOU DON'T MEAN ME ANY HARM, WHY ARE YOU DOING THIS?

LANE060: I WANT TO TALK TO YOU. I SUPPOSE I HAD TO SAY WHAT I DID TO GET YOUR ATTENTION. AND IT WORKED.

HEYJUN: HOW OLD ARE YOU TO BE ON THAT SITE? IF YOU ARE A KILLER, YOU MUST BE OLD.

LANE060: I'M NOT OLD. I'M THE SAME AGE AS YOU, JUST LIVING A LITTLE DIFFERENTLY.

HEYJUN: I'M SO CONFUSED... THIS CAN'T BE REAL.

LANE060: THE MONSTERS CLUB IS VERY REAL. OUR MEMBERS ARE ALL AGES. BUT ANYHOW, IT WAS NICE SPEAKING TO YOU FOR THE FIRST TIME. YOU SEEM FUN. I'LL BE BACK SOON. BUT BEFORE I GO, I WANT TO TELL YOU SOMETHING.

HEYJUN: TELL ME WHAT, YOU'RE GOING TO KILL ME AFTER ALL?

LANE060: NO, I WON'T KILL YOU. BUT I WILL KILL YOUR FAMILY.

HEYJUN: WHAT???

138

File   Edit   Search   Help

LANE060: I MEAN, IF YOU STOP TALKING TO ME
AGAIN. I NEED YOU TO START SPEAKING TO ME ON
HERE AND IF YOU DON'T REPLY, I WILL START
TAKING OUT THOSE AROUND YOU.

HEYJUN: SO, YOU ARE A KILLER, JUST NOT THE
KILLER OF ME YET. YOU ARE SERIOUS.

LANE060: INDEED, I AM. IT IS ALL I ASK OF
YOU. TO TALK TO ME ON HERE. NOT EVERY DAY,
JUST WHEN YOU CAN. BUT IF YOU DON'T RESPOND,
I WILL PLAY THIS GAME UNTIL YOU DO.

HEYJUN: I CAN'T EXACTLY SAY NO TO THAT, CAN
I?

LANE060: NOT REALLY, BUT I'M NOT ASKING TOO
MUCH. BE HAPPY YOU'VE GOT ME, AS MOST OF THE
KILLERS ON OUR SITE WOULD HAVE DONE FAR
WORSE TO YOU BY NOW. I'M OFF NOW, BUT I WILL
BE BACK SOMETIME THIS WEEK. IT IS UP TO YOU
TO DECIDE YOUR FATE. SEE YOU LATER, JUNIE
HAN.

He logged off. So now I couldn't even delete the chat log portal. I sat back in my seat and sighed. One mistake had cost me so much, but I couldn't put my family in danger. I needed to find a way to see who this person was, but if they could break through my security, it meant they were seriously good at this. I tried to find his address to no avail. I realised I was playing with a master. I tried to stay calm, but knowing this guy gave out Yamazaki's address pained me so much I could barely function. I had to stay calm and assess the situation, even if that meant coming on here all the time to hear from this lunatic. I had to do it to stay alive.

Chapter Eighteen

When you distance yourself from reality like I had, when something like this spills out from your online life into your real life, it feels surreal. Losing that much control. Everything I'd worked for had broken apart. Or was close to it. This Lane was had stepped out of the dark web and into the real world. He was here, and he was watching me. A genuine killer. I couldn't switch off my computer to escape him. Or use a firewall for protection. I was vulnerable from all angles, and it was something I had never experienced before.

Over the weekend since I'd ran out on Theodore, I'd done nothing try not to think about what had happened with this Lane guy, and for once, I was looking forward to going to school to get away from my computer for a few hours and not have to be reminded of what was going on.

'Oh, Junie. You're up. I wanted to say I'll be back late tonight since I have to stay late in the office. Will you be alright making your own dinner?' My mother said as I crashed into her at the bottom of the stairs.

'Of course. I have so many times now, I don't know why you even need to say it.' I replied, stuffing my bag full of books.

'Oh, somebody is grouchy this morning. Anyhow, I had to say because your dad is doing the same.'

I didn't reply and we headed to the car, not long after dropping me off. I'd managed to look as though I was in good spirits on the car journey, so thankfully avoided any questioning. I was soon able to lose myself in school, and later that day, I found myself in my usual place, in the hope Theodore would come to me as I took a cigarette break so I could apologise to him. I had not answered any of his messages; I'd just not been up to coming up with an excuse.

As I stared off into the distance, thinking he'd maybe given up on me, I soon heard a familiar voice by my side, and I felt marginally lighter.

'Hey, you're here.' Theodore said.

I turned to him, blowing out a puff of smoke. The sight of his reddened cheeks from the cold air comforted me.

'I knew you would come soon enough, so I didn't bother coming to see you.' I said.

'Coming to see me?' He quizzed, leaning against the wall.

'Yes. To say sorry about rushing off like I did. Not replying to you either.'

'Don't worry about it, I got the message that something came up and you had no time.' His smile was so warm, but I could tell it did bother him. Since when did I start to care so much about Theodore. It was all coming on so fast.

'I'm glad, because that was the case. I'm sorry. I feel bad for not contacting you, but a lot happened.'

Indeed, I'm being stalked by some serial killer who sent out the address of my closest friend, causing him to be killed. I'm sure you'll understand. I couldn't stop myself from thinking it.

'Don't apologise, I'm glad you seem alright. But you do owe me one thing from this.'

'What is that?' I laughed.

'Another date.'

'That does not seem like much of a penalty. I'm up for it.'

He blushed at my honesty. 'You were really serious about that?'

'Of course. Why wouldn't I be?'

'I don't know. I'm just annoyed at myself for taking so long to ask you out when you are being so open about the possible future of liking someone. I know it may not happen but the fact you are even doing this makes me happy.'

Just as he said that the school bell rang, and we parted ways. But later at the school gates he collared me, and we picked up our conversation again. It was strange; I could feel everyone looking at us with curiosity, and oddly, it made me feel good. It was what I needed right now to change the topic from why I was gone to why is Junie Han talking to Theodore so much. Theodore was popular after all and although my fake image I had created of myself wasn't far off either, he was one of the school's heartthrob's, so me being with him really did make me stand out.

'So, our next date then. Sunday?' He said.

I nodded. 'Sounds good. At the beach front?'

'Yes! That would be great. We can get some ice cream and talk a little more. It has been so long after all. Even if it is freezing.'

'Anytime is good for ice cream.' As I stared at him, I felt guilty. 'I really am sorry, Theodore. About the other day.'

'I told you I understand. Is everything okay? I meant to ask, but I didn't want to push it.'

'Yeah, it is fine now.' I lied. 'I feel really bad though for leaving you like that.'

'Don't worry about it. If anything, you can make it up to me on our next date.'

'Sure, it will be nice to start getting out again.' I smiled.

'Glad I can be of service.' Just as he said that, his friends started calling him. 'I'd better be off; I'm going to have a match. Do you want to come?'

'I best get home. Have fun.'

'I will. Take care, Junie. I'll text you before our date.' I nodded back. As he went off with his friends, I wondered what I was even doing.

Was I really going to get invested with Theodore? I knew this was just a distraction, but for the first time today, it felt good talking to him. He had such a nice, calm aura. So different than I remembered. It was good for me. To at least have one light-hearted situation right now. I had to look it that way. Because the if I had to talk to this killer guy online, I needed at least one escape. It was strange, I was genuinely being nice for once in my life. Who was I becoming?

Chapter Nineteen

Switching on my computer for the first time of the new week had never been so nerve-racking but I had to get this talk over with, so I logged on, seeing a message from Lane already waiting for me. I gulped as I opened it and saw what awaited me.

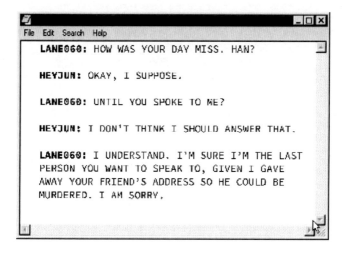

LANE060: HOW WAS YOUR DAY MISS. HAN?

HEYJUN: OKAY, I SUPPOSE.

LANE060: UNTIL YOU SPOKE TO ME?

HEYJUN: I DON'T THINK I SHOULD ANSWER THAT.

LANE060: I UNDERSTAND. I'M SURE I'M THE LAST PERSON YOU WANT TO SPEAK TO, GIVEN I GAVE AWAY YOUR FRIEND'S ADDRESS SO HE COULD BE MURDERED. I AM SORRY.

My hand froze over the keyboard as I looked over those words. Seeing this person so openly talk about it chilled and angered me, and I couldn't do anything about it. Because even if I were to get this guy traced either myself or by the police,

I could get in a lot of trouble myself. This person knew I was stuck in a corner, so they were free to talk to me like this. So openly and with little care.

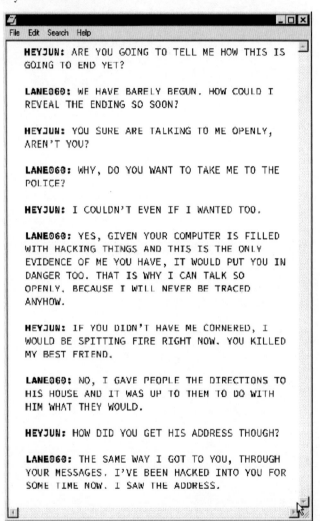

HEYJUN: ARE YOU GOING TO TELL ME HOW THIS IS GOING TO END YET?

LANE060: WE HAVE BARELY BEGUN. HOW COULD I REVEAL THE ENDING SO SOON?

HEYJUN: YOU SURE ARE TALKING TO ME OPENLY, AREN'T YOU?

LANE060: WHY, DO YOU WANT TO TAKE ME TO THE POLICE?

HEYJUN: I COULDN'T EVEN IF I WANTED TOO.

LANE060: YES, GIVEN YOUR COMPUTER IS FILLED WITH HACKING THINGS AND THIS IS THE ONLY EVIDENCE OF ME YOU HAVE, IT WOULD PUT YOU IN DANGER TOO. THAT IS WHY I CAN TALK SO OPENLY, BECAUSE I WILL NEVER BE TRACED ANYHOW.

HEYJUN: IF YOU DIDN'T HAVE ME CORNERED, I WOULD BE SPITTING FIRE RIGHT NOW. YOU KILLED MY BEST FRIEND.

LANE060: NO, I GAVE PEOPLE THE DIRECTIONS TO HIS HOUSE AND IT WAS UP TO THEM TO DO WITH HIM WHAT THEY WOULD.

HEYJUN: HOW DID YOU GET HIS ADDRESS THOUGH?

LANE060: THE SAME WAY I GOT TO YOU, THROUGH YOUR MESSAGES. I'VE BEEN HACKED INTO YOU FOR SOME TIME NOW. I SAW THE ADDRESS.

Lotté Jean Elliott

File   Edit   Search   Help

LANE060: YET YOU SEEM SO COOL ABOUT THIS?

HEYJUN: WELL, I HAVE TO BE. YOU THREATENED TO KILL MY FAMILY. WHAT CAN I DO, GO AND RAGE TO THE WORLD?

LANE060: THAT IS TRUE, AND THEODORE HAWK-SILBERSTON IS INCLUDED IN THAT BY THE WAY.

HEYJUN: HOW DO YOU KNOW ABOUT THEODORE?

LANE060: I AM WATCHING YOU. I SAW YOUR DATE AND YOUR FAKE SMILES. DOES HE KNOW YOUR TRUE SIDE, THE HACKER GIRL THAT LOVES STEALING MONEY FROM PEOPLE? I LEARNED SO MUCH ABOUT YOU IN THOSE MESSAGES WITH YAMAZAKI. YOU SEEM TO BE NOTHING LIKE HER IN REAL LIFE. THAT IS ALSO WHY I'M SO CURIOUS OF YOU. YOU SEEM TO HAVE A LOT OF SECRETS.

HEYJUN: PLEASE LEAVE HIM OUT OF THIS. AND OF COURSE, I AM DIFFERENT. IF YOU ARE WATCHING ME IN REAL LIFE AND SAW WATCH THOSE MESSAGES, YOU WOULD UNDERSTAND WHY. ANYWAY, WHAT IS IT YOU EVEN WANT TO TALK ABOUT?

LANE060: NOTHING TODAY. I WAS JUST TESTING TO SEE IF YOU WOULD COME ONLINE. GOOD GIRL. YOUR FAMILY IS SAFE, AS IS MR. THEODORE. FOR NOW.

HEYJUN: HOW LONG ARE WE GOING TO BE DOING THIS FOR?

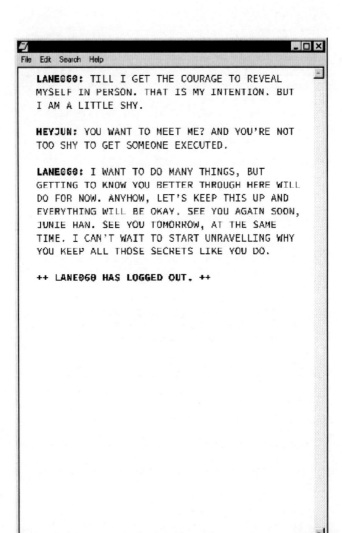

LANE060: TILL I GET THE COURAGE TO REVEAL
MYSELF IN PERSON. THAT IS MY INTENTION. BUT
I AM A LITTLE SHY.

HEYJUN: YOU WANT TO MEET ME? AND YOU'RE NOT
TOO SHY TO GET SOMEONE EXECUTED.

LANE060: I WANT TO DO MANY THINGS, BUT
GETTING TO KNOW YOU BETTER THROUGH HERE WILL
DO FOR NOW. ANYHOW, LET'S KEEP THIS UP AND
EVERYTHING WILL BE OKAY. SEE YOU AGAIN SOON,
JUNIE HAN. SEE YOU TOMORROW, AT THE SAME
TIME. I CAN'T WAIT TO START UNRAVELLING WHY
YOU KEEP ALL THOSE SECRETS LIKE YOU DO.

++ LANE060 HAS LOGGED OUT. ++

After he logged out, I felt sick to my stomach. I slouched back in my chair, now knowing he wanted to meet me in person at some point. But what would he do? Did he like me, or did he want to kill me? Whatever the reason, my head felt like it would explode from anger of a guy who spoke with me so casually after having my best friend killed. It was horrendous. I had to keep my cool, I had to lure him out and stop him in a way that I wouldn't be caught. However, until that day came, I had to keep playing along to keep my family and Theodore safe.

As I sat there moping in the hell that had become of my life, another chat box popped open, and this time, it was a familiar one.

'Reign?' I gasped wide eyed as he typed a message and it soon popped up.

REIGN: JUNIE, ARE YOU HERE?

HEYJUN: YES, HEY REIGN. HOW'S IT GOING?

REIGN: WELL, TO BE HONEST, I THOUGHT YOU WERE DEAD.

HEYJUN: HUH, HOW COME? BECAUSE I NEVER POSTED ON SERPAN?

REIGN: NO, HAVEN'T YOU SEEN THE SCREENSHOTS ON OUR FORUM FROM THE MONSTERS CLUB?

HEYJUN: NO?

REIGN: IT SEEMS SOMEONE TRIED TO MAKE OUT YOU WERE DEAD.

A second later, he sent over image attachments. They were screenshots of a message someone called HexHax had posted on the forum. It was about me.

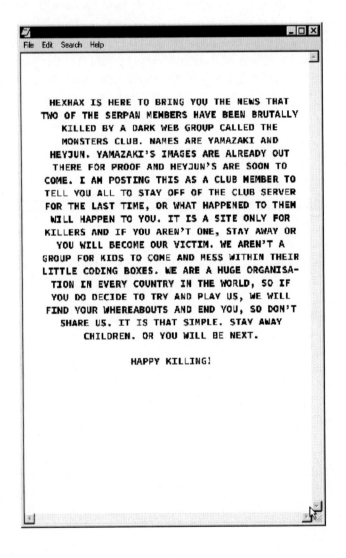

Finishing the message, I wanted to throw up. I was to be a victim like Yamazaki. Heck, they'd made it look like I already had been killed. Had this guy I was talking to have supposed to have killed me, but hadn't? It was strange seeing this. But even worse knowing my days really could be numbered.

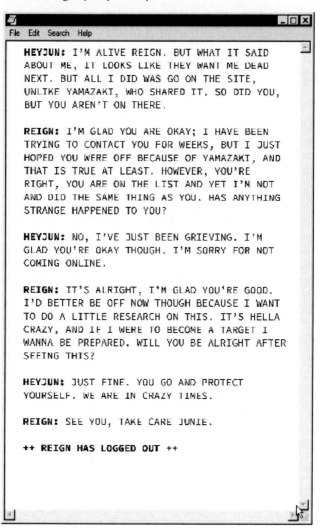

This was all a mess. This Lane guy had singled me out, and I was the only one he was preying on. I went to close down the computer but, just before I did, a new message popped up.

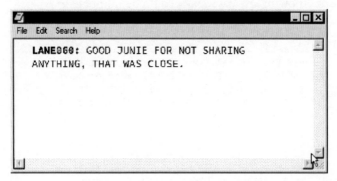

That was all he said before he logged off again. I knew I had to be careful with my words now. But why would someone be faking my death? This situation got wilder with each hour that passed by.

Chapter Twenty

It becomes hard to live a normal life with a psychopath watching your every move. I was so paranoid because of the message the HexHax person had sent. I kept double-checking everything wherever I went the next morning. I checked the doors and windows multiple times, making sure they were locked tight. It wasn't long before my mother noticed my strange behaviour as I waited with her while she got ready for work. Something I never did unless I was going to school, but since I only went one day a week now, being awake at that time was odd. If people were after me, I had to make sure everything was secure when my parents were out.

'You've checked that door lock about a hundred times now. What is up with you this morning?' My mother asked from the table, looking at me like I was going mad as she ate a piece of toast.

I applied a fake laugh. 'I was just checking it.'

She narrowed her eyes in confusion, finished her toast and dusting off the crumbs from her skirt before getting up. 'Well, I'll leave you to it. I have a huge meeting today, so I need to get there a little earlier. You'll be alright, yeah?'

'I'm alone most days,' I sighed. 'I don't know why you keep needing to ask me that.'

'I'm just being caring.' She came and kissed my cheek. 'Anyway,

I'll see you tonight. Remember to do some schoolwork. This isn't a vacation.'

After she left, I checked the locks and windows a couple more times. This was all so frustrating. I just wanted my old life back. The one where the fake me roamed in normal society and my real self came alive on the web. But now both of those sides were merging. And to top it all off, I had a possible killer after me.

I supposed this was my karma for all those years of taking people down. Revenge for the paranoia I brought them when I revealed their secrets while saving my own skin. Ela was a rare case where it hadn't mattered in the end, but most of the people I had targeted had never recovered from what I'd done to them. Maybe this was my payback from the universe for being such a selfish girl.

I never used to be this way, so conniving and secretive. Ready to take someone out if they dared play me. However, going to Dallington and seeing all backstabbing and fakery, I realised that I would have to be ruthless in order to survive and escape. And as time went by, I only grew crueller. I wasn't the only one like this at school. However, I was certainly one who would go darker than most to keep my secrets. I couldn't change now.

I told myself to take a deep breath before I headed upstairs and got showered and ready for the day. I had to distract myself in some way. If I kept thinking about what was going on, I would lose my mind, and my mask of normality had already slipped too far. I couldn't risk it arousing any more suspicion. As I finished getting ready, I dropped my phone down the side of my bed. As I went to retrieve it, my finger got caught on the side of a brown box. My breath caught in my throat as I realised what it was. It was where I'd hidden things Yamazaki had sent me.

As we'd grown closer, we'd started sending each other items. Sharing our addresses had been the ultimate display of trust. We needed that if I was going to move in with him, after all. We'd also video-chatted into the late hours so many times and comforted each other through our worst moments. As I opened the box, a tear fell down my cheek as I saw the items he'd sent me; from our funny letter exchanges to his favourite anime figurines, as well as other cute items.

Even during my depression, I still hadn't mourned him and now this was all surrounding me. I was stuck having to act like everything was okay; plus have casual conversations with the person who'd organised his murder. And until I'd figured out a way to get justice, I'd have to keep up the charade.

My finger traced over a letter Yamazaki had sent me and a tear spilled onto the page. It was so hard to keep silent. Yet I had to do so if I was to keep myself safe as well avenge him. I placed the letter back into the box and pushed it away. Continuing to stare at this stuff would only make things worse.

I climbed back into bed, where I slept for a while, then woke following a nightmare. My body was so cold and sweaty that I had to go and take another shower to calm myself down. I realised it was the afternoon, now and if I didn't get my schoolwork done my mother would kill me. Not knowing the cause of my depression only made her leniency stretch so far.

As I sat there failing to focus on my textbooks, the doorbell went. I jumped at the sound, but quickly composed myself and went down to see who it was. There was nobody behind the frosted pane of the door. I saw no one there as I opened it either. Instead, an object lay on the doorstep. It took a moment for my eyes my eyes to register what it was. A brown boxed package. But on top of it was something written that made my heart stop.

Words in black marker scrawled along the brown crinkled top. From Lane060.

I didn't know what to think or what to do as I stared down at the mysterious package and looked at the familiar username staring back at me. Lane060. The person controlling my life right now had left a package for me at my doorstep, confirming this person did know where I live. Something I didn't want to believe, but was now forced to accept.

I somehow managed to keep my composure as I looked down to the box and scanned the front garden to make sure nobody was there. Nothing. My skin prickled with goosebumps, but I picked it up and brought it inside. Which may have been a stupid idea, as it could have been anything. However, as I slammed the door shut and braced myself to see what was inside.

I took the box to the kitchen, placing it on the table as I sat in front of it. I felt numb as I read over the username again, and did nothing but stare at the package for a good few minutes before I could force my hand to open it. I ran my fingers along the box before I finally got the courage to pull off the tape to reveal a small letter and pouch-like bag.

Before I looked at the contents of the pouch, I took a few deep breaths and opened the letter.

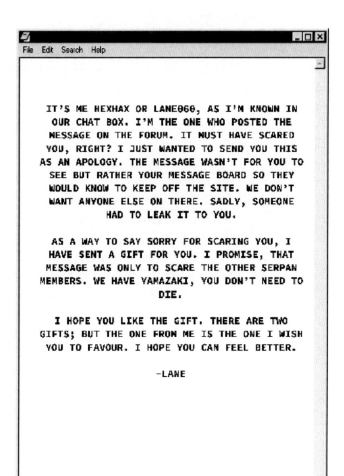

IT'S ME HEXHAX OR LANE060, AS I'M KNOWN IN
OUR CHAT BOX. I'M THE ONE WHO POSTED THE
MESSAGE ON THE FORUM. IT MUST HAVE SCARED
YOU, RIGHT? I JUST WANTED TO SEND YOU THIS
AS AN APOLOGY. THE MESSAGE WASN'T FOR YOU TO
SEE BUT RATHER YOUR MESSAGE BOARD SO THEY
WOULD KNOW TO KEEP OFF THE SITE. WE DON'T
WANT ANYONE ELSE ON THERE. SADLY, SOMEONE
HAD TO LEAK IT TO YOU.

AS A WAY TO SAY SORRY FOR SCARING YOU, I
HAVE SENT A GIFT FOR YOU. I PROMISE, THAT
MESSAGE WAS ONLY TO SCARE THE OTHER SERPAN
MEMBERS. WE HAVE YAMAZAKI, YOU DON'T NEED TO
DIE.

I HOPE YOU LIKE THE GIFT. THERE ARE TWO
GIFTS; BUT THE ONE FROM ME IS THE ONE I WISH
YOU TO FAVOUR. I HOPE YOU CAN FEEL BETTER.

-LANE

I dropped the letter and looked at the box. What was I supposed to think of this? Why was he sending this to me as if it was going to make things better? He said it was a lie to scare the forum, yet Yamazaki was actually dead. And to Lane, pretending I was dead was OK, and a gift made it better. Who's mind worked like that? Was this really all because Lane was intrigued by me? It was all too strange.

I pulled the pouch and opened it, pulling out two necklaces. One was completely black and had a small chain with a star. The other one made my eyes bulge out of my head. I recognised it as one that belonged to somebody I'd just lost.

I held the necklace up against the kitchen window light and felt the Y with my fingertips. A letter Y with thorns entwined around the it. This was Yamazaki's. Every time we had chatted via video, I'd seen it dangling around his neck. Lane wasn't playing at all; he was deadly serious. He'd given me this as a reminder of what would happen if I dared play him. He was still threatening me. I wanted the world to swallow me up. How could this be real?

Chapter Twenty-One

For the next few days, I did nothing but sleep. It was hard to do much else due to fear and the desire to ignore both the world and forget what my life had become. I'd not stopped clutching Yamazaki's necklace since the moment I'd received it, and cried a thousand tears over the next few days. Lane had gotten this necklace from Yamazaki's murderer, which told me that the two were in contact. And that Lane may have had more input than simply letting out his address.

As I lay in bed looking at the necklace, rage surged through me, and I decided to message Lane to see what the heck he was playing at. I turned on my computer and opened up the chat box.

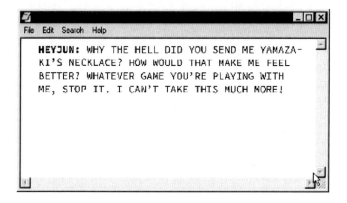

HEYJUN: WHY THE HELL DID YOU SEND ME YAMAZA-KI'S NECKLACE? HOW WOULD THAT MAKE ME FEEL BETTER? WHATEVER GAME YOU'RE PLAYING WITH ME, STOP IT. I CAN'T TAKE THIS MUCH MORE!

I waited for a few moments, but no response came. I violently switched off my computer and jumped back onto my bed, feeling suffocated. I needed someone to let everything out to. But that was impossible. Spilling my guts would endanger both me and my family. Either way, I had nobody. However, today I needed somebody.

Before I knew it, my hand was at my phone and I was dialling Theodore's number. Maybe he was the best person to tell. A person I wasn't that close with, but close enough to be able to talk to without putting anyone at risk. After a few rings, he picked up, and I let out a sigh of relief.

'Theodore, it's Junie. Can I talk to you?'

Theodore's voice seemed to lighten up. 'Sure. Is everything okay?'

'Not really. I need to talk to someone, anyone, about something. Right now. Could you meet me?'

'I'm just about to head into class…' I let out a huff on the other end. 'But I suppose I could, it's only Maths. I don't mind skipping it. Where should I meet you?'

We agreed on a place, and I rushed to get dressed and go to meet him. I needed to let my feelings out before I exploded or fell into despair. I couldn't let this Lane guy destroy me. He'd done enough damage. I wouldn't let him win.

I met Theodore at the back of the local park, and he was already waiting for me there. His face was full of concern. I realised what a mess I looked. I hadn't even combed my hair. He pulled me to a nearby bench.

'Junie! What's wrong?"

'Not really…'

As my cheeks filled with redness from the chill, he pulled out a scarf from his bag and placed it around my neck. 'You'll get a cold. What is going on? You look like hell.'

'I'm in hell. So much is going on and I can't take holding it all in. I'm barely keeping it together, I'll lose it again if I don't tell someone.'

'You can tell me anything. I don't mind.' He tried to reassure me.

I looked at him dead in the eyes, knowing I was playing a dangerous game, but I had to say something. 'I know this is random and I'm sorry. I must look crazy.'

'It hardly matters.' He replied, stroking my arm. 'I just want to know what is wrong. I might be able to help.'

I took a deep breath and began. 'Look, you can't tell anybody what I'm about to say. It's a very dangerous situation.'

He nodded. 'I won't. I promise.'

'It has to do with my depression a while back. But now, I have something else going on and it's far worse. You're about to learn a strange fact about my life that not even my family knows. I can't believe I'm about to talk about it.'

Theodore gulped. 'You're freaking me out. Tell me what it is, Junie.'

'Okay. I'll go back a little, as to why I missed all that school; I suppose you need to know the reason for that. What really caused my depression? It was to do something nobody knows about me.'

'What was it?'

It took me a few seconds to get the words out. 'In basic terms, I'm a hacker and my best friend was recently murdered after we went on an illegal site together. A site created for killers to go and talk and share photos of their victims. One of them killed him for exposing this site.'

Theodore stared at me blankly for a few seconds as he took in my statement. He sat back half confused, half shocked. 'Your hacker friend was killed after going on a site for murderers?'

'Yes. He was from Japan and to be honest, he was my only friend I have ever been able to be myself around. When he died, I felt like my world ended. And I couldn't even tell anybody about it as it would've meant confessing to a lot of criminal activity.'

'I must say, this is a shock. Studious Junie, an illegal hacker…'

I sat back and sighed. 'That isn't the end of it. His death has led to another issue, which is causing me even more grief.'

'Your friend dying and you not being able to do anything isn't the end?'

'No. It was one of the murderers on that site that killed him because he exposed it, and now one of the killer's on that site is stalking me as well.'

Theodore gasped. 'What?! Is this real?'

I sighed. 'I wish I could say no, but it's true. And this person isn't giving much away about what he wants to do with me. I don't know what to do. He just sent me this necklace that belonged to my dead friend…' I pulled out the necklace that I was now wearing and showed him the Y.

He didn't seem to know how to respond. 'I don't know what to say. This all sounds like some crazy TV show. But this person after you, have you told the police?'

'Nobody knows.'

His face flushed. 'Are you joking? You must tell the police if this crazy guy is after you and sending memorabilia of your dead friend!'

'I can't tell them because if they find out they'll need access to my computers, and if they find my hacking stuff and all the illegal things I've done, I'll be arrested. I can't tell anybody.' I didn't mention the fact that telling him all this was dangerous. I'd said enough as it was.

Theodore looked into the distance for a moment, still not comprehending how bad this was. 'I can't believe you're a hacker. But most importantly, I think the least of your problems should be about someone finding your hacking stuff. Your life is in danger, Junie.'

'Theodore, if it was that simple, I would have gone to the police, but if they get my stuff, I'll be put away for a long time.'

Theodore huffed. 'Junie! How am I supposed to react to this?

You're telling me all of this, yet I can't do anything for you! You won't go to the police, so what am I supposed to do, sit back and see what this stalker from this crazy site will do to you? Does your family know at least?'

I sighed. 'They know nothing, not about the hacking or the stalker. That is why I had to tell someone; I was losing my mind. At least you know now, so if I go missing, you'll know why.'

Theodore snapped his head my way. 'Junie! You can't say something like that and expect me to do nothing!'

'You can't do anything. If you mess with this it could put my family in danger. He'll hurt them if I tell anyone. The only person that can get me out of this is me. I'm sorry for telling you, but after losing my friend and gaining this stalker, I needed a release.'

I could tell Theodore wanted to run to the police now, but he seemed to understand me. 'I suppose I have to do what you say. But you're in danger, I won't sleep knowing that a murderer is stalking you. What am I supposed to do?'

'I'm so sorry, I feel bad for burdening you now…'

I could feel tears start to well up. It was the release I had needed, but at the same time putting this much negativity on someone else was not what I wanted to do.

Theodore pulled me into a hug. 'At least you told someone. However, we can't let this go on long. You can't risk your life. We'll have to figure something out together. In the meantime, is your home safe?'

'Thank you, Theodore. But I don't want you involved. You can't tell anybody about this. It's dangerous..'

'Don't worry, Junie. I'm here for you. I won't tell a soul and we'll work out how to stop this person, one way or another.' I had to hope his words held truth because, I'd needed to do this.

I felt like a weight had been lifted, but at the same time, I felt like another weight was going to be placed there if Lane found out what I had just done. But even if he was watching me surely, he couldn't hear what I'd said. But still, he was a murderer, and he had always stayed one step ahead of me. The more I thought about it, the more I began to realise I'd made a mistake. I could only hope it didn't end badly. From either Theodore's side or Lane's.

Chapter Twenty-Two

The next day, I pulled my mask back on and wore Yamazaki's necklace to give me the strength I needed to get through school.

'You're looking good today.' My mother said as she parked up outside Dallington. Gazing at me with delight to see me smiling for once. I did feel a little better for having just talked with Theodore. It was the best I had felt in a while. It made faking cheeriness easier.

'I do feel good.' I replied, trying to keep her spirits high, as I held the chain. 'I think things are starting to settle now.'

'I'm glad to hear it. You'll need all that enthusiasm with your final exams coming up. It's so strange to say you'll be heading to university before you know it. Oxford will be your new home. I can't wait!'

'I haven't even got into Oxford yet.' I sighed.

'You will.' She smiled before kissing me on the forehead.

It was strange to hear such a word as university, given it wasn't something I'd thought about in weeks. I'd put the future to the back of my mind while I tried to work out how to survive my present. However, it was something I knew I had to start thinking about again. I had to decide if I was going to play along with my parents' expectations forever or start afresh with a new escape plan on my own. But without the help of Yamazaki, I didn't know if breaking away from them was something I was strong enough to do.

I put it to the back of my mind again as the last thing I needed was more stress. I'd just released some of it and I didn't need to fuel it back up again. I nodded to my mother and headed to school. However, that morning, there was a different taste in the air as I walked into my classroom. Looking around, I noticed everyone looking me as though I'd done something crazy.

I brushed them off and headed over to my group of friends who were sitting huddled around one of their desks. As I approached them, I was greeted by a trio of glares as they turned to me with disgust.

'Hey, what's going on?' I asked out of confusion at the silence. 'What's with the looks?'

Ela got up, turned directly to me and slapped me right on my face. Shocked, I looked at her in disbelief.

'You have some nerve, coming up to me.' Ela snapped.

'What the heck was that for?' I snapped back holding my cheek.

'Playing ignorant won't get you anywhere!' She seethed.

'I have no clue what is going on, Ela.' I said, looking between her and the others, trying to get some understanding as to what was happening.

'Then how about I re-jig your memory, huh?' She placed a school news story in front of me, and my eyes widened. It was a tell-all, revealing the fact I was the one who had shamed her at the party. There was a page with my picture used as the main image and, an article stating that I had tried to embarrass Ela because I was jealous of her. And claim that I was the one truly in charge of the threat list that year. I tried to search for a name; something that revealed who'd written this, but there was nothing.

I gulped. I'd never been exposed like this before, even if the article was only sharing half of the truth about what I'd done.

Whoever had found this out wanted to wreck me.

'I didn't do that' I replied, trying to hold it together. 'Someone's lied about this.'

'Then who did? This does seem true. You disappeared from the party that evening. There was only us four who knew the plan!'

I looked towards Maria and Aisha. 'Are you two trying to say I did this to Ela?'

'We know you did it, Junie. You vanished that night; you were the only one who could have done it.'

'Anybody could have changed that video.'

'But you were the only person not in the room! Why did you leave?'

'I told you...'

'You went home to study? Lies! I spoke to your mother and she said you were with her 'til late. How could you do this to me?!'

Ela threw the article at me and sat down. I didn't understand. Who had found out what I'd done? Even if it the part about my motivation being jealousy was wrong, someone knew a lot. My brow twitched when I realised something seemed familiar about this tactic. To get at me for some reason. Lane had found out Ela's secret. Obviously, he'd got it when reading my messages with Yamazaki. But why had he felt the need to do this? It dawned on me that he'd obviously found out I'd told Theodore, and reality came crashing back down on me.

'I didn't post this, Ela. I swear.' I tried to protest, but she refused to budge.

'How can you lie to me like this?' She began to cry.

'Ela, someone is playing with us. I never did this. They're trying to take the blame off themselves by posting this around the school. I really am innocent.'

'Stop lying!' She yelled back, and the whole class began to pay attention to our conversation.

'Ela, I swear, never in a million years would I have done this.' I so wanted to just tell her what was going on behind the scenes but that was obviously the worse thing I could do. Especially if Lane already knew about Theodore. He was serious. He was everywhere.

'Go away! Don't speak to me again, you bitch!' She yelled. Accusing eyes bore into me. My earlier attempts at a good mood vanished, I rushed out to my hide away spot outside.

Lane had played me in real life, and I knew it was because I talked to Theodore. But how could he possibly have heard that conversation? As tears of anger and frustration streamed down my face, I pulled out my phone and opened the chat box where a message was already waiting for me. I hovered over the it for a second but refused to be scared.

I opened the message and braced myself.

LANE060: YOU WORE HIS NECKLACE IN PUBLIC.

HEYJUN: YAMAZAKI'S?

LANE060: WHO ELSE'S?!

HEYJUN: YOU SENT IT TO ME. WHY WOULDN'T I WEAR IT?

LANE060: I SENT IT FOR YOU TO KEEP, NOT WEAR. THAT IS WHY I SENT THE BLACK ONE. I WANT YOU TO WEAR THAT ONE. YOU SHOULD BE WEARING THAT ONE.

HEYJUN: YOU PUT THEM BOTH IN YOUR STUPID GIFT! I'LL WEAR THE ONE I WANT!

LANE060: STUPID?

HEYJUN: YES, SENDING ME HIS NECKLACE ONLY PROVES YOU HAD MORE TO DO WITH THIS THAN SIMPLY SENDING OUT HIS ADDRESS! YOU WERE INVOLVED IN THE PLANNING!

LANE060: IS THAT WHAT YOU THINK? OR IS THAT WHAT THEODORE TOLD YOU?

HEYJUN: WHAT?

LANE060: I KNOW YOU WENT TO MEET HIM, AND I KNOW YOU TOLD HIM ABOUT WHAT IS GOING ON, EVEN WHEN I TOLD YOU NOT TO. THIS GAME IS SUPPOSED TO BE OUR SECRET.

File   Edit   Search   Help

LANE060: I TOLD YOU. WE ARE EVERYWHERE. AND IN TELLING HIM OUR SECRET, I'M AFRAID YOU'VE BROKEN OUR RULES.

HEYJUN: YOU WROTE THAT STORY ABOUT ELA, DIDN'T YOU? TO GET BACK AT ME. NOW SHE HATES ME.

LANE060: THAT WAS JUST ONE THING I DID. THERE WILL BE ANOTHER TO PROVE YOU SHOULD LISTEN TO HOW SERIOUS I AM ABOUT KEEPING QUIET, JUNIE. YOU AREN'T TO LET ANYBODY KNOW WHAT IS GOING ON. NOW, I WANT YOU TO START WEARING THE BLACK NECKLACE TO PROVE YOU ARE LISTENING AND TAKING ME SERIOUSLY.

HEYJUN: YOU WOULDN'T DARE...

LANE060: I'M AFRAID FOR YOU'VE LEFT ME NO CHOICE. I HAVE TO TAKE ACTION TO MAKE YOU UNDERSTAND.

HEYJUN: YOU TOUCH ANYBODY I'M CLOSE TO AND YOU'LL BE DEAD! I WILL HIT BACK!

++ LANE060 HAS LOGGED OUT ++

'No!' I yelled and threw my phone to the ground. If he hurt anyone, I was going to hurt him back. One way or another, if he dared do anything, I wouldn't sit back and take it. There was not going be another Yamazaki.

Waiting to see if someone you love will die is a very strange feeling. The incident with Ela was bad enough; knowing he was yet to do worse filled me with dread. Not to mention the fact that I was getting tons of hate messages, people thinking I had shamed Ela. My school image, which I'd kept pristine for years, was in tatters. Lane knew what he was doing, and I did see how serious he was. He had destroyed my online and real world lives.

I was running out of options that would end this before it got too out of hand. I could call the police, expose Lane and protect my family. And also condemning myself to prison, and hurting my family with the knowledge that their daughter was a criminal. This scenario filled with me frustration, but I knew I had to decide fast as Lane and The Monsters Club were not messing around.

I lay in bed, twiddling my thumbs. It seemed the only thing I could do was wait. Wait for someone to die. I didn't want this, partly because I didn't want to lose anyone else, but also partly out of selfishness. I couldn't bring myself to reveal my secrets to the world, to see everything I'd built come crashing to the ground.

I was so angry at myself for letting this happen. I had never wished for this. I had been so careful to keep my two worlds' separate. I knew it would all be over if they ever merged. And yet, I still couldn't bring myself to go to the police and end it, even when the life of someone close to me was in danger. My selfishness was now beginning to scare even me.

Then I realised something. It wasn't going to be my family that he would hurt, but rather, he would go after Theodore, because he was the one I'd told. Theodore knew too much; while my parents knew nothing. I also couldn't protect Theodore like I could my parents. I now realised how big of a mistake it had been to tell him this. He was in more danger than I was letting myself believe. Everything was suddenly clicking into place.

I picked up my phone and let out a sigh of relief when he answered, though I noticed his tone was harsh.

'Theodore, I just thought I'd call you...'

'Did you really do that to Ela, Junie?' He interjected.

'No, of course not. It was...' I soon realised talking to him on the phone was a bad idea. Well, in person was bad too, but at least there wouldn't be a recording of the conversation. 'Look, can I meet you? I need to speak with you face to face.'

'Okay, I just hope it isn't true, because that would be a crappy thing to do, Junie.'

'Look, just come to my place and talk to me.'

'Your place?'

'Yes. Now hurry, please. I have a lot to tell you.'

Chapter Twenty-Three

An hour later, Theodore arrived at my door looking half worried, half frustrated with not knowing what was going on. I'd already told him about being a hacker, my best friend dying, my having a stalker, and now I'd called him in a panic asking him to come to see me. Plus, he now thought I'd tried to hurt Ela, which had only confused him even more.

'Is everything alright? I got here as fast as I could.' He said, breathless as he stood at my front door. I quickly pulled him inside, scared somebody could attack at any moment.

'Not really. Everything is going to hell.' I replied, as we stood in the front hall. He took me to sit down at the stairs.

'Junie, you're scaring me. Has something happened? Is this about school?'

I shook my head, wishing it was something as childish as school drama. 'No. Well. About that first: that article was written by my stalker, OK?'

He nodded. 'The situation with Ela? I twigged that on my way here. I'm sorry. I don't know why I didn't think of that first.'

'It's fine. I only just told you about what is going on; you're probably still processing it. That's why I needed to talk to you now. Something terrible's happening, Theodore. I should never have told you about any of this.'

His face went pale. 'What's going on, Junie?'

'This hacker or killer, or whatever person is playing with me, is angry.'

'How so?'

'Because I told you about him and all that was going on, when he didn't want me to.'

'Did you tell him you told me?'

I shook my head. 'Of course not. However, he somehow found out.'

'How could that be possible?'

'He tells me they have ears and eyes everywhere. Whatever that means, but it doesn't matter because he knows and…'

'And what?'

'He may be coming after you because you know.'

Theodore gulped and sat down on the stairs beside me. 'Coming after me, as in…'

I looked at him, filling up with guilt that I had put him in this situation just because I had needed to vent. 'To kill you. I don't know what he wants with me. He says he is playing with me till he meets me. I'm so sorry. I shouldn't have told you about any of this. This club is real. They are hurting people. They are real killers and one of them is messing with me.'

Theodore somehow kept himself calm. 'I don't understand enough of what's happening. Can you show me this site and the guy that is doing this to you?'

'I can't. He tracks everything, so he'll know.'

'It hardly matters at this point, Junie. Just show it to me so I can understand, because right now I'm so confused. Who this person is that is playing with you, or this group? These people that may now want to kill me.'

I didn't want to show him the site. But I had involved him, and he now needed to understand the danger we were both in. I pulled him upstairs and sat him at my computer. It felt like an eternity for it to power up. I then realised I could no longer enter the site; I had deleted all my software. All I had left was the chat box.

'What's wrong?' Theodore asked, concerned when I paused at the computer.

'I forgot that I deleted all my hacking equipment and the sites I use in the dark web, and it would take hours to set it up again.' I soon realised I could at least show him who this Lane person was, and our conversations. 'However, I can show you the chat messages I have been having with Lane, and you can see what he has threatened if I don't play along with him.'

Theodore went pale as he read my conversations with Lane. He could now see the seriousness of the situation.

He turned to me with a horrified expression. 'Junie, this is crazy. I can't believe you haven't gone to the police yet. This guy has got hold of your dead friend's necklace and sent it to you, it shows how real this all is. You could end up dead! He knows where you live.'

'I know that, and I wish I could but if I talk to the police I will be arrested as well. They will need to use my computer to trace this guy and they'll find my illegal equipment. I can't do it. That and the fact I never reported the death of Yamazaki. This situation isn't simple.'

Theodore sat back in, his seat running a hand through his hair, knowing I made sense but unable to come up with a solution. 'What are we going to do? If this guy is after me or your family, what can be done without protection of the police?'

'I'm so sorry for doing this to you. I shouldn't have told you anything.'

Theodore sighed. 'Don't be like that. Keeping this stuff to yourself would only have driven you mad. I want to be here for you. It's just, I don't know what I can do but listen. We can't escape this because, and we don't know how to stop it. We don't know where he is.'

I felt defeated. I'd put my family and Theodore in danger, and it was now starting to hit me as to what had I done by letting it come this far. All I could do is sit and wait and hope we all kept safe. But these people were ruthless, actual killers. How was I going to avoid Lane's punishment for me disobeying him? I couldn't code it out of my life or put up a firewall. This was real life, and I didn't know how to operate in it, because I had never truly lived as my real self in it.

'I really don't know what to do. I think I will have to contact the police, and if I go to jail, then so be it. I can't risk your life or my family's.'

'You can't go to the police.' Theodore snapped. 'You will go to jail for a long time. You've gone too far, and you'll be found out. Without this computer they won't be able to help, and if you do give them it, you'll be in trouble. We have to figure a way out ourselves, Junie.'

I turned to him. 'You shouldn't have anything to do with this. You have just come back in my life, and I've involved you in this. I bet you're wishing you'd stayed away.'

Theodore put his hand on my cheek, making my eyes widen. 'I don't care about this. I would still want to be in your life. I've liked you for so long. I suppose this just makes things move a little faster.'

In that moment, I felt something for the first time. A warmth in my heart. I felt that if he let go of me it would hurt. I pulled him into a hug and cried. And for once, being this way with another person, revealing my flaws to someone who wasn't Yamazaki, felt natural. I didn't care about the fact my mask had fallen; being with him felt nice. Despite everything, he still wanted to be there for me.

'We'll find a way to get through this. We just need to be on guard. We'll not go out at night, and we'll keep our homes secure, okay? We'll figure out a way to find this guy. We should have some cameras installed to see if we can see someone. What do you think?'

'It's a great start.' I replied pulling back to look at him. 'I am so sorry about this. I don't understand how he even heard our conversation. That is what confuses me.'

'We don't know what this person looks like, and if he does live around here, I'm sure he followed you. You won't know what or who to look for. But let us just start somewhere, eh? I'm here for you, Junie. Call me at any moment, I'll do the same for you and if we feel or see anything strange. Then we can call the police and say you have a stalker but keep the messages quiet. It's all we can do right now.'

'I am so sorry…'

'Don't be. Even if this is a strange way to be back in your life, I'm glad to be here with you again.'

We didn't know what was going to happen next, but we thought as long as we kept ourselves on guard, we could do this. But I also knew how dangerous these people were, and so far, they had kept the upper hand. We had to try and get ahead of them. I needed to warn my family in some way that didn't reveal the truth of what was going on.

Me and Theodore went through life as normally as possible, but remained on guard, keeping our eyes wide open. At school, stores and our homes. We were constantly prepared for an attack. I had also managed to get my parents to put up some security cameras by making up a story that I'd seen a burglar one night.

'I can't believe that happened.' My mother said, shivering at the thought as my father put them up at the front of our property. 'This is a private estate. It's supposed to be secure. How could somebody like that have gotten in?'

'We live in a wealthy neighbourhood, of course they would target here.' I replied. I felt bad for scaring my mother like this, but it was for our own protection.

I didn't know what Lane was going to do. If he did try and hurt me or my family, at least the cameras could catch him. I was not going down without a fight. And until this all came to a stop, I could do nothing but live each day as it came.

My mother sighed as my father came down from the ladders. 'Well, at least you saw them. This will make me worry less, but still it gives me the creeps knowing someone tried to get inside our home.'

'We'll be fine with these. Besides, the house is secure. They'll need to do a lot to get in here. I just think this is a good measure to capture anything in the future. Living in a house like this, we should have done it years ago,' my father replied. I was glad he was being so open about this, as he normally was the type to not listen to our concerns.

My father passed by me and took the ladders with him, and not much later I was back in my room, struggling to fill my time with any sane activity. Given I didn't exactly go out after Lane had destroyed my friendships with Ela and the others, I had limited options. I wanted to try and reconcile with them, but there was no chance of that. The damage had been done.

It was strange though. I less scared by what Lane did with the Ela situation, and more bothered by the fact Lane had ruined my reputation. I had worked so hard to hold onto my status in society, and it would be impossible to claw back after something like this. I had never truly considered Ela and the others to be my friends, but they had been vital to keeping up my day to day charade, and maintaining a good position in the real world. My fake image, which I'd thought I could fall back on, was lost. But there was nothing I could do about that. I had to let it go.

I ended up falling asleep out of boredom. I struggled to fill my days without technology. I woke to my phone buzzing at my side. I jumped to check it, and was relieved to see that it was Theodore. I opened the message to see he had sent me a picture of his parents installing cameras, filling me with relief.

I sent him a picture back of me smiling and giving a thumbs up, glad he was safe and taking this all so well. He did the same back, smile again. I couldn't understand how I was feeling like this all of a sudden. I wondered if it was revealing my secrets that had made me feel closer to him. It had been that way with Yamazaki; the more we shared, the more we bonded. Though I knew I couldn't get too close with Theodore. I knew I had to be careful.

I held Yamazaki's necklace and sighed. 'What would you have done in this situation?' I asked.

I could hear Yamazaki's comical and snarky tone replying. 'I would set up one hell of a virus and beam that site down!'

The thought made me laugh and then cry. I wanted to hear his voice again. We used to talk every evening, and even with the huge time difference, he would wait up for me, and we would talk for hours. Helping me out with different things.

I was about to get lost in my emotions again, I suddenly realised something about what I'd just thought. Maybe if I took down that site, it would show these people I wasn't to be messed with either. If I poured a strong virus into their web page, I could capture all the evidence on this site and send it anonymously to the police, that way I wouldn't get caught. It was a dangerous thing, and Lane would know it was me. I could, however, plant a lie that a fake group was taking them over. Maybe, just maybe they would run, and leave me alone.

I got up and stared at my computer. I knew I could be causing more damage than good by doing this. Though maybe it was what was needed to end that site at least. Because even if Lane came after me for doing this, if I made people truly aware of it, these people would lose their platform and would be exposed. I had to try. I was known for making the best viruses that could take down any site. I just needed to collect all the information that I could send to the police, and then take it down.

I may be risking myself even more but I didn't care. I was already in this game, and I was going to start playing on my on terms. I jumped on my computer and began to reinstall my coding devices; I suddenly felt a rush of adrenaline like I used to get every time I opened up the familiar code boxes. I had to at least do something. I wasn't going to let them control me by fear. No matter what happened, I could at least say I tried for Yamazaki. Because I knew if I sat back and didn't do anything, he would be upset with me. That wasn't the girl he knew. I had to do this for him and my family. To expose this evil and to have a chance at keeping myself alive and out of prison. This was my last chance to save my secrets.

Chapter Twenty-Four

It took me all night to reinstall my old programs and configure them to fit the modem of my computer. There were certain ways I liked to work, and if I didn't do it right, I wouldn't feel confident enough in what I was about to do. I was about to put an end to The Monsters Club. After this, it would be down to the police. They could tackle finding these people, and would see that these were actual murderers, not just people trying to be edgy.

Of course, I was putting my family in danger, but then, they already were. No matter what I did, there would be consequences. And I could no longer sit back and let someone else be hurt like Yamazaki. Even if I lost the war, I would win a few battles along the way.

I could feel my ruthless online persona returning to me. My true self. Once I finished with the last program, I began to build the virus. I had to be quick as I knew Lane would probably be watching me, and even though I was doing my best to disguise my programs, he would get through them eventually.

Virus-building was something I had learned from when I first entered this strange online world all those years ago. It was complex and took many different rigid combinations to be able to secure the effectiveness, but once I was happy with the strength and was sure it would be able to break through their strong firewall and kill their site, I soon locked it up and got ready.

But first I needed to make sure I knew what I wanted when I entered the site. I had to screenshot as much as I could before setting the virus off. Then, I was going to post it on our forum and have it be leaked to the world. And share a little of my own story without giving myself away.

I quickly got everything secure before I opened the dark web and typed in the forum and went back to the old post with the website in it. I didn't want to type it in the URL space as it would alert Lane faster as to what I was doing. He could close me down at any moment, and I didn't know when he would be online.

It felt so strange being on here like this, but so right at the same time. I opened up the forum and got everything ready so I could attack the club. I logged into my old page, and just being on this forum again sent chills down my spine. I kept myself focused and moved forward, breaking through barriers and retracing the steps I could to get to The Monsters Club, and thankfully, the old post of that website link was still up.

I clicked on it. At first it took me to an empty landing page but, soon enough, the familiar old red scratched text welcomed me to the horrors that lay inside. Last time, it had taken me quite some time to get inside but now I knew the way around getting into it, I was in quicker than ever. As soon as I broke through the passworded area, I was greeted by a lovely picture of a decapitated boy. I quickly moved past it and tried not to look the site as I bled the virus onto the page. Making sure I left a message behind for them to know they couldn't scare everyone online, and also getting some screenshots of what was shared on here.

After a few moments, it consumed the site and every page you tried to click on held an inescapable message with my note to both stay away from this site and also a message for the users to think again before ever coming back as it was never going to reopen. That it was going to the media and the police, and that their information would be leaked if they did not leave. I had none of that information, but I had to make them see I was serious.

As quick as I'd logged in, I escaped and headed back to the Serpan pin board where I posted a part of my story about how going on that site had killed Yamazaki, and now others were in danger, and that it needed to be exposed. I knew the users here would soon share it to the police anonymously. I wouldn't have to do a thing on that count, and that would be the thing to save me. However, none of this would protect me from Lane when he found out.

After pasting in all the screenshots and having finished the message, I posted it all. I'd decided I was not going to stay long enough to see the results of what people were going to do. Besides, I was sure Lane would tell me. I closed the forum, deleted all of my programs again and sat back in my chair and sighed.

This was going to be interesting to watch. I probably would have a thousand murderers after me now for spreading this site, but I knew I had done the right thing. Hacker or not, I still had to live in the real world as a normal student and girl. And now I was unable to do even that, I'd been forced to take decisive action.

I waited to receive a message from Lane, but one never came. I knew it would come, as would a news report. Something this crazy lurking on the dark web would definitely be headline material. I had to be careful now, more than ever until I found who Lane was and ended this site once and for all. If that was even possible. But I had to try. I refused to be completely defeated. I had played my part and now it was time to watch the destruction commence.

I expected hell to soon greet me but at least the world now knew, I didn't feel so suffocated any more. I had taken back some control.

The next few days were eerily quiet. I told Theodore of what I had done but we'd heard nothing, nor had we seen anything strange. I knew Lane was most likely planning a revenge attack, but still, it was too quiet. The one place that was not silent though was the news.

The site had been leaked all over the national media and people were shocked by all the things I had exposed. No one ever took the dark web seriously until now. Now they had been handed evidence of the existence of true evil. I'd watched videos of people trying to access the site and not gaining any entry because of my virus stopping them. It made me smile to see it had worked for so long, but having not heard a thing from Lane bothered me. Today was the day he usually contacted me, and I was not looking forward to it.

'The world sure is a crazy place. These insane monsters were able to create a site to share pictures of their murder victims. It's disgusting.' I heard my mother say on the phone to someone that evening as I came downstairs for dinner. It was weird to hear her talking about the very site that had crippled me these last few months, and she had no idea she was muttering the reason as to why I had locked myself away. It felt so crazy.

As I walked into the kitchen, she greeted me with a smile. 'I'm going to have to go, Hana. Call me back tomorrow. But yes, the world truly is insane. Stay safe. Bye.' She put the phone down and passed me over a plate. 'Here you go, I made your favourite rice dish.'

'Thanks.' I smiled back, shuddering slightly at her casually discussing The Monsters Club.

'Are you okay? You look pale.' She asked.

I shrugged. 'I'm fine; just hungry.' I began digging into the meal to erase suspicion.

After dinner, I went back to bed and called Theodore. It had been a few days since I'd spoken to him since he'd learned he was in danger as well. I'd been so focused on watching the news that I'd had no time to contact him. Which I knew was a pretty stupid thing, given I'd put him in danger, but since he hadn't called me either I assumed he needed some space. As I knew myself, this was a lot to deal with.

After a few rings he picked up, but the voice on the other end did not match who I was used to hearing on this line.

'Hey, is that Theodore?'

'It may or may not be someone of that name.'

'Uh, is it or not?'

'Who knows.'

'Who is this?' I asked again, having a bad feeling rise in my gut.

'Oh, I'll stop playing now.' It was a strange laugh. 'This is Lane060 and I think we better speak regarding your friend's life right now. You made a big mistake, Junie Han.'

Chapter Twenty-Five

'Why are you speaking from Theodore's phone? What is going on, have you hacked his or my phone?'

The voice was calm on the other end, and rather soft. It sounded young. 'This is Theodore's phone. I am speaking from it.'

My body froze. 'Please, don't tell me…'

A light laugh breathed back. 'No, not yet. But it may come to that if you don't give me a good enough reason as to why you decided to destroy The Monsters Club system, and still not wear my necklace I sent you. You'd better have your speech ready.'

'Speech? You found me out; what am I supposed to say, Lane?'

He froze on the other end for a moment before sighing. 'You sure are sharp these days. Hacking the site like that, what the hell? Are you really trying to gather some courage and play me?'

'I'm not playing you. I never started this. Nor did I want to do what I did.'

'You really are getting brave. Hmm, I suppose it was to do with my threat the other day. When I was mad at you for wearing Yamazaki's necklace instead of mine. Did you get me back because you thought I was going to harm someone around you?'

I sighed. 'What was I supposed to take out of that threat? That you were going to come and say hello?'

'Of course not. I wanted you to get the threat, but I wasn't planning on anything. I just wanted you to wear my necklace. If you did what I asked, everyone would be fine.'

I had to laugh. 'You would kill someone because I wasn't wearing your stupid necklace?'

'Yes.'

'That's insane!'

'Maybe. Anyway, I guess I did to you what you enjoy doing to others; playing mind games to get what you want.' His words made me wonder if he was doing this in part to try and show me who I truly was. For whatever warped reasoning he had. 'But it's too late for that now. You've gone too far, Junie. Taking down our site like that and exposing it to the media. Don't you know that's what got your friend Yamazaki killed?'

'I'm on your hit list anyway. What does it matter to me?'

Lane sighed. 'I've already told you; I won't hurt you, just those around you if you don't listen, which you don't seem to do. Why are you making this situation more complicated than it needs to be? You're putting your friends and family in danger. Just like Theodore here.'

'Please, where is he? Don't hurt him. He has nothing to do with this crap. Nor does my family. Involve me. Target me, leave them alone!'

'Your care for them has come a little late. However, don't worry about Theodore yet. He is fine. Just, shall we say, in storage. Ready and waiting until I decide what to do with him. But for now, I'm going to give you a warning.'

'What is it?'

'Fail to listen to me again and not only will I end him right now, but also your family and everyone around you. You have me angry. Now, I know you want to try and beat me. But you can't. I love playing with you too much and I have a lot of things I want to do. I will give you this one chance to stay off the web and shut your mouth. I will keep Theodore until you can prove to me that you will listen to me, okay?'

'Just don't hurt him, and I'll do anything.' My weakness was showing. I'd known that this would happen, but now feeling it in reality, I wish I'd never done it. But at the same time, I'd had to.

'I won't, but you must do this one task for me and I'll forgive you.'

'What is it?'

'Your school hosts parties a lot, don't they?'

'Yes. What about them?'

I could feel the smirk behind the phone. 'Well, I didn't want to meet you till a specific day but I think now is the time, so I can show you what I mean when I say you must listen. When is your next school party?'

'Not for weeks yet.'

'Then get your parents to host one, I read that they enjoy doing them. Don't they?'

'How do you know that?'

'I know everything about your life, Junie.'

His words shocked me. 'You want to meet me at a party?'

'Yes. If you do this, I'll be able to see how trustworthy you are around your family. If you call the police, then I'll have your family killed. If you just meet me and show me you can do this secretly, and listen to me, I will be happy and I will ease things again. Ease the rope around your friend's neck, that is.'

I felt myself suffocating. I'd brought this on myself, but I had to stay strong to keep Theodore alive. 'Fine. I will do anything you say. But won't meeting me be dangerous? Why would you want me to see your face?'

'You won't. I want you to have a costume party, and have everyone wear masks. It's too early for you to see me, but I want to meet you to get it into your head that I am not joking around. Understand?'

'Okay, just don't hurt him or…'

'Don't threaten me, Junie. If you ever try play me like that again, it won't be pretty. I will get the site back up. You haven't won. Just be glad I can get the members off your back for now. You almost ended up just like Yamazaki.'

I gulped at the name, but I had to go along with him and have this party. Was there any point to what I had done? Who knew. But at least I had tried. Now it was time to deal with the consequences in the real world.

'Fine. I will get it organised. I will message you the date and location when it is done. I will listen, I understand how serious you are now. Please, don't hurt him and keep your promise.'

'Oh, I will, for you. I like you too much to hurt you, but if I must, then so be it. Now, go and get it organised, Junie. I look forward to finally talking to you in person.'

'Lane, what game are you and The Monsters Club playing with me?'

'Junie, you're mistaken. It's not the club playing with you.'

'What?'

'It's only me. I'm a part of the club but I'm the only one playing with you. However, if you go against me, then you'll have both to deal with.'

'Why are you doing this to me? What are you leading towards?'

'I will tell you this. When I started to read through your chats with Yamazaki and how you were online to offline, I knew I had to play with you.'

'What do you mean?'

'I love showing humans how they truly are. It's my passion. People think we're monsters, but at least I'm honest about who I am; a psychopath. You lie so much and hide your true self. Well, I want to slowly bring the real you out into the world. One secret revealed at a time. Now, I have to go, but be prepared. All I want is for people to see the real you. All the evil it is. Good luck, Junie.'

Lane hung up, and I didn't even hear Theodore's voice or gain any idea of where he was. I fell to the ground. I'd known something would happen, but actually dealing with it was different. It was going to be hard to not let my anger get ahead of me when I met this Lane in person. I just had to get my parents to organise a party now, all so I could meet a psychopathic murderer. I really couldn't get out of this. Lane had full control of me both online and now in real life. And now I knew why he was playing with me; he wanted to reveal my secrets to the world. I had to do something to stop him. No matter what, if someone was going to expose me for the person I really was, I would have to stop them. Even if that person was selfish and warped. I had to try and work out a plan, to save everyone and cover my lies.

Chapter Twenty-Six

I don't know how I managed to keep my cool when Theodore's parents called me to say he had never come home, but I didn't even let a tear gloss my cheek. I kept myself focused through knowing I would see him again once I'd had this party for Lane. As I put down the phone, I reminded myself of the fact this was all going to be okay, even if I wanted to collapse.

My body felt so light yet so heavy. I was fooling myself into thinking I was living in a dream and that me and my family weren't under threat. That I had just gotten them to host a party for the fun of it, like they always did. Theodore wasn't missing; I had made myself think he was on holiday or it was back to the old days where we didn't talk. It was the only way I got through it.

My parents had taken to the party idea pretty well, and were surprised that I had suggested it given, I always hated that aspect of my life. But it was also great getting them into thinking that I was trying to get back to my normal life. It helped to distract them from looking into what was really going on, and ultimately, keep them out of danger. As for me, I was in a cage and there was no escape. At least until I saved Theodore first or Lane exposed me, however he planned to do that.

As my friendship with Ela and my other friends had been destroyed, I was surprised to see them come up to me at school and ask me about the charity party my family was hosting. I knew it was to do with the charity aspect and not a sudden eagerness to talk to me again, given their families always came to these things.

I felt a strange pang as they walked away. When I had been part of their friendship group, I never had cared for them. All I had cared for was my online world and trying to keep it a secret. I never believed these people knew me, yet they'd believed I was their friend. Maybe if I'd been a little more myself with them, things may have been different. I now felt some guilt for what I'd done to Ela, even if I'd accidentally helped her get together with Dillan. Lane had made me see that at least.

I was beginning to feel guilt about the various other bad things I'd done in an effort to preserve my image. But I couldn't stop being this way. Not just because I had to try and fight Lane, but still, selfish as it was, I wanted to escape this life. Therefore, conniving Junie wasn't going anywhere anytime soon.

I kept myself focused as I had just as much planning to do for the party as my parents. Since I was the one who had brought up the idea of a party, combined with how busy they were with work, they were relying on me for a lot of the organising. When I wasn't at school, my mother was either calling me to make sure I was arranging things or sat near me making sure I was on a call and organising the event we would be hosting or making sure the venue was big enough for all the guests that were slowly responding to the invites my mother had posted. These parties never failed to bring in the wealthy.

This felt like karma to me since I'd always hated this side of my family's life. The wealthy, overly-privileged side. Hosting a party for charity was of course a great thing but the people that came to these things only came to show off. Even if they were donating, the sentiment behind it was never genuine but rather about who could give the most money, and I hated it. But I had no choice but to endure another one and get this meeting with Lane over with. I knew he must've chosen to meet at a party because he would know how much I hated parties. Knowing this annoyed me even more.

'I'm so excited to be holding a party, it has been so long since we've done it!' My mother had been beaming ever since the day I had brought it up. 'I can't believe how fast we've gotten everything done, not to mention that you're so enthusiastic about doing this. You've always hated parties, whether they were hosted by us, friends or Dallington.'

I tried to make it seem like I was doing it to simply try and get better. 'Yes, well. I thought I would suggest it since it has been a while, and I thought it would be good to do something normal again.' I lied. 'Anyway, I think we have everything in order now. Most of the guests have gotten back to us. The venue and everything is all set up.'

My mother clapped her hands together with delight. 'Now we just have to decide what you're going to wear!'

I laughed, knowing how much she loved to dress me up. My style was a lot plainer than hers, meaning she wouldn't allow me to dress myself for these events.

'I guess I have to leave that to you again, eh?' I said.

'If you so must. Since your style isn't the best, I should handle this. I'm going to look online now for some dresses and a mask. How exciting!'

As my mother danced off, I sat back in my chair and sighed, wondering how I was going to cope on the day. I had messaged Lane to tell him all the information. Now it was sent, there was no going back. I had no choice but to go through with this if I wanted to save Theodore. I hadn't even let myself think about what was going on with him. If I did, I could break. I knew by hacking that site and leaking it there would be repercussions, but now it had happened, I regretted it. Plus, it looked like the police had not done anything with the site. Only the news had mentioned it.

I just had to get through this and hope Theodore was okay.

I had a lot to do to make it up to him for involving him in this craziness. A moment of weakness had made me do this, and now I was in a deeper hole than ever. It was weighing me down now, being reminded every day of Yamazaki, and now Theodore was being held hostage. All this, plus the fact I had to meet Lane face to face; I didn't know how I was going to cope. Yet I had to. For Theodore, my family and Yamazaki. I'd kept going this far; I could carry on for a little while longer. I just had to save Theodore, and get rid of Lane.

As much as meeting Lane was weighing on my mind, trying to pretend like everything was okay was just as tough. My plan to take down the site had failed. The more I thought about it, the more I realised that it was a mistake to use a virtual solution to a real-world problem. However, I needed my *Queen of Coding* persona; she was the only one that could get me through this.

The day of the party came so fast I didn't know what to do with myself. The entire day I spent getting ready into my costume for this meeting; it made me feel sick. Knowing Lane was going to be in the same venue as my family terrified me. I had to play this right or it could end badly for everyone.

I looked at myself in my mirror as I finished putting on the last layer of mascara and saw the reflection of my computer in the background. I'd made up my mind that I was expelling myself from the hacking world forever. What I'd done had been a mistake and I'd caused more harm than good given what I now had to go through with no idea of the outcome. It'd been the hardest few weeks of my life seeing Theodore's family put out pleas to find their son, knowing I had the information they needed but being unable to do anything. It wasn't just about saving myself, it was about saving everybody. Dealing with it was getting to me every day, and I'd barely slept leading up to this party.

My mother arranged my hair in a style that matched my elegant aesthetic for the night and, as usual, she had pulled out no stops to look as over the top as possible. She looked like an aristocrat that had walked out of a Jane Austen novel after we were all ready and gathered at the front of the house.

'You look beautiful, Junie. It's been so long since I've seen you so done up.' My mother said as I stood there uncomfortable in my dress and forced out the enthusiasm.

'Yes, well. Let's get this all over with and raise some money for charity. That's what I'm looking forward to.' I replied, stepping into the car.

The venue was at an old manor house semi-deep into the countryside. Since it was a costume party, my mother had wanted to match our outfits to the vibe of the building, and we were all gathered in the enormous grand hall that stood as wide as it did high. It was one of the oldest buildings around here and was owned by one of my mother's friends, so she got the venue cheaper than most. I felt myself turn pale as I stepped inside. I forced myself to focus and kee an eye on Lane. Even though I had no idea what he looked like, I would notice if anybody was watching me.

It wasn't long before everything was set up and the guests started to pour in. The rich families were simply here to show off as usual, but for the first time it was my last care in the world. They could do what they wished tonight. I just needed to stay alive and keep it together while I went to meet a killer who was holding my friend hostage.

I was doing the event to show Lane I was trustworthy. I wanted to meet him and get it over with so I could find out how Theodore was. The masks made it impossible to tell who was watching you, and my unease became worse as the night progressed.

'Are you alright? You've been shifting about all night, Junie.' My mother said, elbowing me in the side halfway through the party. I could tell I was beginning to show how uncomfortable I was. I tried to compose myself.

'I'm fine, I'm just warm is all. I think I need to cool down outside.'

'Well, that is a better response than your usual groans of annoyance for being here. It seems you have changed after all. Finally grown up, eh?'

My mother looked far too pleased with herself as some of her friends came over and began talking. Their usual boasting. The slience from Lane was starting to alarm me, but just as my mother was getting lost in the conversation with her friends, I felt a buzzing go off in the dress pocket.

Come to the balcony. I'm waiting for you.

I placed my phone in my bag and tried to still my shaking hand, knowing it was finally time to greet a self-confessed psychopath. 'I'm just going outside for a few minutes for some fresh air, I won't be long.'

'Well, don't be, because the gala will begin soon!' My mother brimmed with excitement and I nodded my way over to the balcony entrance on the second floor, where it was much quieter.

A light chill hit my skin as I made my way out onto the open space that overlooked the garden grounds and at first, I couldn't see anybody until I stood near the edge and heard a voice that sent a shiver down my spine.

'Junie. We finally meet.'

Chapter Twenty-Seven

Lane was taller and slimmer than I thought he would be. Even though his face was covered in half a mask I could tell he was around my age. His tone and the smug way he held himself reminded me of the Dallington boys. I could see him smiling as his eyes gleamed triumphantly beneath his mask.

Everything froze in time as I saw him smirk at our first ever meeting. The world didn't feel real, and the music that blared outside from the hall and onto the balcony soon became a distant sound.

'Where is Theodore?' Is all I could say at first. I don't know why I thought he would have been here, but I'd held onto a secret hope. However, it was just me and Lane.

'He is safe.' Lane responded, his voice becoming clearer as he took a few steps forward and was illuminated by the door's light. 'I'm glad you came to see me.'

'I didn't have much choice, did I? You have my friend in captivity.'

He still smiled. 'Don't worry about him. This is about you for now. I just needed you to see me to get it into your mind how real this is. I'm not messing around. I'm here and real. At least this shows you can listen.'

'Look, what I did to the site, I had a moment of madness, okay. I have been listening. I just went a little stir crazy from everything. I haven't even been able to mourn Yamazaki's death.

It is hardly a surprise I would do something like this.'

'Why did you do it?'

'I just said, I had a moment of madness. I just wanted to strike back, and my online persona just went for it, regardless of the consequences for the real-world me. It was dumb.'

Lane laughed. 'You really talk as if you are two people, you know that?'

'Because I was two people.'

'What do you mean?' He quizzed.

'Don't you have your online self and offline self? You must have to put on a fake persona in your daily life, I'm sure of it, or you'd be in prison. The same as I would be.'

'That is true. However, the way you talk about yourself is really strange. That you couldn't stop her from doing the leaking. You are her. You're this online girl as well as this person I'm currently seeing.'

'I know that, and only since this all began have both selves connected. The real and the fake.'

Lane sighed. 'But why did you create such specific people? You can have different sides, but you seem unable to share them equally.'

'It doesn't matter. They are both merging now because of all that has happened. I don't have a true self any more. They are both me. But what do you want with me, Lane? I've shown you I can be trustworthy, and I won't let my hacker self do that again. But please, stop playing. Just tell me, what is going to be the outcome of all this?'

Lane leaned against the balcony. 'I suppose, I could go a little more in depth as to what I want from you. I imagine it would be torturous not knowing.'

'To say the least…'

Lane came to the edge of the balcony in one smooth step. 'It really is your own fault for going on the site. I never would have become this way had you not tempted me when I found out you were a hacker girl. It made me want to learn more about you, and now I can't stop myself. I love the control. It is the killer within me. You need to learn to better protect yourself when prowling the dark web, Junie.'

'I was barely on your site; how did you find me?'

'Because I caught all three of you. It was just lucky timing because I was logged in at the time. Remember, I am a hacker myself, and I built The Monsters Club. The firewall you used can't work everywhere. I made this site so anybody who shouldn't be there could be caught.'

My eyes widened. 'Wait, you built that site, The Monsters Club?'

He seemed to find delight in me acknowledging the fact. 'Yes. I told you, I am not the owner, but I do have big management over it.'

'How is that possible? How are you involved in this? You must only be about my age!'

Lane laughed. 'You can tell my age under this mask?'

'Well…'

'No, you're right. I am actually your age. I got involved for many reasons. Many of us do that use it. It seems some killers like sharing their prizes they have killed, to show off them as a trophy. I don't do that, but the site gives me comfort to talk with people who understand what it is like to…'

I cut him off. 'To be a murderer? So, you have killed people?'

He didn't hesitate. 'Yes, I have.'

'How?'

'What do you mean, how? Well, I plan them out and…'

'I get that! I mean, why? You're so young, how is this possible?'

'There are young killers, Junie.'

I couldn't grasp that he was saying this so effortlessly. As if murder was nothing. He was truly insane. I wasn't perfect, but this was a whole new level of crazy.

'I don't even know what to say to the fact I'm talking to a

killer. A killer that is holding my friend hostage, and arranged the murder of my best friend.' I leaned against the balcony, breathless and struggling to process what was happening.

Lane sighed. 'I understand how crazy it sounds. But now you know I am a killer and I know I can trust you. So, how should we move ahead?'

'That is what I want to know from you.' I sighed.

'I do have ideas. However, you confuse me. I never would usually string out things like this. I would play and then take my prey, but with you, I can't seem to stop playing. At the same time, I don't want to hurt you. I think it is because you are a hacker. It makes me not want to lose you, since pretty hacker girls seemed nonexistant. That, and the fact that your two separate selves intrigue me. Why do you put so much effort in hiding you're a hacker?'

'What can I say to that? This is all in your hands. If I don't play, you'll kill people I care about. This is up to you, as much as I hate to admit it. Either kill me or stop this, please. And does it matter why I choose to hide myself?'

'I can't stop playing. I like talking with you. I want to know more.'

'There has to be some other person you can target!'

Lane took a step forward after I raised my voice. 'Keep your voice down. We don't want anyone hearing us, or another person could get involved with this.'

I looked around, and thankfully the space was still deserted. 'Can't you go back to killing like you used to? What are you gaining from me?'

Lane's smile withered. 'Do you realise what you just said?'

'What?'

'You're telling me to go out and kill others. Do you really not care about hurting other people?'

'That isn't what I meant! But then, I suppose, yes. My emotions are so warped these days and I have so much to focus on, I can only care about my family and friend right now. Emphasis on the singular friend since you ruined it with my school friends and Yamazaki.'

'I know you don't care for them anyway,' Lane laughed. 'I did you a favour. Anyhow, I can't stop playing with you yet. I enjoy speaking with you, but I don't want you to die.'

'Then what, you are going to keep texting me like a creep all the time?' I demanded.

'I guess so.' His laugh filled the space. His amusement was eerie. 'I told you, I want to break you away from some of those secrets. Help you to be yourself.'

'I'd rather you killed me. To end this hell. I can't take much more.' I knew I shouldn't have let out this truth, but it was starting to consume me. I was strong, but only could take such much alone. 'If you did read my messages then you'd know the one thing I worked hardest on was to keep my secrets hidden. You may not understand why, but you don't have to. Just play with me in other ways, not exposing me.'

'Don't say such a thing. I would be sad to lose you before I knew you. Besides, if you knew how I killed people, you wouldn't be saying that.'

'How many people have you killed if you're this young? Why did you start?' I quizzed.

'I'm sure I've lost count now. But it's enough to render me a serial killer. I'm sure you've seen them on the news over the years. I like to space them out. It is how I haven't been found yet. I started young, know that.'

'So, now we have talked. What now? Can you trust in me again?' I asked. I was ready for this to be over with. 'And when will you release Theodore?'

'I do trust you now. And Theodore, he won't be released until I decide how we should end our game. I've only just started playing with you.'

'You're keeping him locked up?'

Lane nodded. 'Until I figure us out. He is okay, don't worry. I'm not starving him. Only, I will if you go against me. I'm sure you should get that by now. This is your last chance to just let things be and we'll be okay. I won't expose your secrets, if you play along with me and just talk to me; your family will be safe as well. However, every time you do mess with me, I will expose another truth, just like with Ela's, or I will hurt someone. It will get worse and you'll lose everything you built up.'

'I've said I will, but for now all you're going to do is carry on like before? If I don't go against you, you'll keep my secrets hidden. Then, what are you doing?'

Lane nodded as he took a step closer to me. 'Yes, until I want this to end. I won't harm you, I just want to speak with you. It's nice, we should speak more about hacking in the future since it is our common denominator. All I want from you is to talk.'

'You really are crazy. Acting as if I'm a friend of yours. But what can I do, if I don't want my family to be hacked to death by you or anyone from that club.' I leaned against the balcony edge, feeling winded. This world was truly insane, but I had to keep playing along and keep playing his weird game to keep my secrets to ourselves.

Lane came and stood right beside me, leaning over the balcony and looked at my frustration. 'Everything will be okay. I'll keep killing, and I won't hurt you. I usually like killing things that are the most attractive to me, but I'm keeping you. I don't live far so we'll see each other a lot, and maybe without the masks one day. I'm going to see where this journey takes us. It will be fun.'

'So you may never release Theodore?'

'I will, one day. Because it will come to an end.' He suddenly stood straight, wiping the dirt off his black tuxedo. 'Anyhow, now we have met, and I trust in you again, I will let the hacking incident go. The site is back up and I've blocked off the police. If they or the media try to get in, it is easy to hold them back. Just don't do it again, then you and your family will be okay. I'll be off now, and I'll see you back at the chat box sometime this week.'

He turned and headed to the door but not before I got my last word. 'You really think I'm going to play along forever, Lane060?'

He barely turned. 'Maybe not. That fact is you will do as you wish. I hope you do keep playing; the future is up to both of us though. See you again, Junie Han.'

He left the balcony and I collapsed from the exhaustion of everything. I couldn't take it any more. This meeting had taken everything to a whole new level that I couldn't handle. Going on one site had changed my life, and I never would do it again as long as I lived. For however much longer that was. I gave into the stress and blacked out.

Chapter Twenty-Eight

I woke up in my own bed, having zero recollection of how I'd even gotten there after recalling passing out on the balcony. I'd never passed out from stress before, and it was surreal. Surreal to not only have met Lane in real life but also just how ordinary he had been. He didn't seem sinister or like a maniac, even though his words made it seem so. I spat out my thoughts and he didn't react with violence. He was too normal. Somehow, that made things worse.

I didn't know how I'd imagined this psycho killer to be, but it certainly wasn't somebody my own age. It was all so wild, but so was this entire tale. I felt like I was drowning. I could handle anything online, but this real-life stuff was too much. Plus, I was no closer to finding Theodore. I didn't even know if I had a future any more. My real life self had fallen, and she had been so hard to keep up.

As I woke up in the warmth of my bedroom, I heard my mother tap gently at the door, then rush towards me when she saw I was awake.

'You're awake, oh thank the lord!' She said, sitting on the side of my bed. 'You passed out at the gala last night and have not woken up since. Are you okay?'

I licked my dry lips and gulped. Even though I wasn't going to tell her what was wrong, she could at least know I had fallen again. Back to my old state in a split second. I felt as weak as I had when I had lost Yamazaki.

'It has happened again. I'm back to square one...' I felt like crying.

'What do you mean, Junie? What has happened?'

'I'm exhausted, mum. With everything.'

'With what? Is it the depression again?' She asked.

'I wish I could explain what is going on, but I can't...' I cried.

'Junie, you did this last time. You can't do it again if you don't tell us what is going on with you. How can we help? What made you pass out last night?'

'Stress.'

'Stress? What is causing such a thing? I thought we had helped you out by not letting you go to school so much?'

I wanted to blurt out everything to stop my mother from worrying but I couldn't. 'I'm sorry, I'm just tired. I think I let this party get to me. It was a lot to host. A lot of people to deal with. I guess I wasn't ready to be doing such a thing again.'

'Is that what it is? The party was too much?'

'I guess so.' I lied.

My mother pulled me into a hug. 'I knew it was strange for you wanting to host this. I suppose you pushed yourself to do something to get back into society. Junie, I can't believe you would do it when you aren't ready to deal with so many people.'

'I'm sorry...'

'Don't be, just don't do it again. When they told me you were passed out on the balcony, I nearly had a heart attack!'

'I won't. I'll take it easy again.'

'Well, get some more rest. Please, don't force yourself to do stuff you aren't ready for like that, okay?' I nodded back and she left the room.

I slammed my head back into my pillow and slept. It was my only way of escaping this strange world I was living in right now. I needed to breathe in peace for however long I could because my mind couldn't take much more of this situation.

I woke up a little while later feeling more refreshed but when I heard my phone buzz beside me, anxiety soon riddled my body and mind with problems again. I took a deep breath and grabbed my phone, and saw a message from Ela, of all people. We hadn't spoken since she'd said she was coming to the party.

 Messages **Ela** Details

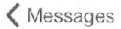

Hey Junie, I thought I would text you after hearing you passed out at the Gala. Are you alright? Ela x

 Text Message   Send

I was shocked by her concern. I felt so bad for what I'd done to her. I was ruining everyones lives for my own sake, and now I was losing everything. I wanted to reply to her, but I felt so bad for what had happened I slammed my phone down, unable to even conjure up a message. I knew hiding from things was not a good idea, but I needed to clear my mind, and talking to her would only make it worse.

I got up from my bed, brushed past my computer, and headed downstairs. My mother was nowhere to be seen. I looked everywhere; both downstairs and outside. I couldn't see her anywhere, and no matter how much I called she didn't reply. I could feel myself starting to panic. I had never felt this way before, but her not being here made me feel so sick that I thought I was going to pass out. My calling soon turned to yells for help, as I began to believe Lane had taken her after I'd fallen asleep. She eventually entered through the front door holding some shopping bags. On seeing me looking flushed in the hallway, she rushed over in a panic, dropping them at the door.

'Mum, I thought I'd lost you…' I cried, unable to control myself. I didn't know what was happening but this panic had taken over and I couldn't get rid of it.

'What is going on, Junie?' My mother gasped.

'I thought I'd lost you…' I buried my face in her neck as she stood there, stunned.

I was at breaking point. Last night had shifted things to a whole new level of reality. I was a mess and so was everything in my life.

My mother sat me on the sofa not long after the spectacle, placed a cup of tea in my hands and gradually calmed me down after my panic. I thought she'd been taken, even though there was no reason to suggest anything bad had happened in the house. The stress had taken me over and my mother was baffled as to why I thought she'd been hurt.

She sat on the sofa facing me, looking into the distance and having no idea how to respond.

'I wish you would tell me what is going on with you, Junie. There has to be something behind what has happened to you this year. Something has changed. I have never seen you like this before. I wish you could talk to me.'

I stared at the ceiling wishing to blurt it out. I wanted to in that moment. Because I knew this was how I would be feeling every day from now on. I gulped and decided I had to at least release something about this situation. Even if it was about my old online self. Something that wouldn't put her in danger, or expose too much about me.

'I will tell you something, Mum. I can't hold it back any more.'

Her eyes gleamed with hope. 'What is it?'

I spat it out. 'I'm a hacker.'

She took a moment to process my words, not understanding what I was trying to say. 'A hacker? What is that supposed to mean?'

'I'm a hacker and the reason as to my bad episode was because one of my hacking friends from online was murdered and I was sent the pictures of his dead body.'

My mother went pale. Never in a million years would she have come up with a reason such as this. Maybe a school issue or a grade problem, but nothing like this.

'Where do I even start with this? You're a hacker and your online friend was killed and his images were sent to you…'

I placed down my mug of tea on the coffee table. 'I know it sounds crazy, but it's the truth. I've hidden this world of mine from you because it was nothing like what you would expect from me.'

'How did you become a hacker?' She quizzed.

'By accident. I found a coding book at school and ended up learning how to code and it took a darker turn…'

'Who is this friend of yours that was killed, Junie?'

'Well, in our online space we often shared different things and us two bonded. Well, something happened as he went too far and was killed for sharing the wrong information. We are dark web hackers, meaning we deal with underground illegal stuff. Because of that, he was found and killed as a warning to everyone else to not share information.'

'Oh my god, Junie! Why on earth would you involve yourself in such a thing as this?!' My mother demanded.

'Because I felt it was the only place I could be myself.'

'What do you mean?'

'Online, I can talk and act as I wish, but in the real world I have to be this pristine, studious daughter. I was forced to act like this in society because of the pressure I felt. I became a hacker to escape reality.'

My mother sat back in her seat and huffed. 'I can't believe any of this. My daughter is a hacker. But this boy that was killed, is that what made you act up like this?'

I nodded. 'Yes, because I was unable to tell anybody how I was feeling. I never got to vent, and it all got to me. That is what caused my depression.'

'All this time I simply thought you were having a bad teenage spell or were stressed because of university. I am so sorry you've been going through this, but at the same time I'm furious with you for involving yourself in such things. I don't even know how to process this.'

If she thought this was bad, she'd be horrified if she knew about Lane. I let out a sigh at the thought and knew it was something I could never tell her. At least I was finally talking about Yamazaki. Even simply breathing his name out into the world relaxed my body. I needed to get this outat least, and try to calm my own mind.

'I'm so sorry. Ever since his death, I've been in a very bad place. But it's my fault for not telling you.'

'Why didn't you just talk to me?' My mother said.

'Because I couldn't let you know about my secret world. I can't take much more silence now though. It was eating me alive. The fact I didn't get to mourn him.'

My mother came and threw me into a hug. 'I can't believe you've felt this way for so long. I'm so sorry.'

'Don't be, I involved myself in this world. It was my own doing.'

She pushed me back and held my tear-stained face. 'And are

you out of it now?'

'Yes, I left it a long time ago. After what happened I realised it was too dangerous and that I needed to get out of it before anything else bad happened.'

'These images, they were definitely of your friend?'

I nodded. 'His massacred body. That was why I couldn't cope, he was my only friend, and he's gone.'

'Your only friend?'

I shrugged. 'My school friends aren't my true friends. I used them to look like I was normal, but I never cared for them.'

'You really thought you couldn't be yourself? Am I that bad of a mother? Is this society that bad?'

Her words made me cry further. 'It's not you, I was the one who couldn't be myself. I shouldn't have taken the route I did, but it felt like an easier option. But now it's over, I will learn to be myself in the real world. Even if for my dead friend, Yamazaki.'

'Yamazaki?'

'He was from Japan.'

'Your only friend was halfway across the world? The internet truly is an amazing place.'

'He was an amazing friend.'

'I'm so sorry you have been through this. I can't even be angry at you. You shouldn't have seen what you did. But now I know this, we can work on getting you better, Junie. I will fix this for you and help you not only get over your friend, but your hardship of not being yourself. I realise this now. I have forced you on a path I chose for you, and for that, I am so sorry.'

'None of it matters now. I feel so much lighter, finally having told someone. It was slowly killing me not being able to mourn him. I will start to accept myself for who I am and be that girl in reality. I promise. This won't ever happen again. I will never go online again, either.' It was a half lie and half truth. I wasn't going to be that much of myself but releasing part of this problem did help to calm me.

'Junie, I love you. I hope you know that. I know how much I work and it makes it seem like me and your father are distant, but you are my everything. That is why I get overly pushy. I'm sorry.'

'Enough with the sorry, you have just helped me be able to breathe again by listening to me. We will get through it together and move forward. I promise. I'm never hacking again.'

I felt a little more rested, but I knew there was a long way to go before this was over. This had all gone too far. I would have to act quickly now. I didn't think Lane would find out about my confession to my mother, but after Theodore, I couldn't be sure. I had to end this situation before my selfishness hurt anyone else.

Chapter Twenty-Nine

The world had never felt so distant. I felt like I was living in a matrix as I got on with my normal life. Or the new version of it. Since my mother knew part of the reason why I'd been depressed we'd began working on ways to get better and start my new life off right. My new life of being myself in reality and doing what I wanted.

We focused on small tasks, one at a time. The first was slowly coming back to school, which was going to be the hardest. Everywhere I went, I saw missing posters with Theodore's face on them, and I knew very well who had him but I couldn't say anything. I didn't even care about the fact Ela had turned much of the school against me.

I could cope with that right now because it was my karma for doing what I did to her in the first place. It was Theodore that hurt me the most. I had to learn to block it all out and gain new breathing techniques to learn to control my panic attacks; a new thing my mother had instructed me to do to stop my constant worrying about everything. I was moving forward, but it wasn't easy.

We'd add two new school days to my schedule and for the most part they were okay, aside from the awkward glances between me and my old friends. I spent most of my time in my secret spot outside where I could smoke and ignore old memories of me and Theodore there, the short time it had been.

I was getting better at blocking things out, but the weekly conversations with Lane would bring it all back to the forefront of my mind. I worked hard to ignore everything, but then I was forced to chat with him and keep him from killing anybody around me and stop him from revealing my darkest secrets. I knew it couldn't go on long term. Every time I was getting better, he would pop up and I would be back at square one. I had no choice but to deal with it.

One day, whilst back at school, I was called to the headmaster's office and was greeted by two policemen sitting either side of him. My heart dropped as I entered the room, thinking my mother had told them about my hacking, but I was shocked when they brought up an accusation made by a friend.

'Hello, Junie. How are you today?' The headmaster asked. 'I'm sorry to have had to call you here.'

'Yes, well. I'm confused as to why I'm here.' I said glancing between him and the officers.

'Well, we've been interviewing students and a comment has come up in regard to your recent relationship with Theodore Hawk-Silberston. It seems you may have some information which could be helpful to the police in regard to his disappearance.'

I went pale at his words. What had he meant by recent relationship, and how did they know about it? 'I don't know what you mean, sir?'

'Have you built a recent relationship with Theodore?'

I knew I couldn't lie about it if somebody had spoken about seeing us together. 'Uh, yes, we began talking again recently. But we were childhood friends.'

'I see. Why would that friendship be rekindled all of a sudden now though?'

'Are you assuming something?'

The headmaster rested against the table. 'You don't have to

answer me, Junie. I'm just asking you a few questions. However, I brought you here to let you know the police will need to speak with you about Theodore's disappearance.'

'Why? I have no idea where he could be.'

'It's okay. We just need to speak with you.' One of the policemen interjected. 'But we will come to your house to do so and have your guardian present. We wanted to let you know about that here.'

'What's going on? What has someone said to make you want to speak with me? You're acting like I'm guilty.'

'We aren't meaning that. It's just that we received some information today and need to let you know that we want to interview you. An accusation has been levelled against you which we wish to discuss further.'

I shut my mouth, knowing someone had tried to frame me for some reason. Either that or said something strange because their reaction made it seem like I was a bad guy. They soon let me go, telling me they would call my parents to arrange a date to come around.

I stormed out into the hall wondering who would have targeted me like this. Someone had said my name for a reason, and I knew who. Her middle name was payback.

Ela was the only person who had seen me with Theodore for long amounts of time, it had to be her. It was her. Could Ela really have gone that low to pay me back for what I'd done to her? I stormed to our gym class and saw her standing there. I approached her and slammed the locker door shut, alerting her.

'What the heck?!' she yelped, before she simmered down when she saw me.

'You told the headmaster that I'd been hanging around with Theodore recently.' I said outright. She shrugged.

'He asked me a question, I answered.'

'Do you realise you made it seem like I'd something to do with Theodore's disappearance, Ela? What accusation have you given them enough to interview me?'

'Did I?' She said with little tone.

'Are you really doing this?'

'Doing what?' She replied slamming her door shut.

'Using this to get back at me for what happened to you? I told you, it's all a lie!'

Ela scoffed. 'I'm not doing anything. But maybe it is strange how you were hanging out with him all of a sudden and now he's gone, isn't it?'

'You bitch… I could go to jail for you making up such an accusation. You've framed me.'

'Then maybe in the future you should learn to keep secrets to yourself and maybe I would do the same.' Ela barged past me and I was ready to attack. But I held myself back. I never knew she could go so low. It was bad. I'd forgotten how ruthless Ela Allard could be.

That week the police came round to my house to quiz me over Theodore's disappearance. Ela had leaked the fact we'd been getting close lately and they had to see me to understand why it was and how it could relate to his sudden absence. I never knew she could be so petty, even though I'd done it to her. She had accused me of something terrible, to frame someone was on another level. I had to remain calm so not make myself out to be worse, so when I told my parents what was going on, they were shocked.

It wasn't long before the police got to the point. 'Miss Han, we've a few questions to ask if that's okay with you. It's about the disappearance of Theodore Hawk-Silberston. He's your friend, correct?'

'Yes.' I replied simply.

'Yes, he is your friend or yes, you know about his disappearance?'

'Yes, he's my friend.'

'Okay, I see. How long have you been in contact now?'

'Not very long. We started talking after catching up at Ela's party.'

The officers both exchanged a glance which I knew was because Ela had accused me of something. 'And in this new meeting, has anything odd happened?'

'Odd?'

'Yes, have you noticed anything about Theodore that could give us some insight into his disappearance.'

I shrugged. 'I've no idea what's happened.'

'Are you sure?'

'Yes, why wouldn't I be?'

One of the officers let out a short breath and I saw the accusation coming next. 'I'm afraid we've had an accusation that you may know more about his disappearance than you are alluding too.'

'An accusation?' My mother interjected.

'Yes, it seems someone believes Junie's sudden involvement with him holds strange ties as to why he may be lost.'

'Who made such an accusation?!' My father demanded.

'It doesn't matter who. Why someone would think your reunion with Mr. Hawk-Silberston would be strange?'

'I know who you're talking about and that girl has framed me on purpose.'

'Excuse me?'

'She's angry at me for something she believes I did, even though I did nothing wrong, and is doing this to get back at me. Making me seem crazy.'

The officer sighed again. 'Miss Han, are you saying the person gave us a false accusation?'

'Yes, I had nothing to do with this. Ask anybody about how she's mad at me right now, and look at her history, she enjoys hurting people. Especially if she believes she's been wronged.'

The officers exchanged a glance before writing something down and I groaned internally hoping it had worked for now. I looked over to my parents who didn't have a clue what to think but as long as they believed it was a lie, it was all that mattered.

'I think we need to re-evaluate if you're making this claim. I wasn't aware of such a fight.'

'She wouldn't tell you that, she wants me to look bad.' I added.

'What fight?' My mother enquired, who was confused by everything.

'It doesn't matter, what matters is clearing my name of any suspicion. All I did was begin to talk to Theodore more but I've no idea what's happened to him.'

'And this is your final statement?'

I nodded. 'Yes.'

'Okay, we will need to investigate this further. We're not accusing you Miss Han. All we're doing is making sure we follow every lead. His disappearance has been very sudden, and we need to follow everything we can get.'

'I understand, but that accusation is taken out of context.'

'Why would someone accuse you of foul play?' My father asked.

'It's a long story. It's not what you think.'

The two officers stood. 'We'll be back in touch if we need to. Thank you for your time.'

After they left, my parents didn't seem to know what to say about the random happening. It was so out of the blue, and was all Lane's doing for making Ela act this way. It boiled my blood.

'I'm sorry about that. It's all over nothing.'

'It was certainly a surprise to see them at my door this morning. I'm so confused.'

'Don't even think about it, Mum. I want to find Theodore as much as the next person but what has happened here is all a mistake.'

'I certainly hope it is. Anyhow, we'll just have to see how it unfolds.'

'Okay.'

'Junie, do you really not know where Theodore is?' My mother asked.

'I really don't, Mum. I wish I did, he was a good friend to me.' I walked off and slumped into my bed wondering when life would give me a break for five minutes. Every day it seemed to escalate, and I didn't know how much more I could take. I was used to lying but every day a new worry was added to the pile and it would only going to take so long before I'd explode.

Later that day, as if the morning hadn't been enough of a task, it was time for my forced talk with Lane. I logged into the computer at the usual time and he was already waiting for me but today, even more so than usual, I was in no mood to talk. He was the one who was causing all my problems, and now I had the police sniffing around, it only added another rotten cherry on top of a bitter cake.

LANE060: HELLO, WELCOME BACK TO ANOTHER EPISODE OF JUNIE HAN TALKING WITH A KILLER.

HEYJUN: CAN WE KEEP THIS SHORT?

LANE060: SHORT? YOU'RE ALWAYS SHORT. I'M USUALLY THE ONE FILLING IN THE BLANKS WITH HUMOUR. JUST LIKE NOW, AND THE LACK OF APPRECIATION FOR MY SARCASM IS UPSETTING.

HEYJUN: YES, THEY'RE SHORT BECAUSE I HARDLY WANT TO TALK TO A PERSON WHO THINKS IT'S FUNNY TO MAKE JOKES ABOUT DEATH.

LANE060: WHAT'S UP WITH YOU TODAY?

HEYJUN: EVEN MORE CRAP, AS USUAL.

LANE060: SUCH AS?

HEYJUN: WELL, IF YOU MUST KNOW, BECAUSE OF YOU MESSING ELA AND LEAKING THE TRUTH ABOUT WHAT I DID TO HER, SHE'S DECIDED TO GET PAYBACK ON ME BY TIPPING OFF THE POLICE ABOUT THE FACT I HAD RECENTLY BECOME THEO-DORE'S FRIEND AND INSTNUATED I'D SOMETHING TO DO WITH HIS DISAPPEARANCE JUST BECAUSE I WAS TALKING TO HIM MORE. THE BITCH HAS JUST CAUSED MORE HASSLE FOR ME.

LANE060: I SEE...

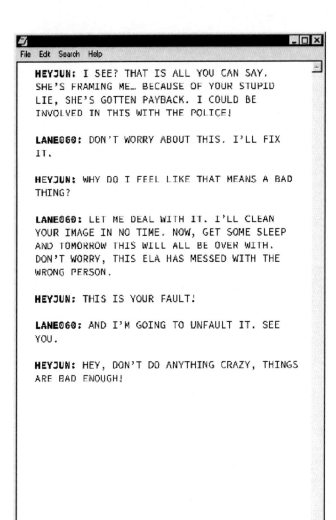

HEYJUN: I SEE? THAT IS ALL YOU CAN SAY. SHE'S FRAMING ME... BECAUSE OF YOUR STUPID LIE, SHE'S GOTTEN PAYBACK. I COULD BE INVOLVED IN THIS WITH THE POLICE!

LANE060: DON'T WORRY ABOUT THIS. I'LL FIX IT.

HEYJUN: WHY DO I FEEL LIKE THAT MEANS A BAD THING?

LANE060: LET ME DEAL WITH IT. I'LL CLEAN YOUR IMAGE IN NO TIME. NOW, GET SOME SLEEP AND TOMORROW THIS WILL ALL BE OVER WITH. DON'T WORRY, THIS ELA HAS MESSED WITH THE WRONG PERSON.

HEYJUN: THIS IS YOUR FAULT!

LANE060: AND I'M GOING TO UNFAULT IT. SEE YOU.

HEYJUN: HEY, DON'T DO ANYTHING CRAZY, THINGS ARE BAD ENOUGH!

Lane left the chat and I wished I hadn't breathed a word. I shut down my computer with a sigh. It was going to come to a bad end. I just knew it.

Chapter Thirty

I woke up the next day with a knot in my stomach. I never knew what awaited me any more. Every day was different and I couldn't prepare myself. With what Lane had said the day before, I knew that once again something bad was coming. He was the king of hitting me with bad things out of nowhere so I prepared myself for the worst.

'How are you this morning?' My father asked me as I hit the bottom step. It was strange to see him in the morning since he always got the early train to work in central London.

'What are you doing home?'

'I've decided to take you to school this morning.'

'How come?'

'I want to talk to your headmaster.'

'What for?'

'Just to make sure everything is okay. Someone accusing you of wrongdoing after some argument isn't a thing to let go of easily. I want them to know I pay a lot of money to keep this school going. And for this to happen to you, to have police at my home, I want to find out who this student is who framed you so I can have them expelled.'

I placed my school bag on the kitchen table as I followed him inside. 'Dad, don't do this. I'm not telling you who it is because there's no point. I'm fine and know I'm not guilty of anything. It will backfire on her.'

'I don't care if it will backfire, the fact I had police here means I can't let this rest.'

'Please, let it rest. You'll only make things worse. Where's Mum?'

'She already left because I said I would take you.'

'No!'

'Junie, don't you see how serious this is? Someone can't accuse you like this and get away with it.'

'And they won't get away with it, let the police handle her lies. Please.'

He thought it over as he did up his tie. I knew he just wanted to protect me, but this would only make things worse. 'Fine, I'll let it go for now but if they do it again, I'm dealing with it.'

'Fine. Just take me to school but don't do anything else.'

'Alright. I'm so angry though. Whoever accused you, I'll ruin them if I ever find out who they are.'

As he stormed out the room to put on his blazer, I leaned against the table. Now I had two things to worry about: what Lane and now my father were going to do. Ela had better hoped neither of them got near her, otherwise it would be her end.

As soon as I arrived at school, the air felt heavy. I was waiting for something bad to happen. Thankfully, he didn't stay and soon drove off but I could see it took all of his energy not to storm to the headmaster's office and complain. I went straight to my locker and sighed into it as I grabbed my sports kit for the morning class. My body felt so weak and yet I had javelin practice. It was going to be torturous as I tried to fake-care about anything.

Faking anything had once been second nature. Passing down the hall at the same time as the teacher I paid to fake my grades never used to take any energy. Being the pretty version of myself everyone had loved at one time had been so easy; and yet after all that had happened, I couldn't force a fake smile. It took so much energy to lie that I'd forgotten what it had once felt like when it came so easily to me.

As I passed down the hall to the changing room for class, nobody cared about me now the whole Ela situation had settled. However, it didn't mean people didn't give me side glances any more. Had it been me a few months ago I would've done anything to change the situation, but it was out of my control and for once in my life the last thing I cared about was my reputation. I'd other important secrets to guard for a change; Dallington couldn't bother me now.

I arrived at the half-empty changing room and hurriedly dressed to miss my ex-friends who would only fill the room with tension. I'd never put much effort into sports but I thought I could use it to vent out some frustration. Throwing some long sticks into the ground; I was going to send my anger with it.

I walked out into the hall where everyone was already waiting to be let inside at the gym's entrance. It was strange because it was never normally locked this late in the morning as the janitor normally cleaned there before practice.

I caught eyes with Maria and Aisha for a moment, but Ela was nowhere to be seen. They rolled their eyes at me before turning back to the group beside them.

'Why is the gym closed?' Our teacher said, breezing past us a moment later.

'We don't know.' Aisha interjected. 'Can you open it already, it's freezing out here!'

'I don't have the key,' Ms. Woodacre said, trying to unlock it before scouting a janitor. 'Excuse me, could you open the gym?'

The man came over, surprised. 'That's strange; I had it open earlier.'

He unlocked the door and swung it open. Everyone poured in but before my foot hit the step, a chorus of yells erupted in front of me, fixing my body in place.

It was in the gymnasium I saw what Lane had done. The screams of my fellow classmates filled the hall as they rushed out of the gym. I braced myself as I took the few step forwards before heading inside to discover the reason for the screams.

'There's a dead body in there!' Screamed one of the students as they all bled out the gym.

Ela was stuck against the wall, her body a pin cushion of javelin poles, stapled to the wall with blood splattered on every surface around her. I froze at the sight of her, everyone screaming and the blood pulsing in my ears. Before I could take a step back the light flickered and a blink later, I passed out.

Chapter Thirty-One

I woke in the nurse's office with a sore arm after falling so suddenly and passing out. I lay in the bed for a good few moments, staring at the ceiling, pretending what I'd seen was a dream. It had to be. Ela couldn't have been impaled to the wall, her dead body left out like some disgusting trophy. There was no way this could be real but in my heart I knew it was, and I knew who was responsible.

'Junie, you're awake?' A voice called from my side and I tore my gaze away from the ceiling to see Ms. Hawthorne looking at me with concern. She was completely pale and sickly looking as she came to my side. 'How are you?'

I shrugged. 'I don't know. Was that real?'

She sighed, sitting on the facing bed. 'I'm sorry to say it was, yes.'

'How...'

'We don't know, yet.'

'How long have I been passed out?'

'About two hours. The police are here now. I told your family not to worry and that I'd take you home once you'd woken up. I didn't want to get them too concerned yet as to what you'd seen.'

'Thank you.' Is all I could breathe as I turned back to the ceiling. I'd caused this. Ela's death. Yes, she'd been the one to start it with the accusation that triggered Lane to act, but it was all my own doing. I shouldn't have opened my mouth, and now she'd died a gruesome death. I couldn't begin to feel like it was real.

'I'm so sorry you had to see that. I don't understand what's going on lately. This and the loss of Theodore, what is happening? This school seems to have become tainted. Nothing like this has ever happened before.'

The mention of Theodore made me nauseous and Ms. Hawthorne passed me a bucket as I puked out all my sinful secrets. Two people lost; one dead and the other close to it if I dared mess up. Every hour things were getting worse and if I said the wrong thing it would keep happening. Lane wasn't playing.

I felt like I'd purged all my energy at the sight of Ela's body. Ms. Hawthorne gave me time to rest before driving me home a little later in the day. School was called off and the police started their investigation. I watched the academy close in the distance and wondered where Lane was lurking. I had the answers for so many problems and I couldn't give them.

The drive home was quiet but as we neared home, Ms. Hawthorne told me to call her if I needed to talk. She said that my parents wouldn't be long, having decided to leave work early after all. I agreed before going inside and locking myself in my bedroom. My body felt numb, stunned by what had happened. I sat on the side of my bed and stared into the distance, unable to compute anything. It was the first time I'd ever seen such gore in real life outside of the dark web and all I wanted to do was vomit.

I was part of the mess now, so even if I wanted to go to the police, I would be in trouble for withholding evidence about all the craziness from the start. I was a player in the game. How much longer was it going to continue once Lane had taken it to the next level? I never gotten to tell Ela the truth and the guilt over what I'd done to her at that party was starting to play in my mind again. I was never one to feel guilty but after all that had happened, it sliced at my heart like a razor blade.

I lifted my eyes to my computer. The place that started it all, from the loss of Yamazaki to Ela's death in my real world. Everything was merging, and I had to do something to stop it. I couldn't live on a knife's edge wondering what Lane would do next. I had to play him back. This was my last option. I realised now the only way out was to reawaken my hacker side, that ruthless girl who would do anything to save her secrets.

As the tears poured down my cheeks, I switched on the computer, ready to start my own game. This was the last straw. I opened the chat box and began a new phase. I was surprised when he replied right away.

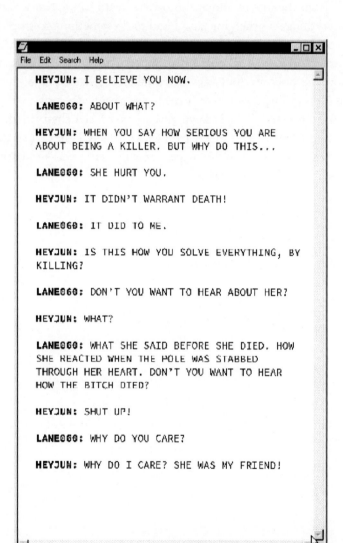

HEYJUN: I BELIEVE YOU NOW.

LANE060: ABOUT WHAT?

HEYJUN: WHEN YOU SAY HOW SERIOUS YOU ARE ABOUT BEING A KILLER. BUT WHY DO THIS...

LANE060: SHE HURT YOU.

HEYJUN: IT DIDN'T WARRANT DEATH!

LANE060: IT DID TO ME.

HEYJUN: IS THIS HOW YOU SOLVE EVERYTHING, BY KILLING?

LANE060: DON'T YOU WANT TO HEAR ABOUT HER?

HEYJUN: WHAT?

LANE060: WHAT SHE SAID BEFORE SHE DIED. HOW SHE REACTED WHEN THE POLE WAS STABBED THROUGH HER HEART. DON'T YOU WANT TO HEAR HOW THE BITCH DIED?

HEYJUN: SHUT UP!

LANE060: WHY DO YOU CARE?

HEYJUN: WHY DO I CARE? SHE WAS MY FRIEND!

LANE060: A FRIEND YOU ALMOST DESTROYED. A FRIEND YOU'VE LIED TO ALL YOUR LIFE. WHO TRUSTED YOU AND YET YOU TRIED TO HURT THEIR REPUTATION JUST TO SAVE THAT STUPID SECRET OF YOURS? THAT ONE YOU NEVER CARED ABOUT ANYWAY? THAT FRIEND?

HEYJUN: I KNOW WHAT I'VE DONE, BUT I'D NEVER KILL SOMEONE TO SAVE MYSELF!

LANE060: ARE YOU SURE ABOUT THAT? AREN'T YOU LETTING THEODORE SUFFER TO SAVE YOURSELF BY NOT GOING TO THE POLICE BECAUSE YOU'RE SCARED OF EXPOSING YOUR ILLEGAL ACTIVITIES?

HEYJUN: STOP TRYING TO PLAY MIND GAMES WITH ME. YOU KNOW THAT'S BECAUSE IF I DO SOME-THING, YOU'D HARM HIM.

LANE060: WHATEVER, AT LEAST SHE GOT THE MESSAGE. SHE WOULD'VE BEEN FINE HAD SHE NOT BOTHERED YOU LIKE THAT.

HEYJUN: YOU'RE GOING TO HELL!

LANE060: I'M SURE THERE'LL BE A NICE SPACE NEXT TO ME FOR YOU.

HEYJUN: GET OUT OF MY LIFE!!!

LANE060: OH, LITTLE JUNIE, THIS IS ONLY THE START. I'VE HARDLY BEGUN.

HEYJUN: THEN I'LL END IT.

I shut down the computer after this last sentence, knowing it would annoy him. But I couldn't hear it anymore. It all had to end. If I kept testing him, another person I knew would either die or be taken away from me. I had to end this now, and I would have to do it myself. I had to meet Lane again and finish it once and for all. And that meant either my body being found or his. I just couldn't lose another person.

It was time I brought out the darkest part of me, the one only Lane and Yamazaki knew. The one I'd tried to bury so deep, deeper than all of my secrets combined. Eviller than Lane realised. It was time to end it.

Lane texted me not long after I'd ended our conversation and I soon responded demanding to meet up with him. It was the only way it was going to end. I'd a plan, but needed to see him in person again to play it out.

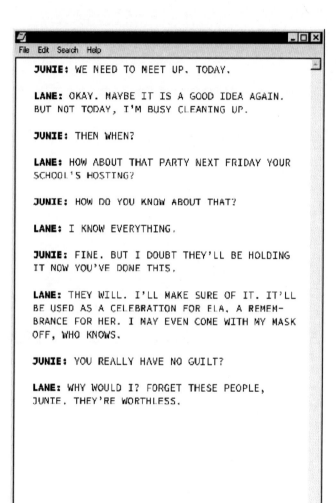

JUNIE: WE NEED TO MEET UP, TODAY.

LANE: OKAY. MAYBE IT IS A GOOD IDEA AGAIN. BUT NOT TODAY, I'M BUSY CLEANING UP.

JUNIE: THEN WHEN?

LANE: HOW ABOUT THAT PARTY NEXT FRIDAY YOUR SCHOOL'S HOSTING?

JUNIE: HOW DO YOU KNOW ABOUT THAT?

LANE: I KNOW EVERYTHING.

JUNIE: FINE. BUT I DOUBT THEY'LL BE HOLDING IT NOW YOU'VE DONE THIS.

LANE: THEY WILL. I'LL MAKE SURE OF IT. IT'LL BE USED AS A CELEBRATION FOR ELA. A REMEM-BRANCE FOR HER. I MAY EVEN COME WITH MY MASK OFF, WHO KNOWS.

JUNIE: YOU REALLY HAVE NO GUILT?

LANE: WHY WOULD I? FORGET THESE PEOPLE, JUNIE. THEY'RE WORTHLESS.

I wanted to punch back that he was the worthless one, but I didn't need to make the situation any worse for myself. I had no choice but to hold the meeting there. At least it would be in a public setting. I kept myself calm, focused on anything but what had happened to keep myself going.

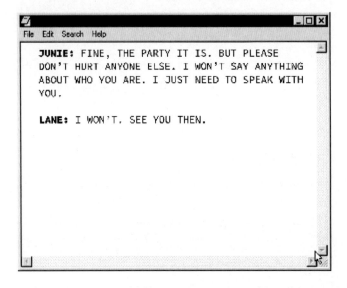

I closed my phone with a sigh, knowing it was dangerous but so was everything in my life right now. It didn't matter, I was living in hell so I may as well face it in person.

Chapter Thirty-Two

The week before the party was hell. Two students had both been lost in some way and as a result Dallington Academy was swarming with police. I knew they were still looking at me in some way as a person of interest. Even more so now, since it was Ela who had tipped them off in the first place. It made me look guilty and I knew behind the scenes they'd be working to get me somehow, so I had to be extra careful. That and the fact I didn't even know how I was going to handle meeting Lane again. But one way or another it was coming to an abrupt and final end.

The party was still going ahead, so I stayed away from people for most of the week until the day. I was glad I only had to attend school for such a short time, otherwise it would've made hiding the truth even more difficult. I was so fragile at the moment and my mind felt like it could collapse at any time. When things had become too much, I used to have at least one person to vent my emotions. But now I had nobody and it felt like it would all seep out at any moment.

Normally, the school would be buzzing with the new seasonal event and someone would've been chosen to navigate the threat list position. Except this time, the school mourned Ela while silently hoping for news of Theodore. Nobody was full of mischief or smiles. I'd never seen the school so glum. The party was being held in memory of Ela and to raise money to find Theodore; two things I held the answers to.

When the event arrived, I readied myself, stomach growing with a sickness the entire car journey to the venue. My mother hadn't left me alone since hearing of Ela's death and I only managed to escape this time as the parties were separated into adults and students as always. As we arrived at the building, I said my goodbyes to my mother and headed inside. I felt unwelcome in the student area and the place was already filled with the faces of my fellows.

People were smiling, enjoying themselves, but others still held the same sadness as at school. I looked at the main stage where a huge picture of Ela stood. I gulped; a reminder of where I'd shamed her. I saw Dillan standing beside it, looking into the image until one of his friends pulled him away. He caught my gaze for a second before he was pulled away. A glare leaving me behind.

I sighed my way into the event, turning my attention to my purpose there. I would endure all the stares to meet Lane again. I tried to pick him out in the crowd but given I only knew his body and not his face, he was hard to differentiate against all the youthful people dancing in the centre of the crowd. I was at the edge of my sanity, forced to sit in a party dress, to make things even worse.

I moved to stand by the edge of the room and get a better look at the crowd, but as the room was so dim and the lights flooded only the centre, it was difficult to tell. Then a familiar voice caught me suddenly from my side.

'Hey, Junie. Long time no speak.' Said Maria, standing nervously and picking at her hands as I turned to meet her. It was weird to see her again as we hadn't spoken in so long, and even though I wasn't in a great mood, I forced a smile.

'Hey, Maria. How've you been?'

She came forward, ignoring my question. Eyes filling with tears. 'I'm sorry for avoiding you, Junie.'

'It's okay. I understand.' I replied as she threw me into a hug, before pulling back and smiling. It took me by surprise given not long ago she'd been glaring at me like everyone else.

'I can't believe this has happened... She's gone.'

'I know, I still haven't processed it.'

'I know you two left on bad terms, but I think we can come together at such a dark time as this. I've missed you.'

'I've missed you too.' I lied but I was thankful she'd at least checked on me. Everyone else had left me to rot, still clinging to the lie.

'Aisha is still wary of you, but don't take it to heart. She doesn't process things well.'

'It's fine. I just hope you two are okay. I think Dillan wants me dead.'

'He's just sad and is clinging on to her anger for hating you. Are you okay?' She asked.

I shrugged. 'As good as I can be.'

'Well, how about I'll go and get us a drink and we can talk some more, huh? I'm sure it would do us some good to put our differences aside now.' I nodded and she soon floated off. It was strange talking to Maria again. But I didn't hold it against her being on Ela's side at the time, they believed what seemed true and I couldn't do anything about it. I was somewhat happy she'd at least spoken to me, though I knew she was only doing this because Maria always needed a leader. And since Aisha was the same, she'd looked for guidance in me.

I turned my attention back to the crowd but couldn't see any strange figures who stood out. Lane had been tall and very slim, but without knowing what he looked like it hardly mattered. I wondered how he'd be there tonight given it wasn't a masked party. But surely, he wouldn't show his face, it would be dangerous. Then again, the guy never failed to surprise.

I began to circle the room like a vulture, analysing each person without trying to seem strange in doing so. But it was no good, so I moved by the back entrance knowing I would have to let him come to me. It was frustrating because I needed it to be over. I needed to see him to let him know it was going to end there or, if he refused, my hidden, dark self was going to come out.

Then as I was standing back at the entrance, Maria returned with two drinks and another person. She seemed livelier than before, though I didn't recognise the person she was with.

'Hey, Junie. Have you met Lane?'

I froze at the mention of his name, knowing when I turned my eyes to him, it would be the evil face that had been torturing my life. And all the while Lane stared back at me with a smile, I forced myself to remain calm. It took me a few seconds of quiet breathing before I dared see his maskless face.

He was extremely and unsettlingly handsome, which I'd never expected of a person like him. You expect evil to be as ugly as their soul but Lane was another level of handsome with his beaming hazel eyes and intensely sharp cheekbones. It didn't match the evil I knew existed behind those eyes. The one who had Yamazaki assassinated and brutally murdered Ela.

I didn't know how to respond, so Lane chirped up first, extending his hand to me. 'Hey, nice to meet you.'

I shook his hand so Maria wouldn't suspect anything. His palm was as cold as his eyes.

'Who're you?' I asked, quickly pulling away.

Maria smiled. 'I just got talking to him at the drinks stand. Apparently, he knew Ela. He's come to support the event for her. Isn't that nice?'

Lane nodded. 'Yes, I knew her very well. Since we were kids. I can't believe this has happened. I had to come and celebrate her life. What a brutal way to pass.'

His lie made me want to vomit but I remained calm as I knew he was testing me. Trying to shock me with such an open appearance and he'd obviously spoken to Maria to antagonise me further. But I wouldn't let him win.

'Oh, yes. Now I remember that name. Ela had talked about a Lane.' I said, adding a hint of sarcasm to my tone.

'She had?' Maria replied wide-eyed.

'Yes. Some puny kid from her childhood that never used to leave her alone.' Lane lightly rolled his eyes at my statement.

'I've never heard her say that. Never mind, it's nice to meet a secret friend of hers. I can't believe she never told us about you, given how handsome you are. How come she kept you on the quiet?'

Maria's strange statement didn't bother me as much as it should've, as I knew it was time to talk. 'Uh, actually. I wish to talk to Junie for a second, do you mind giving us a minute?' Lane said.

Maria shrugged. 'Sure, but what for?'

'Nothing special. It won't be long. I just heard Ela talk a lot about Junie, and I would love to hear about Ela from Junie's point of view since they were so close.'

Lane suddenly pushed past Maria and latched his hand around my wrist tightly and began dragging me away. He pulled me up some stairs and guided me to the open balcony that overlooked the back of the venue. When we got to the top, I threw off the hand that had caused so much chaos, feeling disgusted.

'Get your filthy hands off of me.' I said, not caring how sharp my words were. 'You sure have a nerve.'

Lane laughed. 'What? I thought I'd just use her as a tool to talk to you to make our introduction seem natural in public. You like lying to people. I thought you'd enjoy it.'

'Please stop...'

He tutted. 'I'm not doing anything; it's the people around you that are causing this to happen to you. All of this craziness.'

'How is it them?!'

'Can't you see why I want to take them all out? Because they made you become this dual person. Had you not been this way and were you able to be yourself, you wouldn't have become a hacker and we wouldn't have met. It's their fault this is happening.'

His words stunned me because they held truth. It was the first time I'd heard him say such a thing, blaming those around me for why I couldn't be myself. But it was also my own doing for caring so much about other people's opinions that I hid myself like I did. They couldn't take all the blame. I was the lost one.

'It doesn't matter. None of it does anymore. I only want you to stop and leave me and those around me the hell alone. You said you'd only harm people if I didn't listen to you. Well, I've been following your orders, and yet, you've killed Ela.'

Lane lay against the railing. 'You know that isn't going to happen. This won't stop, and I killed her because she tried to expose you.'

'You're the one who leaked what I did to her!' I placed my hand against the brick and sighed. Looking down at the courtyard, wishing the night wind would sweep me away. 'Why have you shown yourself to me like this?'

Lane shrugged. 'I trust you, and even if you try to out me, I'm well protected. There's no point in a mask this time. At least you know my face now. I can tell it's shocked you. I know I don't fit the murderous image of a killer you wanted to see.'

'You're right. You don't. But if you are this way, why would you do what you do?'

'What do you mean by this way?' He laughed.

'You know what I mean.'

'Because I'm handsome? Beauty doesn't determine a character, Junie.'

'I suppose not. But what a life you've wasted.'

Lane sighed. 'I've lived a pretty good life. I enjoy it.'

'Why do you enjoy killing people?'

'Because sometimes death is needed...' As soon as he said it and I looked over the balcony, something inside me snapped. This was the moment to bring her out; my plan.

I couldn't take it anymore. He was right, sometimes death was needed, and I knew the only way to get rid of a psychopath was to do something crazy in response. What I was about to do was crazy but it was my last option of escape.

I looked around, turned to him, saw the chance and took it. 'You're right, Lane.'

'I am?' He said, surprised by my response.

'Yes, you're right. That death is sometimes needed.'

'I'm glad you think so.'

'And tonight, you're included in that statistic!' It took him a moment to compute what I said, though before he could, I shoved him. He tripped, managing to lose his balance enough that I should easily push him over the edge of the building. I didn't look as it happened. I turned and ran. I didn't need to know what'd happened. I was a killer. Just as he had his dark ways, so had I. I hadn't gotten so far in life with the secrets I carried by being good. There was more to my hacker ways. To get what I wanted I would go low, and as he slipped over the edge, he'd seen the truest version of me.

Chapter Thirty-Three

I rushed through the crowd and made my way to the front of the building, taking a deep breath to try and calm myself. I couldn't believe what I'd just done but when I heard the screaming crowd commence, I knew that was my cue to leave. Lane had been hurt and I fled the scene, before calling a taxi home. Just hoping nobody had seen what I'd done.

I couldn't stop shaking. The taxi driver kept peering at me through the mirror, probably wondering why I looked so pale and out of sorts. I just needed to get home and calm myself down, take a deep breath and forge my strategy of lies if anything came from it. It had happened so quickly. I wasn't sure if anyone had seen me or not.

It wasn't a great feeling, especially as my inner rage began to take over. I fought against the girl hiding so deep down within me, who only needed to surface when I needed to reach to the darkest lengths to save myself. She'd forgotten the world existed and now I was questioning whether people were there or not. I had played my own game to get rid of Lane and time would tell if my actions were worth it.

It felt like the longest drive home of my life, and when we finally arrived, I found myself standing outside the house. I waited there a few minutes, knowing my parents would be surprised to see me when they got home. I didn't want to think of an excuse. Didn't want to step inside. I waited until they returned and braced myself to tell them everything that had happened. But I couldn't summon the strength and the tears began to flow.

An uncontrollable swell of emotions burst from me, I fell to the doorstep as all my frustrations poured forth. I wanted it all to end, to return back to normal with Yamazaki there, and even my old fake face if it would make things easier. It was all too much. I'd come to a point of no return. I couldn't take any more death or control. It felt like my lungs had been drained of breath.

I didn't know how much time passed, sitting at our doorstep in my designer dress, unable to feel the cold because I'd been so caught up in myself. The car pulled into the drive way and I looked up to my mother. I heard my mother gasp at the sight of me looking a complete mess and sitting there on the doorstep.

'Junie, what on earth are you doing back here?' She half-yelled as she lifted me up in shock. 'I've been looking for you everywhere!'

I wiped my eyes and tried to compose myself, but nothing could hide my emotions. 'Everything is so messed up mum. I can't take it anymore.'

She pulled me inside, slamming the door shut behind us and dragged me into the living space where my dad rose from his chair in shock.

'What has happened?' He said panicked as I cried.

'I don't know. Junie disappeared tonight from the venue and I've come home to find her here, looking worse for wear.' My mother cried.

'Junie, what has happened?' My dad said, sitting beside me as I tried my best to calm down.

'So many things...' I said through teary gasps.

'Many things? Have you been hurt?'

'I don't know. I don't know anything. What has happened to my life?!'

'What are you talking about, Junie? I can't help you if you don't explain it to us?'

My dad let out a sigh. I wasn't making any sense and I couldn't get my thoughts straight. The truth was too wild to believe and if they knew what I'd done, who knew how they'd respond. Luckily, I didn't have to give a response as, not much later, the sirens came .

I jumped up at the sound with a gasp. 'No, I can't believe it.' My parents looked at each other in shock as I cried.

'What the heck has happened tonight, Junie?!' My father shouted, turning to me as the police lights flashed outside.

My mother gasped, heading to the window as the knock came at the door.

Sitting in the waiting area of the police station, waiting to be questioned with mascara running down my cheeks, was never a look I had intended on wearing. I was at a loss for words. I felt so numb. More at the fact that I had seemingly been caught, than what I had done to Lane.

It wasn't long before I was sat in an interrogation room. I had not been charged with anything yet, but they wanted to talk with me over what had happened to Lane. It seems somebody had seen me after all and reported a girl in a gold dress running away after he had fallen from the balcony.

It was the same officers who had questioned me over Theodore, and they didn't look pleased to see me. Theodore's disappearance, Ela's death and now Lane: I got a feeling that they were linking me with them all. Being caught in three different scenarios didn't make someone look great. However, as we were getting ready for the questioning, a strange scene broke the moment before it could begin, when I heard a familiar voice shouting from the hallway as one of the officers was about to close the door. A voice that made my heart sink.

'Junie was not responsible for this!' Lane called from the hall. He was standing, and his tuxedo was torn in a few places, and he had a bruise laying neatly on his forehead. But he was not as injured as he should have been from the fall. Then our eyes met, and I wanted to throw up. 'There she is, Junie did not do this!' Lane said as he was helped to my side.

'How...' I gasped as he limped to the door.

'Junie, I'm sorry about this. There seems to have been a mix up. They think it was you who threw me over the side of the building. I've told them it was only an accident.'

'You really just fell?' The officer asked.

'Yes, I slipped and went over the rail.'

'Weren't you two talking?'

'No. I was alone and fell.' Lane added.

'What sort of mix up is this?' The officer replied, rubbing his bald head.

'I guess it must've been confusing but I'm fine, I was alone.'

'Really?'

'Of course. Now can we leave?' Lane replied.

'I see no reason why not. This has been a very confusing night. I am sorry, Miss Han, but we were told you were seen fleeing the scene.'

'Come on, Junie. Let's go.' Lane said, and I didn't dare deny him given he had both saved me and he had a look in his eye that read don't play me again. I stood up and paced beside him as the officers helped us out to the front.

'Shouldn't you wait for your parents?' The officer called to me. 'They're on their way here.'

'We'll get a taxi.' Lane called back and we left as fast as we had come. Me wondering when I'd wake up from this dream.

It wasn't long before we were sitting outside the police station and waiting for a taxi home. I had just attempted to kill him, and he was now sitting beside me, smiling as if this was all okay. He had been bruised pretty badly and had a few cuts on his face and body but other than that, he was fine, and I couldn't understand how.

'It's a beautiful night, eh?' Lane spoke up and I turned to see him gleaming at me with a dimpled smile.

'Why are you smiling at me?' I asked. Not knowing what else to say.

'Because tonight has been fun.'

'I just tried to kill you...'

Lane shushed me. 'Shh... nobody needs to know that.'

'Why aren't you mad at me?' I asked. 'Is it because of where we are, and you don't want to be caught doing anything to me by a police station? I guess so.'

'You think what you did bothers me?' Lane laughed.

'Of course. You should have died...'

His next words confused me even more. 'You got ahead of me... I never expected that. Do you realise it has made me like you even more?'

'What?'

'You're so smart. I was dumb back there. I never saw that coming.'

'You're crazy...' I sighed.

'Crazy for you.' He joked and let out a deep laugh, but he recoiled back in pain as he did so, clenching his stomach. 'But you did get me good, I will give you that.'

'How did you survive that?'

'When you pushed me, I slid down the edge and didn't fall right off. Thus, no splatter and only some injuries.'

'You must have the best luck ever.' I couldn't believe we were talking so casually about this, but I didn't know how else to handle this madness any more. It was surreal.

'I guess so.'

'So, what happens now then?' I asked.

'What do you mean?'

'I know you'll want pay back for this.'

'How so?'

'I tried to kill you!'

'I told you, I liked it.'

'I don't understand what that means!'

'I like how your brain works against fear. Most people would continue to only listen to me in this situation, but you broke and tried to end it. I liked that about you. The hacking you did a few weeks back was different. This is more my style.'

'You make no sense.'

'It doesn't need to make sense. Why does anything in life need too?'

'Because if things don't make sense, we can't come to logical conclusions.'

Lane huffed. 'Forget all that logical crap. There is no logic to anything. We as humans all hide things, do bad stuff. We're not special.'

'It isn't that I need logic. I just want to understand why you are doing this. What do you want from me, Lane, it can't just be to purge out my secrets and show me to the world?'

Lane sighed. 'It was that at the start, but now this has happened, you've changed your course. You really must know?'

'Yes!'

Lane looked around. Urging me to calm down. 'Look, I will tell you. If you let me stay at your place tonight. I will tell you everything if you take me to your hacking station. I want to learn what it's like to be you.'

I was going to call him crazy, but that felt redundant now. I knew I wasn't going to get out of this though, and I wanted to finally get some answers. But I couldn't let a killer stay at my house.

'I can't let you be near my family.'

'Then no truth.' He repeated.

'Why this?'

'You wanted to talk, didn't you? It is the best space to be, in your natural habitat.'

'With my family around some killer? I don't think so!'

'Fine. Carry on pondering. Oh, here's the taxi.'

As he slowly stood up, holding his stomach, he smiled at me. 'Don't worry, I'm not going to retaliate because of this. It's invested me even more if anything. Now, let's go. I will head home, and you do so as well. A lot has happened lately. We'll have to talk more some other time.'

We got into the taxi. Most people would think I was crazy for sitting next to a psychopath so easily, but I couldn't break out of this web now, I was so entwined, I couldn't even think properly. Ela was dead. Theodore was in captivity. My family were under threat. And I had almost killed someone. What was going to be next? I was so far detached from reality at this moment, life no longer felt real.

Chapter Thirty-Four

I lay in bed the next day, still in my party dress and with mascara down my cheeks. I felt like I was living in some strange matrix. Last night I had almost killed someone. I was on the edge. I needed him gone. But I knew he wasn't going anywhere now. Once again, I had made the wrong move.

I turned and screamed into my pillow at the thought. A person had died, and Theodore was missing. Who else could be next? I had to get this guy away from everyone, and I knew I couldn't put off the police any longer. I had to deal with the fact I would go to jail and get this over with. After sitting in that taxi with Lane and finally having seen his face, and after what he had done to Ela, I knew I had to do something to save Theodore. I couldn't be selfish any longer. I had to expose this.

I pulled out my phone and my fingers hovered over calling the police, but I couldn't do it. The number felt far past being able to help me now. I had to do this myself somehow. And the only way was to get rid of him. Through death. I'd failed once but I had to try again. I didn't want to do this but since I couldn't bring myself to call the police, this had to happen. It was selfish. But this was my only way.

·····

Can we meet again?

So soon?

I just want to speak with you.

I'm a little injured right now so you'll have to come to me, okay? I actually have a message for you myself

Fine. Where?

How about the place I'm holding Theodore?

Okay.

See you then, Junie.

📷   Text Message   Send

I felt sick to my stomach. Why would he bring me there? I just knew there was going to be a message behind this. It was a reminder not to go against him. I'd hurt Lane but I had a feeling even though he loved me for it, this next meeting he was going to tell me not to do it again.

I gathered my courage and headed to the location he sent me after I'd showered and changed, not even telling my parents I was going out. I first snuck to the kitchen to grab a knife and hide it in my jeans. After the incident the previous night, I could tell they were at their wits end with me, but it wouldn't matter anyway if I didn't come back alive.

The location wasn't far from my house either and took only a few minutes to get there by taxi. It was an abandoned building, an ideal setting for a horror movie showdown. I felt like a monster myself, given I had hurt so many people. I had to end it once and for all.

I couldn't tell anybody what was going on, it was too late. I'd let it go so far and I was even guiltier now I'd taken it to such an extreme. I stood outside the building with the knife in my jeans and headed inside, not knowing what waited for me. Lane being semi-injured gave me a slight advantage. I remembered that Lane said this was where Theodore was being held right now, and the thought stopped me in my tracks. I pulled out my phone and read the message again, knowing I may have to kill Lane in front of Theodore. The thought made me feel sick, but I had to save him. I couldn't let another person die because of my selfishness.

I built up the courage and continued inside, looking everywhere for Lane. 'Lane, I'm here, where are you?' I shouted into the rotting room, but the place was so dark I couldn't see far into it.

Silence greeted me, but after walking further inside a huge light switched on and the sight of two people greeted me. One was the now all too familiar Lane. The other Theodore, who was swinging from the roof.

'Theodore!' I yelled. It looked like he'd been hanged.

Lane laughed. 'Don't worry, he's fine, just having fun up in the air, is all.'

Theodore was unresponsive. I glared at Lane. 'Let him down!'

'Not yet.'

'What are you doing? I came to see you. Why do you have Theodore out here?'

'Because this is your punishment.'

'What?'

'For trying to kill me.'

'I thought you didn't care?'

Lane stood tall. 'I told you it made me like you even more, but I can't have you try such a thing again. Okay?'

I nodded. 'I won't. I listened to you last time and I will again. Please, just let him down.'

Lane nodded and brought the rope back down. I stepped forward to go to Theodore. He was painfully thin, and looked half dead laying there on the floor now. As I looked him over, Lane pointed a knife my way.

'Even though I'm injured, I can still hurt you. Leave him.'

I froze in place. 'Fine. I get the message.'

'Good. Now, it's time to say goodbye.'

Lane moved forward and went to place the knife to lifeless Theodore's neck. 'What are you doing?!'

'Delivering the message.'

'You've told me it!'

'Yes, but the final issue is to make sure you listen, and I have to kill him to do that.'

'Do that and I'll kill you!' I raged.

'I'm sure you will try. But I advise against it.'

'I've done everything you've said!'

My words seemed to annoy him, and he pointed the knife back towards me. 'Trying to kill me is hardly listening!'

'I thought you didn't care?!'

He let out a cackle of a laugh. 'I don't! But I need to make it clear to you not to do it again, is all.'

'I said I won't. Just don't hurt him.'

'I have to. To really cement the message into your mind. I'm sorry, but this is your own doing.'

Lane turned back to Theodore and motioned towards him with the knife, picking him up by his tatty collar and getting ready to make the cut at his neck. I lunged forward and fell on top of Lane, who laughed as the blade fell from his hand and to the side of us. But strangely, everything paused there. He didn't move to get it back or hurt either of us. Instead, he lay on his back, clutching his stomach and laughing hysterically.

I sat in place, confused by his response. 'What's so funny?'

'You're so funny,' He cried with laughter. 'You take everything I say so seriously.'

'And why wouldn't I? You speared my friend's body to the wall of my gymnasium.'

His face straightened as I said that and he sat up sharply, staring into my eyes. 'I'm not going to hurt him. I was only playing with you.'

'What?'

'I was testing you there, and it made me see how much Theodore means to you. It seems like he will be a good tool for me.'

'Tool?' I quizzed.

'Yes.' Suddenly he was close to my face, holding my chin. 'To make sure you never pull such a stunt again. I found it fun, to see you act as cold as me. But try it again and his flesh will be peeled layer by layer with you watching. This is my warning.'

I shook off his hand. 'You make no sense. One minute you're

happy with this and the next you threaten me?'

'You did try to kill me. I still have to make sure you won't perform such an act again. Though you don't seem to be scared given what I just did.'

'After everything you've done, I couldn't feel any worse than I already do,' I replied.

Lane sat back. 'I suppose I would feel the same if I was in your position.'

'Then why do it to me? Why are you playing me like this? What are we going to gain? This has to come to an end sometime. But then again, I guess it is because you are a killer and like the thrill of playing with your prey.'

'I will admit, it was that at first but the more I have gotten to speak with you, the more I like you. It satisfies me, even talking with you like this. I won't kill you, but I can't leave you alone either. I told you I wanted to reveal your secrets, to bring your world crashing down. However, it's more than that now. I want to do more than make you be your true, selfish self in public.'

I dug my hands into the dirt below, looking at Theodore. 'I wouldn't care about this if you only played with me, and left my family out of it.'

'I do only want to play with you. But people around you keep playing. Don't you see, they are the bad guys. They made you hide your true self. Can't you see that is what I am here to do?'

'Showcase me?'

'Yes. To bring you out of hiding and showcase you to the public! I want you to be yourself.'

"You're doing this, hurting people just so I can be selfish in public? All of this!'

'I know these two images you hold of yourself. The pristine image to the world and the hacker queen, which is the real you. I've slowly started to bring her out by doing what I have. I didn't want to go this extreme, but I have had to do so to finally get you to start being yourself. I had to go to these lengths because it's been so hard to lure you out.'

'You've... this is what you are doing? Trying to make me be my hacker self in real life?'

He nodded. 'Yup.'

'That's it? That is your plan?'

'I watched your for so long. I had to do it. You want to be yourself, right? Well, I'm forcing the truth out of you.'

'By killing my friends?'

'Sometimes you must eliminate people to become who you are.'

'I don't need you to do this. I am this way for a reason, to be able to escape this place! You doing this isn't going to help me! Besides, by killing Yamazaki, the only person who truly knew me, you destroyed my chances of ever being myself in the real world.'

'And so, think of this as an apology. I'm helping you to fully become yourself by getting rid of obstacles!'

This guy really believed what he was saying. I was in shock that this was the reason he was doing this. Playing these crazy games with me so I could be myself. I'd never felt so much anger before. He'd hurt so many people because of this. I'd lost Yamazaki, Ela, and even the control I had over my own life. I looked over to Theodore who was lightly breathing, and I broke. This was all it was about. He tried to help me become myself by killing the people he thought were suppressing me. It was ridiculous and it was ending now before he took anyone else.

I felt for the knife in the back of my jeans and sighed. 'All of this turmoil isn't going to end until you get a reason to kill my family. That is what you're waiting for, aren't you? To get to the people who suppress me most. This won't end until they're dead and you think I've been released. I can't let that happen.'

'I'm here to help you. I answered your cries. I've seen everything about how you feel.'

'How?'

'Through your webcams, cameras, following you. I know everything about how you feel. Don't you get it?'

'Get what?'

'I shared the link to The Monsters Club in the first place with Reign of Serpan. I did this because I found you long ago, and I finally knew this was the time to get things started between us. That is the type of killer I am. I like helping people become themselves. Think of me as a helpful killer.'

'You've done all of this?'

He smiled. 'Yes. To help you be yourself.'

All this time Lane had watched me and set this all up. I couldn't believe what I was hearing. 'You know nothing of how to help me. How dare you feel you have the right to do any of this. You had Yamazaki killed first and slowly played and watched more people around me so you could knock them down one by one. How could you think I would be thankful for this?'

'Because you can't do it yourself.'

'You killed my best friend for nothing!' I yelled. 'I was going to be myself when I got to Japan. You've ruined my life!'

'I'm here to make it better. Forget Yamazaki. Look. I'll let you in on one truth if it will calm you down and help you accept this.' He paused before sighing. 'Yamazaki isn't actually dead.'

I sat back and froze. 'What did you just say?'

'He isn't dead. That was all a setup. I faked it for you. It wasn't Reign who told you he was dead. It was me. Only you saw that page.'

'Are you kidding me right now?' I felt like my breath was caught in my throat.

'No. I had to do this to get him away from you, but I couldn't get to Japan and no one would kill him for me. Serial killers all have their own agendas, you see. It was a lie and now you know this, you can forgive me, right?'

My whole world froze in time. Yamazaki was alive and Lane

had played me like this. Made me hurt and grieve all this time. This was the last straw. Lane was dead.

'I'll kill you...'

'Don't think like that...'

'You're dead!' I yelled and lunged for him, but he grabbed my arm with such force I thought the bone would break.

'Don't do this. I'm here to save you from yourself.'

'I don't need a pig like you to save me.' Pain seared through my arm and for the first time I saw his brutal manner in person. His face wasn't sweet anymore. It was angry and twisted.

'You really don't want to try and kill me. If you try again, I'm not going to be as nice.' He said viciously.

A bout of laughter erupted from me. 'You don't understand, Lane.'

'Understand what?'

'You know nothing about me.'

'Yes, I do.'

'So you know I'm a killer too?'

Lane scoffed. 'Your feeble attempts to kill me hardly make you a killer.'

'No. When I was younger, I killed a girl.'

'What?'

'You'd never have known because nobody else does. I framed someone else.'

'You're lying...'

'No, I'm not. And it was no accident. I killed that girl because she learned too much and wanted to blab. You see, I have a third persona, more evil than the hacker. I never wanted to unleash that one again. But you left me no choice!' Lane froze at my statement and it gave me enough time to break out of his grip. I pulled out a knife and stabbed him between the ribs. He yelped, releasing my arm as I lunged at him a second time.

'You stabbed me...' He breathed through a gasp of pain. 'How...'

'I took my knife and did it, like you do. Fool.' I pulled him closer to me and pressed my mouth against his ear. 'Don't you understand, Lane? A cold bitch like me doesn't need saving. You don't know me. You never had, or you would have expected it would come to this. Now die.'

At this point, I was glad Theodore was passed out; I did not want him to see this. I never wanted my life to come to this. To become a murderer for a second time. I didn't want to be like Lane and The Monsters Club, but the anger raged through me and once I started, I couldn't stop. The blood was everywhere, a red lake forming around us. This was the girl I became when I was forced into a corner.

I dropped the knife as Lane looked up at me with what little remaining energy he had left. I never wanted to believe this would be the outcome, but it had reached the point of it being me or him. And I refused to let him beat me.

'You really are crazy...' He uttered his last words just before his eyes went dull. I didn't feel anything for him as he stopped breathing.

I headed over to Theodore, who was still out of it, and fell down by him. I had to hope he didn't see any of that. I held his face, pulled out my phone and called the police.

'Yes, hello. I need an ambulance, please. There has been an attack.'

Chapter Thirty-Five

Coming up with a story as to what happened was pretty easy. I was a good liar, after all. All that had happened over the last few weeks worked out well for me. I told them that I'd had a stalker who was targeting those around me, and I only found out when he kidnapped me and took me to the abandoned building where he'd been holding Theodore.

I had been rescued from the place not long after Lane's death. Seeing his dead body being taken away filled me with delight. It was strange though, it was a long time since I'd experienced death up close. Not since I'd killed that girl. Something I had buried for many years and would take with me to my grave. Just like this.

As soon as the questioning started, I began spinning my alibi. Once I got home, I could make a compilation of messages that would align with my story. Thankfully, that was all the police would need. Lane had started to harm those around me who he didn't like or believed I didn't like, and that was the reasoning as to Theodore's disappearance and Ela's death. I handed them the messages and told them I didn't know it was him until he kidnapped me. It worked perfectly, as all my lies did. They believed me and, I could go back to my pristine image.

Nobody could believe this had happened to me. After a few days of rest, flowers kept coming to my house non-stop, and it was like I had gotten my old lie of a life back in an instant. I wondered, however, if what I'd told my mother about Yamazaki could have jeopardised this, but she never even brought it up. Lane was gone and I could now take control of my life again.

Theodore had been recovering in hospital from both his injuries and being half starved. The image of his gaunt figure still haunted me, and I'd been unable to speak with him since his family found out all that had happened. In all of this, the one thing I hadn't even gotten a chance to think about was the fact Lane said Yamazaki was alive. I hadn't been able to speak to him and confirm it yet. Partly because my mother barely left me alone for five minutes, but also, part of me was afraid to; if he actually was dead, it would be like losing him all over again.

I lay in bed for several days, pondering about my future. It was hard to deal with all the mistakes I had made. So much death and craziness from one website hacking. It was amazing how life could change overnight, but I had to accept that this was my fate. It was all my own doing, after all.

I wanted to cry and scream but I'd already done that so much from all the guilt that I felt dried out. I looked at my dressing table and saw the picture of Yamazaki I had placed there. I needed to speak to him, I needed to make sure he was okay.

Eventually, I gave in. I decided to go and see Theodore, but first I needed to speak with Yamazaki. I took my chance while my mother was sleeping. I rushed to my computer and prayed that he would be there.

I opened all my old coding sources and booted up the chat box. I needed to manually remove the block Lane had placed on all my devices to prevent me communicating with Yamazaki. I had never even thought of checking this, and as I opened the source and removed the bug from my apps, everything cleared, and his name popped up with a green light. My eyes widened.

'He's alive...' I gasped.

I hadn't dared fully believe what Lane had told me. It took me a few moments to stop shivering, because if this came out to be false, I would break again.

As I logged into the refreshed chat box, his name popped up and I soon typed out a message, my hands shaking just hoping for a reply.

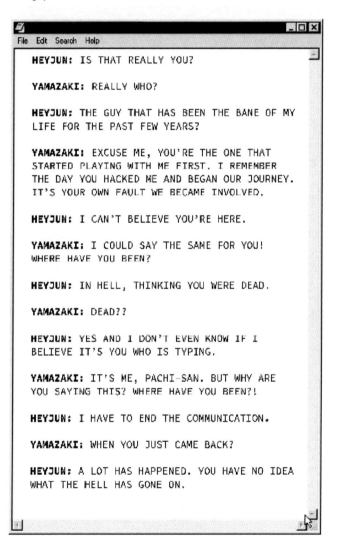

HEYJUN: IS THAT REALLY YOU?

YAMAZAKI: REALLY WHO?

HEYJUN: THE GUY THAT HAS BEEN THE BANE OF MY LIFE FOR THE PAST FEW YEARS?

YAMAZAKI: EXCUSE ME, YOU'RE THE ONE THAT STARTED PLAYING WITH ME FIRST. I REMEMBER THE DAY YOU HACKED ME AND BEGAN OUR JOURNEY. IT'S YOUR OWN FAULT WE BECAME INVOLVED.

HEYJUN: I CAN'T BELIEVE YOU'RE HERE.

YAMAZAKI: I COULD SAY THE SAME FOR YOU! WHERE HAVE YOU BEEN?

HEYJUN: IN HELL, THINKING YOU WERE DEAD.

YAMAZAKI: DEAD??

HEYJUN: YES AND I DON'T EVEN KNOW IF I BELIEVE IT'S YOU WHO IS TYPING.

YAMAZAKI: IT'S ME, PACHI-SAN. BUT WHY ARE YOU SAYING THIS? WHERE HAVE YOU BEEN?!

HEYJUN: I HAVE TO END THE COMMUNICATION.

YAMAZAKI: WHEN YOU JUST CAME BACK?

HEYJUN: A LOT HAS HAPPENED. YOU HAVE NO IDEA WHAT THE HELL HAS GONE ON.

File   Edit   Search   Help

YAMAZAKI: THEN TELL ME? WHY HAVE YOU BEEN
GONE?

HEYJUN: I CAN'T BRING IT UP AGAIN. I'M
SORRY. JUST KNOW THAT I'M GLAD YOU'RE ALIVE.

YAMAZAKI: JUNIE, TELL ME WHY YOU HAVE BEEN
GONE?

HEYJUN: I'D BETTER GO NOW.

YAMAZAKI: JUNIE!

HEYJUN: I CAN'T BELIEVE YOU'RE ALIVE.

YAMAZAKI: IF YOU DON'T TELL ME WHAT IS GOING
ON, I WILL COME TO YOU.

HEYJUN: YOU CAN'T...

YAMAZAKI: TELL ME...

HEYJUN: GOODBYE.

YAMAZAKI: THAT'S IT. I'M COMING TO YOU.

HEYJUN: PLEASE, DON'T. I WILL EXPLAIN ALL TO
YOU. JUST NOT RIGHT NOW. I NEEDED TO KNOW IT
WAS YOU. THAT YOU'RE ALIVE. I WILL GET BACK
TO YOU. ONLY GIVE ME SOME TIME. PLEASE,
YAMAZAKI.

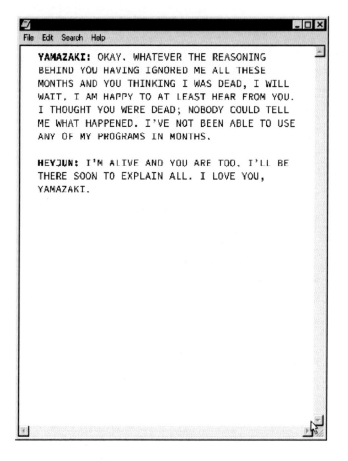

YAMAZAKI: OKAY. WHATEVER THE REASONING
BEHIND YOU HAVING IGNORED ME ALL THESE
MONTHS AND YOU THINKING I WAS DEAD, I WILL
WAIT. I AM HAPPY TO AT LEAST HEAR FROM YOU.
I THOUGHT YOU WERE DEAD; NOBODY COULD TELL
ME WHAT HAPPENED. I'VE NOT BEEN ABLE TO USE
ANY OF MY PROGRAMS IN MONTHS.

HEYJUN: I'M ALIVE AND YOU ARE TOO. I'LL BE
THERE SOON TO EXPLAIN ALL. I LOVE YOU,
YAMAZAKI.

Before he could respond to my last words, I logged off and sat back in my seat. I'd never uttered such words to him before. Yet it felt right. And now this wall had fallen, I couldn't lose him again. I would tell him everything, but not here, not now or online. I was ending that. It was time for us to finally meet. When this was all over. I had to settle things with Theodore first, and then this life I hated was ending once and for all.

Chapter Thirty-Six

Later that day we got a call from Theodore's mother who told us he had finally woken up from his coma. I felt sick at the thought, knowing that he knew everything up to a certain point, and I'd lied about what had truly gone on. He'd been through so much, but I needed to get to him, both to make sure he kept quiet about everything that he knew of. I had no idea what Lane had done to him, and had no idea what frame of mind he'd be in. I knew after everything he'd been through, worrying about myself was wrong, but if I was caught in a lie, it would be the end of me.

We arranged a time for me to visit. My mother took me to the hospital, where she hesitated as we pulled up to the entrance. She was nervous about me going anywhere these days.

'Are you sure you don't want me to come in?' She asked.

I nodded. 'I'm positive. It will only make you think about what has happened more if you see him. I need to talk to him alone, anyhow.'

'Okay, you're right. Be careful.'

'I will. Thank you, Mum.' She nodded, and I rushed out of the car. It felt like it took me an eternity to get to his room. When I arrived and saw him propped up in bed, asleep, I froze at the door and wanted to cry.

My nails dug onto the side of the white door frame as I took in his battered appearance. His face was covered in bruises and his body was starting to gain a little weight, but he was still so slim compared to the Theodore he had been. I felt sick to my stomach for having let that happen for so long. And yet, here I was to make sure he kept our secret. I did care about him, as much as I was able to for someone who wasn't Yamazaki. It was just that my evil side was unable to rest until I knew I had tied up all the loose ends, and this was the last thing I needed to settle. I had to make sure he was okay and that he would keep what had happened a secret.

I slowly walked inside and stopped by his bed. In that moment, I wished I could take all his suffering away. I did still care, my kind self was here somewhere. I stroked his hair, and he suddenly shook awake and turned to me. We froze in time, his eyes on mine and the tears poured.

'Junie?' Theodore snapped awake and gasped.

'Hi...' I barely mumbled back. Seeing him this way had my insides so twisted with guilt I felt bad even speaking around him. As if my words were tainted, and could only cause more hurt.

In those moments, we did nothing but hold each other's gaze. I so wanted to know what he was thinking when he looked at me. When he saw the pain behind my eyes for hurting him. For being selfish and letting him suffer just so my hacking activities would be hidden. How selfish I was. I'd never felt so exposed.

'I'm so glad to see you. This feels like a dream.' He spoke up after a few moments. His voice was so hoarse his words felt rough.

'I had to come and see you as soon as I knew you were awake. Where's your mum?'

'She's getting some rest. I can't believe it's you.' He took my hand from his face and entwined it with mine. 'How are you?

'Forget about me. How are you?'

Theodore lay his head back and sighed. 'I'm doing okay, a

little in pain.'

'Pain that is all my fault...'

'Don't say that... this all was that bastard's fault.' Theodore sighed.

The tears fell. 'Yes, but I let this happen to you because I didn't want my past to be revealed.'

'Whatever the past is, I won't hate you.'

'You should.'

'I can't even if I wished.' Theodore pulled himself up. 'Junie, I know this has to come to an end. Even if we never even really started anything in the first place. But know, no matter what, I'm here for you.'

'And I'm here for you. However, what do you mean come to an end?'

'We can't see each other again.'

'Huh?'

'You know why.'

'I mean, sure, I understand Theodore but..'

'But nothing, what I went through and all your secrets.. this is all too much to recover from.'

'I understand that. I'm so sorry I involved you.'

'Junie, these secrets…'

'What is it?'

'I can't stand this. However…'

'However, what?'

'I have to tell people what happened... I know you've lied.'

The atmosphere in the room shrunk as he said this. It was what I'd waited for, and it had come true so fast. 'What lie, Theodore?'

'My mother told me some story saying Lane was your stalker. Which may be partially true, but you didn't tell people about what happened, who he was or that website?'

'I couldn't. I'd go to jail.'

'I know you killed him.'

'How?'

'I was awake and heard everything.'

'Everything?'

He nodded. 'Yes. I know you've killed before.'

Our eyes froze, my expression darkening. The one thing dangerous for him to hear, and he heard it. This was bad. 'You were awake?'

'Yes, barely but I saw and heard everything. How have you killed before?'

'It was an accident when I was younger. Some girl threatened me, okay?'

'Junie!'

'Look, forget about that. You can't tell anybody the truth of this situation. I had to lie so I didn't go to jail.'

'They told me about Ela. I have to tell the truth.'

'You can't!' I snapped. I could feel my mind darkening.

'Junie, calm down. What's wrong with you? Can't you see, holding these lies like you do, they're destroying you. What you did to Ela and so many others; you're a monster. Just like this Lane guy was.'

'Lane lied to you, everyone did.'

'You need help. Your obsession with saving yourself is hurting people, it's dangerous!'

I dug my nails into his bruised arm. 'Stop talking, Theodore. Don't ruin your future.'

He flinched in pain. 'Junie, I'm sorry, but I can't hide the truth. You're destroying yourself, and others.'

'You don't understand, nobody does! Why I do this, why I go to such lengths, because nobody gives a damn in this society. Stop pretending you care; everyone lies. You can't do this!'

'I have to. When the police come to talk to me, I'm going to. You need help.'

'Don't say such things to me.'

'Why? You need to hear some truth for once in your life.

How did you become this person?'

'Why are you believing what so much of this Lane guy told you? He was a murderer, Theodore.'

'And so are you.'

I let go of him and sighed. This was sad, what I had to do next. 'I suppose then, you won't get a chance to speak to them. Goodbye, Theodore.'

'What?'

I stood, grabbed his pillow and pushed it into his face. He tried to scream, but he was so weak it was impossible for him to break away, even from tiny me. I held it until I could feel his breathing stop under the fabric, and I went completely out of it myself. I was numb, knowing that this was the end of these games, that my time here was up. I had to get out of here. This society poisoned me and brought out nothing but evil.

I removed the pillow, saw his limp body and left. It was time to leave. Leave everything in this life behind. I swallowed the guilt I felt about Theodore and Ela. I was the wrong person to mess with. This had to be the way it ended.

Chapter Thirty-Seven

I stood outside the hospital letting the rain cool me. I had one option left and that was to flee. I'd gone too far and knew if I went back home and tried to act like everything was okay, I'd be discovered. I had to leave town. Leave the country, and that meant there was only one place left for me.

I formed a plan on the way home, to get a taxi, sneak inside and withdraw all of my hacking money, head to the airport, book the quickest flight to Japan and go into hiding. It was the only option left. I'd killed Theodore; someone I'd briefly felt something for, and I was now too numb to care any more. I followed the plan and left.

Before I did, I had one last mission to complete. Destroy the place that held so many of my secrets and burn it to the ground. It was an extreme action but I'd created an extreme case for myself. I'd gone too far. Let myself become a monster. It was like I'd now become a member of The Monsters Club, and I was at the point where I could go the whole way.

I got into a taxi and headed to Dallington. It was a Sunday so there would be nobody there, the perfect time to burn the hell-hole to the ground. I could taste the dangerous girl inside me, brewing with each passing moment as we neared school. This hadn't been how I'd intended to leave for Japan, a criminal that everyone was going to be looking for. I was going to hold a label in society, which would've been my greatest fear last year but now I only cared about getting away from here. It was time I buried this life. I was going to start afresh but I couldn't until I'd burned down the place I despised and that had held so many of my secrets over the years.

Getting exposed now didn't matter, and doing this helped give me some peace to end this chapter to my life. This school had made a monster out of me ever since I had joined, and I needed to kill it along with all my past lies. I felt for the lighter in my pocket, and sighed the closer we grew to the premises, holding onto the plastic for dear life. There were gas canisters that lay at the back of the property, making this all the more easy.

I hoped everyone around me could understand why I kept these secrets. I'd only wanted to survive in a society that had wanted to suppress me and force me to be what other people wanted. I hadn't planned to be a monster, but I had to hide. Not just my hacking life, or to keep the future I wanted but the true reason; to hide this girl that was a killer inside me.

I made the taxi driver wait a good distance away so I had a getaway car when the school exploded into fire. I ran up to the main entrance, sneaking under the front gates and heading to the back of the school where the tennis court lay with the storage unit for the gas canisters. I knew I had only a short time to do it to escape the explosion. I cracked open the lock with a dirtied old statue that lay near the court, and headed to my destination.

I imagined Ela looking at me with disgust, Theodore stunned that I was this person and my parents unable to imagine me being this kind of girl. When did this happen to their daughter? When did she become a monster? Not even Lane had known because I'd never spoken about her to anybody but Yamazaki. I'd told him over the phone; which must be why Lane hadn't known about it. The killer was deep inside of me. That was why Yamazaki was the only person I cared about, because he knew the true me and did not judge it. I'd tried so hard to escape her, and when Lane was playing me, I refused to let her come out. But in the end, I'd had no choice. In fact, she felt at home with The Monsters Club, and I couldn't stop her. Sometimes our emotions control us, and it's impossible to stop them.

I snuck into the storage unit, flicked open my lighter and threw it near one of the canisters before running for my life. I managed to get to the taxi before the explosion started. I looked back to see it rip through the field to the school building in a matter of seconds as the burst of flames reached a great height. The taxi driver looked back, shocked, but he drove forward and I sat back into the seat. It didn't matter if anybody saw me now.

I felt a weight lifted doing this. The source of so much trouble was gone and even though my evil was exposed, I felt relieved. My body felt so free. I didn't care anymore; I was finally escaping this world and heading to Japan.

I went home to get my things before leaving and asked the taxi driver to wait again. I rushed up to my bedroom, packed as much as I could into a bag, pouring all of my money into a secret credit card I had for my hacking money and quickly booked a flight to Japan. As I waited for the ticket to process, I took in my bedroom one last time. I considered the life I'd built in here; the secret one. I was sorry to my family for this. The room felt so empty now; a tainted space of rage and evil thoughts I'd let consume me. I'm sorry. So sorry.

After doing so, it felt like a bitter escape, knowing I was finally leaving this room and would probably never return. I looked at my computer with sadness and thought of The Monsters Club, before deleting all of my tools. I didn't even tell Yamazaki I was coming in case I was traced. I deleted everything and smashed the hard drive onto my bedroom floor to make sure nobody found out. It would be funny to see how he reacted to me. After years of talking, seeing each other in person for the first time yet knowing all of each other's secrets.

I wrote a note to my parents, apologising for everything that was going to come from this but I had to leave, I couldn't breathe here anymore. I grabbed my bag, passport, took my money and got in the taxi to head my new life.

'Are you ready to go? You seem to be having an eventful day.' The taxi driver laughed as I slid into the taxi seat, not even glancing at my house.

I smiled as I shut the door. 'I'm having the best day ever. Please, take me to the airport.'

Chapter Thirty-Eight

I arrived in Japan with a new version of myself. Well, she was old but reinvented at best. However, she was going to start afresh and live the free life she'd always wanted. Not that I had a choice any more, I didn't ever intend to go back to England. This was what I'd always wanted after all, and why I had put such effort in to keep my secrets; to escape.

All I had to locate Yamazaki's address was his IP. He thought he'd covered it so well but in reality, I'd had the things for years, I only hoped he still lived at this place or I was going to be stuck here alone and a criminal. I was a criminal anyhow being a hacker, but murder was a whole other level. I decoded the IP and found the exact address, headed to a taxi and handed it to them. I could speak a little Japanese because of Yamazaki and it was just enough to get me by and away from the airport.

It felt so strange being here. I'd wanted this for so long, and I started to feel a little sick at the thought I'd finally achieved it. For how long I'd be here before being found I didn't know but my main thing right now was finding Yamazaki and fully confirming he was alive. I hadn't even given him a true thought because I wanted to hold onto the hope this was real, and I was soon going to see him. I only hoped he was home.

As the taxi I had caught pulled away from the airport, a sickness started to crawl up my skin. This was all starting to feel real the further away I hid from the world I'd left burning.

So many of my secrets I'd worked so hard to keep hidden would come out, and I worried for how my family were going to deal with this. I did feel bad about leaving them this way, but I wouldn't be able to handle facing them once they knew I was killer. How could you handle the fact your daughter was not who you once thought they were? It's a thought I wouldn't want to have to deal with in person.

I looked out the window and took in the pristine scenery of Tokyo. The place I'd been working so hard to come to in the future, and yet now I was here after committing such dark acts, it felt strange yet right to be here. I was going to be fine either way. I had to keep up positive thinking and hiding. I'd gotten this far, I couldn't let this all fail now. At least until I saw Yamazaki in the flesh and I could feel content.

After a short drive through the busy city, the driver pulled up to a lone street that lay bundled in by numerous tall building, looking like apartments. Is this where Yamazaki lived? It oddly fitted the image I'd had in my mind of his place and after the driver left me standing there with my taxi, I started to get excited to finally see him in person. I wondered how awkward it would be finally meeting. This Monsters Club had almost ruined everything for me, but at least I had Yamazaki. I was soon standing in front of his apartment and my nerves grew as to how he was going react to me being here. Yamazaki was the only person that knew everything about me, so I knew this was the only place left for me.

It took me a few minutes before I finally gained the confidence to ring the bell. Silence lingered before a bunch of profanity and noise came from behind the door. It opened after a few seconds and there he stood, all dyed blonde hair of him. My eyes widened just as his did. It didn't seem to take him long to know who this strange girl was standing at his door.

Yamazaki dropped his bowl of noodles stunned. 'Pachi-san, it can't be you...'

I didn't even know what to do other than cry. It felt surreal. After six years, I was meeting him in real life for the first time. It was bizarre and the fact he wasn't dead made this all crazier.

I laughed through my tears. 'I don't appreciate being called Pachi-san, as usual. However, today I will let it be considering I can't believe it's actually you either.'

Yamazaki came forward with wide eyes. Analysing me like he was trying to believe it was me. 'That sounds like her. But how can this be real; how can Junie Han be standing at my apartment door?'

'I can't believe you're alive.' I sniffled.

'Same to you. You've haven't spoken to me for months!'

'You really don't know what happened?'

He shrugged. 'One day you just stopped speaking to me and I couldn't contact you on anything. In fact, I lost the ability to use any of my stuff. It's all been fried and the fact my hacking skills can't get back access to anything has really messed with my ego.'

'I think now is the time to talk about it.' I added.

Yamazaki gulped, unable to take me seriously. That I was here. 'I can't believe you're here. I don't even know what to say.'

'Do you mind me being here?' I asked.

'I want you here!' He said, holding me by my arms. 'I can't tell you how much I missed you. Now, come inside and tell me where you've been, tell me everything!'

'I have so much to tell you, Yamazaki. Only you will understand me. It's bad. This has been a terrible journey but you're the only person who can get it.'

Yamazaki smiled in spite of this statement. 'I'm always here for you, Junie. It's been this way from the beginning. Now, I'll make us both some ramen since you spoiled my other pot. This feels like a dream.'

As we came inside and I tried to pinch myself and make sure this was real, my burner phone buzzed. Once it had only

Yamazaki who had access to it other than the now dead Lane. I felt sick pulling it out of my pocket but as I did so, what I saw shocked me. A link from Lane's messages, I clicked and it which led me to a post on The Monsters Club.

There it was, The Monsters Club as bright as ever along with a picture of Lane. His dead body. It was here. My post was up. I was finally part of The Monsters Club.

'Please welcome our latest killer to the crew; and one of our first female killers!'

If you enjoyed *The Monsters Club*, you might also enjoy Emma Whitehall's YA Fantasy, *Clockwork Magpies*, available now at Northodox.co.uk

Acknowledgements

Support is everything. First, I want to thank my family, Susan, Leonard, Francesca, and Alexander Kerridge, who have always listened to my story ideas with so much enthusiasm. They keep the life within my books and inspire me to continue with each new story I write.

To my Grandparents who tragically lost both of their lives to the Covid pandemic. They were huge supporters of my writing and eagerly awaited each new book that came. They may have not got to see this one out in the world, but I know they'd be so happy. I was blessed to have them in my life and each new book will have a part of their soul with it. As my grandmother's last words were to me, 'Keep writing.' That is exactly what I will do.

I want to say a huge thank you to the readers of my books. You are the lifeblood of stories and I always appreciate every single person who gives my fictional worlds a chance. You inspire me to keep writing every day and your support means the world.

In the end, if you have a dream. Always keep going!

NORTHODOX
PRESS

HOME OF NORTHERN VOICES

 FACEBOOK.COM/NORTHODOXPRESS

 TWITER.COM/NORTHODOXPRESS

 INSTAGRAM.COM/NORTHODOXPRESS

 NORTHODOX.CO.UK

SUBMISSIONS ARE OPEN!
WRITER & DEBUT AUTHOR [ ]
NOVELS & SHORT FICTION [ ]
FROM OR LIVING IN THE NORTH [ ]

UNDER THE BRIDGE

A LIVERPOOL MYSTERY

JACK BYRNE

WHEN SECRETS
RESURFACE

THE PAST
REACHES OUT

A NORTHERN STEAMPUNK ADVENTURE

CLOCKWORK MAGPIES

EMMA WHITEHALL

LOTTE JEAN ELLIOTT
THE
MONSTERS
CLUB
POPULARITY MEET PANDEMONIUM

JOSEPH DARLINGTON

EVERY SECRET HAS A MELTING POINT

THE GIRL
BENEATH
THE ICE

CATHERINE WIMPENEY

HER
SISTER'S
SHADOW

A PSYCHOLOGICAL THRILLER

THE PAST NEVER DIES

THE SILENT BROTHER

SIMON VAN DER VELDE